M.S. Power was born in Dublin and educated in Ireland and France. He has worked in the United States as a television producer and now lives in Galloway, Scotland. He has been a full-time writer since 1983, publishing a number of novels including CHILDREN OF THE NORTH, which was televised on BBC2.

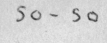

50 - 50

The Stalker's Apprentice

M.S. Power

First published in 1993
by MAINSTREAM PUBLISHING CO. (EDINBURGH) LTD

First published in paperback in 1994
by HEADLINE BOOK PUBLISHING

A HEADLINE FEATURE paperback

10 9 8 7 6 5 4 3 2 1

ISBN 0 7472 4719 6

Typeset by
Letterpart Limited, Reigate, Surrey
Printed and bound in Great Britain by
Cox & Wyman Ltd, Reading, Berks

HEADLINE BOOK PUBLISHING
A division of Hodder Headline PLC
338 Euston Road
London NW1 3BH

For the most loyal of friends
Sean O'Neill
remembering those years in
Merrion Square, Ballyfermot,
Charneux, and Blackwood

. . . for tis the eternal law
That first in beauty should be first in might.

John Keats
Hyperion Book II

BOOK 1

One

So, there I was in the dock, looking as meek and remorseful as possible, and as far a cry away as I could manage from the ruthless killer the stupid tabloids had already labelled me. What with my dad hanging himself and me being up for murder, they really had something to gloat over.

I did everything my barrister told me. I wore my good, dark grey suit, a white shirt with buttoned-down collar, and a navy tie with thin, discreet yellow stripes criss-crossing it. I put gel in my hair to keep it from flopping over my eyes, and some white ointment on my spots to hide them a bit. I kept my head bowed most of the time, and when I did look up I had contrition written all over my face.

I felt quite sorry for Mr Rutherford, my barrister. He tried so hard, dragging up psychological background stuff and all, but he was fighting a losing battle from the start. That's not why I felt sorry for him, though. I was sorry for the poor guy because he'd been screwing my mother for nearly a year and, knowing my mother, if he didn't get me off, he'd have a hard task getting between her sheets again. She could be very vindictive, my mother.

I felt really hurt when the judge said I was evil through and through. Very unfair, I thought. And when Mrs Hayes, giving evidence against me, had the cheek to say she knew from the start that I was born evil, I wanted to stop proceedings and ask the judge if people *could* be born evil, or be born good for that matter. It's an important question, one that I'll have to think about. I don't *feel* evil or anything, but if I *am* evil then it's down to God, isn't it? Down to Him if He made a balls of things.

Anyway, when the judge passed sentence I was relieved that the whole thing was over and done with. I gave him a little nod, and a smile, and left the court quietly. No harm in being polite.

The policemen who escorted me were quite jolly on the whole, dull men with no earthly hope of promotion but kindly enough. They looked concerned as the van drove through the jeering crowd outside the court, and perhaps they shared my bewilderment that my actions could arouse such crass hostility in strangers. What did they know about anything?

One of the policemen offered me a cigarette, but I refused. 'Don't smoke, eh?' he asked.

'No. I don't smoke,' I told him. 'It's a filthy habit and very injurious to your health.' And those were the only words I spoke on the way to prison.

★ ★ ★

And now I'm lying on my cot in my cell. I'm lying on my side with my knees pulled up, my head resting on my arm. It's quite cosy really. Nothing like what I expected, and I've all the time in the world to do what I like best: think. Really think. Building up images, creating situations. I can think about Karen and have her here with me if I want, and I can take her along with me when I'm transferred which I will be, I'm told, in a few days. Some where secure, whatever that's supposed to mean. It all seems pretty secure to me right here. Or maybe I'll decide not to think about her at all. She's dead, after all, and there's something a bit morbid about brooding on the dead, and one thing I'm not is morbid.

When I was on remand I had this priest come and visit, part of his ministry, he told me, to come and give comfort to Catholics. It's all very well organised. All religions catered for, even some of the really exotic ones, I hear. Anyway, he asked me if I wanted to go to confession, to make my peace with God like as if they were going to hang me or something. He looked quite hurt when I declined, as if he'd failed in his duty. I couldn't see the point of it. If God is all that clever he already *knows* what I've done, and I wasn't about to tell Father Ferguson (that was his name) about my misdeeds just so he could get some weird kick out of it. You have to be wary of priests, you know. They go funny, not having sex, although I suppose a lot of them do. You can usually tell the ones that are still celibate: they have an awful wasted look in their eyes, and they're the ones you have to watch out for, Jesuits in particular. My mother had a pet Jesuit, you know. Used to come to the house a lot after Dad removed himself by the neck. I don't think they did any more than just talk, but I wouldn't swear to that. But I'll give him the benefit of the doubt since the last time I saw him his eyes were still wasted. In any case, I suspect Mr Rutherford was giving my mother as much as she could handle if the racket they made was anything to go by. I broke a mirror once and didn't say anything about it. I kept it hidden until I heard them at it and then put it on the floor and scattered the shards of glass about in a careful, haphazard pattern. 'That fell off the wall while you two were humping,' I told them when they came down. Mr Rutherford, who didn't really know me then, not well anyway, got all embarrassed and blew a lot, but all my mother was worried about was the supposed seven years of bad luck attached to such a catastrophe. Some lady my mother is. She's got this paranoia about class too. Not much more morality than an alley cat but very class-conscious. We had some builders in once, putting a fancy conservatory extension on to the dining-room. There was one in particular, he might have been the glazier, about twenty-five, and handsome enough in a Greco-Turkish way, and I could see by the way she kept giving him little sidelong glances that she'd have given a lot to lay him. I found it amusing since old

6

Turkoman thought he was on to a sure thing, and kept giving these white-toothed leers, but I knew my mother wouldn't touch him with a bargepole. Working class, you see. *Ethnic* working class which was worse. I really admired my mother for being able to control her libido like that. And, of course, it was the class thing that made her dislike Karen. A common little piece, she called her. And she was right. But it was precisely her commonness that appealed to me, and my mother could never understand that.

Two

I had just left school when my late father (RIP, as I think of him – but kindly) hanged himself. As befitted the only child of parents with pretensions I had been shipped off to boarding school, to Downside to be exact, a bastion of Benedictine learning. And I loved every minute of it. Those entrusted with our formation were dab hands, big on *education* as opposed to teaching. Mind you, I had a couple of things going for me. To begin with, I found the whole business of learning something of a doddle since I have both a photographic and highly retentive memory. This meant that I could while away the hours in class, daydreaming while others toiled, and it took only a few days of intensive cramming for me to breeze through any exams they set me. This made me the darling of the teachers who regularly held me up as an example; it also put my welfare in jeopardy since, as anyone who has been to boarding school knows, it can be fatal to be admired by teachers, and were it not for my other asset I would, no doubt, have been given a difficult passage by my fellow pupils. That asset? Well, I have been endowed with quite the most enormous penis you can imagine, a gigantic organ, something to boggle the mind. Even dormant it far outstrips your average tackle; when awakened it is a king among genitalia. It caused considerable consternation when making its debut in the showers: juniors recoiled from it, seniors drooled in jealousy. And from that remarkable unveiling I was given *status*. I was also given a wide berth, even when dressed. It was almost as though I carried a Luger Parabella in my belt, and was the deadliest shot in town. Bless it, it permitted me to lead a charmed existence, and indulge in a sort of Borgia patronage, those favoured only too willing to perform pesky tasks for me, believing themselves to be phallically protected. Not that I abused my position. I'm not that sort of person. The furthest I ever went was, on occasion, as a special treat for a job well done, to allow some callow, awed junior to stroke it, to tickle its stomach as it lay on its back, so to speak.

Meanwhile, while I was having the time of my life and thinking how really good it was to be alive, giving no serious consideration as to what I was going to do with the rest of my life, RIP was up to his neck in it. I better explain that my dad was a really nice man, a real gentleman, always calm and considerate, and ready to listen. Not many people do that now, do they – listen. They might *hear* you but they don't listen to you. That's what I find anyway. But my dad did, and just by talking to him problems seemed to solve themselves. I think the right word to describe him is meek. He was quite small, and thin, not at all good-looking, but he had these terrific twinkly eyes that put you in good humour just by looking into them. He and his partner, Francis Twiston-Jones, shared a practice in Harley Street. They were gynaecologists, and bloody good ones too, very popular with the nobility. My mother says there are more aristocratic arses bouncing about the polo-fields because of RIP than because of any other gynaecologist in Britain. Anyway, some old cow who was probably too old to be having a baby in the first place, lost it, and started saying RIP had been trying to have it off with her. I don't think anyone really believed her, but you know what rumours are like, and soon poor old RIP was being seen as some horny old lecher. Snidey little bits started appearing in the tabloids although no names were mentioned. It went on for about a month, and RIP started staying at home a lot. To be fair, my mother was really good about it. Very solicitous. She perked up quite a bit too, and started looking at him in a new light. But it all got to be too much for RIP, and one afternoon, while my mother was out getting her hair done, and I was seeing about tickets for a trip to Greece RIP had promised me, he hung himself.

As luck would have it I was first home, and found him dangling in the stairwell. The only thing I really remember about it now is that his eyes were popping out of their sockets, and they'd stopped twinkling.

After the funeral, and after the will had been proven, my mother sold the house in Sloan Mews and we moved to Ritherdon Road in Balham. That's where we have the conservatory I was telling you about, and interior design by Panache, and a kitchen by David Fortune. RIP left quite a lot of money, and a pile of shares. My mother got most of it, of course, but I got fifty thousand and his collection of coins, so I was well pleased. My mother got his BMW, but she gave it to me since she can't drive. I didn't use it all that much. No point. Spend most of your time looking for parking or worrying about getting clamped or if some lout is going to scratch the paintwork. Anyway, the Tube is far more interesting, as I found out. It was on the morning Tube from Balham to Warren Street that I first saw Karen. And that wouldn't have happened if chance hadn't taken a hand in things, if the Victoria line from Stockwell hadn't been closed for some reason making me carry on all the way on the Northern line through Kennington. I was still feeling pretty disgruntled at this altera-tion to my routine travel arrangements when the train stopped at Waterloo and Karen got on. She sat directly opposite me: even that seemed to be down to destiny since it was the only seat available, and only then because this other woman made her gum-chewing brat of a son stand up, letting Karen sit.

At first – for the first few minutes, that is – I found myself looking at her in only a casual way: the way you eye people in the Tube because you've nothing better to do, really. She was wearing a big, multicoloured, loose-fitting sweater over faded blue jeans, and her long blonde hair, the colour of white sand, tumbled over her face as she read *Smash Hits*, mouthing the words with wide, unlipsticked lips. Then I started to think about her in a practical way: that she'd make a pretty satisfactory lay. Then I began to feel the kind of desire that could be seen as aberrant. Perhaps it was because she was so used to people looking at her that my staring made no impact on her. Or perhaps she had trained herself to ignore the unsolicited attention of prying eyes. In any case she behaved as if she was alone in the carriage, behaved quite naturally, and had, to my mind, an air of total innocence. Once she lifted the magazine a little and peered closer at the photograph of some pop star, George Michael I believe it was, and I became that unshaven fellow, staring back at her from the page with alien eyes, seeing her as unknown, forbidden territory, inviting exploration. Like some lonesome Peeping Tom unable to credit his good fortune, I dared not blink, determined to soak up every detail of her.

And I think it was at the moment when she finally

stood up and left the train at Leicester Square that I began to work on the fantasy that she wasn't a stranger at all.

Needless to add, it was the Northern Line and not the Piccadilly that had the pleasure of my full custom from then on.

Three

It had always been assumed that I'd go to university, but what with RIP's suicide, and moving house, and my mother's blatant hinting that she needed me round her for a while, until she picked up the pieces, as she put it, university was put to one side and, through friends of friends, I got a job as a reader in a publishing house run by a vindictive midget called Consuella Kelly. It suited me fine, although I was surprised I didn't seem to need any special qualifications apart from being able to read. I was given my own office, although I use that term lightly since it was a cubby-hole under the stairs, a converted toilet, I suspect. It had a desk, a chair and a bookcase. There was no window so the light burned as long as I was in it, making it stuffy. One of the first things I did, stamping my territory, was to buy one of those NO SMOKING signs and stick it on the door.

What I was expected to do was read through the piles of unsolicited manuscripts, write a report on them, and pass them on to one of the senior editors –

mostly, it struck me, time-warped Sloane Rangers who wore long skirts and fairisle pullovers and who sat on the floor a lot. You'd really be amazed at the garbage people send in: there must be whole tribes of frustrated Jilly Coopers squatting in the Cotswolds. But every bundle of trash had to be sifted through just in case that elusive bestseller was lurking there. I soon got the knack of things, got the hang of speed reading – very useful when you learn to skip the moronic spewings. All the manuscripts had letters attached, and you could usually tell from these what you were in for. I used to groan at the ones which started, 'Dear Sir or Madam, I know this isn't perfect but . . .' That meant it was a right load of crap, and I'd take considerable glee is saying so in my report. In fact, I really enjoyed doing those reports, making them little gems, relishing the sense of power I possessed as I scorned the years of labour some prat had submitted. Indeed, my reports soon came to be recognised as small masterpieces, and would be passed around, admired and chuckled over, until it got to the stage when editors would stick their heads into my office and ask if I had anything jolly for them to read. That was a very popular word in 1991: jolly. 'Anything jolly for me today, Marcus?'

I'd been there about eight months when, out of the blue, when I was truly least expecting anything worthwhile, *A Letter from Chile* found its way on to my desk. It was a bleak, miserable, drizzly Wednesday morning, and I was in a foul mood. My mother had kept me up half the night telling me how her bridge partner, Billy Dunlop, was a total idiot, always overbidding, and why she continued to play with him she could not understand.

'Get someone else,' I suggested logically.

'Oh, I couldn't do *that*,' my mother said.

'Why not?'

'You don't *do* that.'

'Why not?'

'You just don't *do* it, dear. That's all.'

And some bastard had been in my office during the evening and dropped a half-smoked cigarette into my coffee mug. It was a mug I'd bought myself, one I was particularly fond of, one that *seemed* to make the coffee taste better, a black one with a golden M painted on it in Gothic script. This infuriated me to such an extent that I had no hesitation in smashing it, even knowing that I'd have to make do with one of the disgusting plastic mugs for the rest of the day. And I hadn't seen Karen on the way to work that morning, which really pissed me off. I'd been seeing a lot of her. Every Monday, Tuesday, Thursday and Friday I saw her. She didn't use the Underground on Wednesdays or Saturdays. I knew about Saturdays because, even though I didn't have to go to work I went up on the Tube anyway for a couple of weeks just to see if she was on it. She wasn't, so I had to content myself with my four-day-a-week observations. I stopped sitting near her. I used to take up a vantage point further down the carriage and watch her from there. For some reason I didn't want her to notice me. Not yet anyway. I still didn't know who she was or where she lived or where she worked, but I was learning small things about her. I knew, for instance, that she had a pretty limited wardrobe, and that she had a routine about what she wore. Mondays was the sweater and jeans. Tuesday a short black skirt and blouse. Thursday was the jeans again but with a fluffy, angora sweater, a greeny-blue one. Friday was the black skirt again with a different colour of blouse. She changed her hair at random, sometimes leaving it free the way I'd first seen it and the way I liked it best, sometimes piling it up on top of her head, sometimes in a ponytail which didn't suit her at all. I knew, too, that she had a girlfriend called Sharon because one morning there was this other girl with her, and when she got up to leave at Piccadilly she said, 'Bye, Sharon', and Sharon just said, 'See you later', which disappointed me as I thought she might have given away her name. What else did I know? Yes, that she had a charm bracelet with a broken catch because one morning she spent the whole journey trying to fix it but had to give up and toss it into her handbag. And that she used Impulse because she gave herself a little spray of it when she thought no one was looking. All the while I was planning our first meeting, what I'd say, what she'd say, where we'd go on our first date – dinner I thought, which made me wonder what she'd eat.

Anyway, that's as far as I'd got on that lousy

Wednesday morning. I'd just noticed the fag end in my coffee mug when Carl Duffy, Camp Carl from the delivery room, came in with my daily load of garbage. I was very rude to him, snarling instead of having our usual witty morning chat (he could be *very* funny, Carl could), clearly hurting him, making him give me the sort of look he probably gave a favourite pick-up after a lover's tiff.

There were five manuscripts that morning. Three were professionally bound so I knew the authors had been browsing the pages of something like the *Guide to Submitting Manuscripts Act*. You know the sort of thing, one of those pamphlets brought out by ladies who dabble in writing between collecting for Guide Dogs or the Lifeboats, or Piccaninnies as they used to be called before Race Relations got out of hand. 'Editors are very busy people and if you want your manuscript to be considered it must be presented in such a way that . . .' – bullshit like that. One of the others was, Jesus, it must have been over a thousand pages long and I was in no mood that morning to wade through any such epic. That left the fifth. I've no idea why it caught my eye. It was no different from hundreds of others I'd condemned. It looked to be a couple of hundred typed pages in a clear plastic folder. I picked it up. Through the plastic I read *A Letter from Chile*, by Helmut Kranze. Nothing very extraordinary in that although the title was catchy enough. I turned the page. 'For John Speed'. I turned another page. 'And in vapour reached the dismal dome, no cheerful breeze this sullen region knows'. Oh, Christ. I felt my enthusiasm waver, yet turned another page. 'From the moment I could first think reasonably I knew I would kill somebody.' I perked up. I also felt a curious shiver run down my spine. 'I did not, of course, know which person I would kill or how many, but I recognised there was the compulsion to murder in my genes.' Incredibly, I found myself shaking. Deliberately I stopped reading and closed the manuscript. I leaned back in my chair, swinging on the back legs, and closed my eyes. Nothing but the words 'compulsion to murder' came into my consciousness. I sat forward and took a sip of milky coffee from the wretched plastic mug. I stared at the manuscript, feeling decidedly odd. I can only say that something, some mad imp within my brain, told me that this book was meant implicitly for me, although I am aware that this is quite an outlandish claim. Nevertheless, that was the sensation that overwhelmed me. I put the manuscript in my brief-case, whirling the two small combination locks carefully, making certain each showed a different selection of numbers. Then, in an effort to dismiss my disquiet, I pulled one of the bound efforts towards me. *Betty's Christmas Party*. Oh, shit.

I went home by taxi that evening. I sat in it clutching my briefcase as if it contained treasure beyond compare, still wrapped in that strange, tingling sense of excitement. To tell the truth I was also a little scared.

It was as though I understood exactly what Helmut Kranze meant, as if I too had experienced those precise insights. Indeed, sitting there as the taxi juddered its way through the rush-hour traffic, it came to me how close I had been to killing someone already. At the time, if I had analysed it at all, I would have dismissed it, I'm sure, as a puerile whim, a daydream. But now, crossing Chelsea Bridge, it came back to me so clearly I wondered if, perhaps, had I not been gazumped, I might not have gone through with it. It was my final winter term at school, about three weeks before Christmas, and the subject of my wrath was Bertie Earnshaw, a right little shit who spent his time picking his nose and chewing over the diggings. A fat, flame-haired brute, he was forever farting, even attempting obscene melodies with his arsehole. As some of us carried the whiff of aftershave about our persons so Bertie Earnshaw wafted noxious gas. He was a bully of the worst sort, cowering when faced with anyone who could best him and then taking his cowardice out on some puny junior. One morning during Latin (*The Iliad* was being translated, badly, I remember) I decided, quite simply, to kill him. I saw no wrong in it whatever. It was as if, as I coolly plotted his extermination, my conscience had been numbed. Calmly, methodically, for I am, after all, a methodical person, I wrote down the possibilities:

1.   A severe tap on the head with a heavy hammer;

make it look like accident; push down stone spiral stairs from library to dormitories above?
2.   Drown in lake? How to get him there – dodgy. Have to be dead or unconscious first. Could I lug that fat corpse all the way to the lake by myself? Unseen? Unlikely.
3.   Poison? Too risky. Might wipe out half the bloody school. Cause a bit of a stir.
4.   Suffocation? No. Bastard would struggle and make too much noise.
5.   Garrotting? Make it look like suicide? A definite possibility. Swing the shit from the bell tower. For Whom the Bell and all that!

I had just about settled on strangulation when the bastard beat me to it, falling from a tree while pilfering apples in the out-of-bounds orchard, and breaking his stupid neck. Well, not breaking it precisely, but damaging it enough for him to be whisked off to hospital and out of my reach.

And now, thinking about it, as the taxi-driver called over his shoulder, 'Number ninety-nine you said, mate?', to which I answered, 'Yes,' coldly, since I dislike being called mate, it dawned on me that I had really intended to go through with that killing. It hadn't been a puerile fantasy. It had been nothing short of murder with malice well and truly afore-thought.

'Thanks, mate,' the driver said as I paid him.

'Don't call me mate.'

He looked taken aback. 'Sorry, guv.'
I let that go.

'Marcus, dear, you look quite awful. Aren't you well?'

I turned from my mother and peered at myself in the hall mirror. I didn't look too great. My face was unusually pale, and bluish about the jowls as though I hadn't shaved (I have very dark hair and have to shave twice a day, and I do this meticulously -- like dirty shoes, an unshaven face is a dead giveaway of someone down on their luck), and my eyes looked bloodshot, and had dark lines under them. I sniffed. 'Must be coming down with something. Some bug.'

'I hope not,' my mother said.

'I'll make myself a drink and go to bed.'

'You *can't* go to bed *now*.'

'Why not, for heaven's sake?'

My mother came closer and lowered her voice. 'Patricia and Richard are here,' she whispered, nodding slightly towards the sitting-room. 'With Heather,' she added, making that name sound significant.

'Oh, shit.'

'Marcus!'

Well, what did she expect? Just because she'd mapped out Heather as an acceptable wife for me didn't mean I had to agree, did it? Not that I'd anything against Heather. She was, as they say, a jolly good sort. *Very* into horses. So much so that she'd picked up some of their habits. Like when she laughed she'd throw back her head and sound like a mare in heat neighing.

'Marcus, darling,' Patricia Brazier-Young said, coming to me and pecking me on the cheek.

'Marcus, dear chap,' Richard Brazier-Young said, giving me his banker's handshake, friendly enough but not *too* encouraging.

'Hello, Marcus.'

'Hello, Heather.'

'Marcus thinks he might have a bug or something,' my mother explained, saying it with a certain reproach as if she suspected I'd deliberately gone out and netted the venomous insect. 'But—'

'Yes,' I interrupted quickly. 'You'll have to excuse me, I'm afraid. I feel really rotten. I just told Mother I'm going to make myself a hot drink and go straight to bed.'

Mother glared at me.

I stared innocently back.

'Very sensible,' Richard Brazier-Young stated. 'What you need is hot milk, whisky and a little sugar. Sweat it out of you.'

'Hot lemon, cloves and honey,' Patricia Brazier-Young prescribed.

'Yes,' I agreed to both.

'And a couple of aspirin,' the banker added.

'Anadin,' his wife preferred.

'Solpadeine,' Heather recommended.

'Yes,' I said again.

'Not *all* of them,' my mother put in sarcastically.

'No, Mother,' I said, with as evil a grin as I could summon.

Alone in my room, tucked up in bed, propped up on four feather pillows inherited from my grandmother, and a large Jack Daniels on the table beside me, I raised my knees, using them as a lectern, opened the manuscript and started reading again.

'From the moment I could first think reasonably I knew I would kill somebody. I did not, of course, know which person I would kill nor how many, but I recognised there was the compulsion to murder in my genes . . .'

Four

It was June, a glorious Friday morning, almost eight months since I'd first seen her, when I finally discovered Karen's name, appropriately enough in the Underground. I also got a bit of a shock that fine morning because when I stepped into the carriage and saw her, she had a child of about two sitting on her lap. That really threw me. I mean, I'm not stupid or anything, and I didn't expect her to be a virgin (let's be honest, there's not too many of those about nowadays, are there?) but I had her down as one in my dreams. And now there she was with that dribbling brat snuggling up to her. Oddly enough, I wasn't angry, just thoroughly hurt. No, that's not true. I was bloody furious, but it was that cold, dismal fury that only pain can bring, the smouldering kind that is most dangerous, and it made me do something which could have ruined everything, but fortunately didn't: I moved from my discreet vantage point and pushed my way down the carriage until I stood directly over her, holding on to the rail above my head, using my arm to shield my face. And then, just as I was feeling at my most abject, my luck changed. An old woman, sitting beside Karen, started to play with the baby's foot, and said something to Karen. I turned my head sideways, trying desperately to ear in on the conversation.

'He's such a dear little boy,' the old biddy said, gushing away in the manner old women do when their own families have grown up and left them to fend for themselves.

Karen smiled, showing a narrow gap between her front teeth, and bounced the baby on her knees. 'He's a girl actually,' she said. I don't know why it was but her voice came as something of a surprise. I suppose it was because I liked to imagine her with a husky, sensuous one that the flat, southeast London ('sarf-east', as I later learned she pronounced it) caught me on the hop. It shouldn't have since I knew she was pretty working class, and that was a big part of why I liked her. I'm not saying that I saw myself as a sort of Svengali or anything, not even that Shavian doctor in *Pygmalion*, but it was part of my plan to teach her things, one of them being how to talk nicely. And dress prettily, with taste. And I'd take her to concerts and the opera, maybe even the ballet although I'm not all that keen on ballet, something too poncy about the men for my taste. And art galleries. And as I would explain the Manets and the Monets she'd cling to my arm and stare up at me in wide-eyed wonder, and worship me. But that was all in the future.

'Oh, dear. I'm so *sorry*,' the old woman said, apologising directly to the child as if it cared. 'I'm very *silly*.' She tugged at the booted little foot some more. 'And what is your name, pet?' she asked, and really looked as if she expected the child to answer.

Like she was a ventriloquist, Karen answered. 'Karen.' Then she gazed down at the child and asked, 'That's your name, isn't it? Karen Burgess.'

'That's a lovely name,' the old woman conceded, although she didn't really seem all that enthusiastic.

'She's called after me,' Karen volunteered. 'I'm your Auntie Karen, isn't that right?'

I'm not even going to try to explain the relief I felt at hearing her say that. I could once more get back to the business of seducing this virgin in my dreams, after we'd known each other for a while, of course. And I knew her name at last.

When I left the train and walked the rest of the way to the office there was a spring in my step. It was all so curious. I honestly hadn't realised what a difference knowing her name would make. In a flash we had become more intimate, and it mattered not one whit that, still, she was quite unaware of my existence. Indeed, that was precisely how I wanted it. As I waited to cross the road near the office, another couple of sentences from Kranze's manuscript filled my consciousness: 'It is imperative, you see, that the stalker remain unknown to the victim. He must be a creature of the shadows, unseen, unheard, and, insofar as is possible, an insubstantial being.' And that's exactly what I was. For the time being anyway.

I should, of course, have passed the manuscript of *A Letter from Chile* to one of the editors, but I didn't. It was *my* book, and no one but myself was going to see it. Absurdly, I even felt a curious envy towards the John Speed character to whom the book was dedicated – I'd certainly have to find out who he was. I did contemplate sending the manuscript back to Kranze with a devastatingly cruel assessment, one which would, hopefully, make him toss it into the wastebasket and forget it. But such is the arrogance of authors there was always the risk he wouldn't believe me, and send it to some other publisher, and I couldn't have that. I decided on delaying tactics. I would write him a charming letter, saying that I had enjoyed his novel. That it had, in my opinion, potential (that's always a good word to use), and that, if he was willing to allow me, I would hang on to the manuscript for a while and see if I couldn't, perhaps, assist him in improving it. I did point out that publishing is a very, *very* slow business, and that he must not be discouraged if he didn't hear from me for a while. I thought that would give me a few months anyway. Then there could be another encouraging letter. Then, possibly, a visit to his home (he lived in Cricklewood – Cricklewood, for God's sake!) to discuss the work.

Then another couple of letters, and so on.

Mind you, I had mixed feelings about meeting Kranze. On the one hand, I wanted to. Desperately. I really wanted to talk to the person who had got so close to my being, to my soul. On the other hand, and I'm being truthful about this, I was scared. He might see through me, recognise me for what I was, and that was the last thing I wanted. I had to remain as insubstantial a being as he recommended. There was also the fact that he might disappoint me, turn out to be just some nut who'd happened to write a really good book instead of the wise old Freudian I had by now created in my mind, and if that turned out to be the case it would have made me somewhat ridiculous, wouldn't it?

So, that day, I wrote him a short, business-like note, acknowledging receipt of his manuscript and stating simply that I would be in touch with him as soon as I had had a chance to read it. That should keep him happy for a bit. I posted the letter myself at lunch-time instead of sending it out through the office system. As it left my fingers and tumbled into the box, a small shiver went through me. It was as though I had just committed myself to something, irrevocably.

'You must, above all, leave nothing to chance, but if chance offers you the unexpected opportunity to fulfil some element of your plan you must be ready to seize it, and manipulate it to your needs.' That

31

was what Kranze wrote. I didn't like the construction of the sentence much. Too – well, too pretentious, I felt, but I understood exactly what he meant. And chance, or fate, or destiny, or whatever you like to call it, offered me just such an opportunity that very afternoon.

When I got back to the office, the gaunt, bespectacled Nick Putty was leaning his buttocks on my desk, looking mournful as usual.

'Hi, Nick,' I said cheerfully. I liked him. He was in his forties, a melancholy creature, clinging to the remnants of his hippy youth. He was also the only editor for whom I had any respect, the only *real* editor in the place if you want my opinion.

'Marcus,' he replied with a nod.

'And what can I do for you?'

'Just thought I'd tell you I'm leaving.'

'What? Oh, shit. Why?'

'I'm bored. Time to move on.'

There was no answer to that, so I let it pass. 'Won't be the same without you,' I said, meaning it.

'Yeah, I know. The whole place will collapse.'

'No, I really mean it. You're the only decent editor here.'

He gave a small chuckle. 'Tell that to the Dragon Lady, why don't you,' which was how the midget Kelly was usually referred to.

'Fuck her.'

'No thanks.' He grinned. 'Anyway, Kate and me – you've not met Kate, have you?'

32

I shook my head.

'Well, we're having a few friends in tomorrow evening for a drink. Thought you might like to come.'

'Sure. I'd like that.'

He nodded. 'Got a pen?'

'On the desk.'

He scribbled something down on the edge of a manuscript. 'That's the address.'

I leaned over. 'Where the hell is New Cross Gate?'

'Off the Old Kent Road.'

'You live *there*?'

'Only decent place left in London to live, Marcus. About eight?'

'Fine. Look forward to it.'

'Casual.'

I eyed his jeans and scuffed, slip-on shoes, his Marks and Spencer shirt and cheap zip-up jacket. 'Really?' I asked, pretending to be surprised.

'Cheeky bastard,' he called me.

So, the next evening, appropriately dressed in a pale green sports shirt and black trousers, I took the Tube to New Cross Gate. I brought a bottle of Jack Daniels with me, just in case. Nobody ever seems to keep Jack Daniels in the house, and it's the only spirit I enjoy drinking. I also had a few carnations for Nick's wife, Kate. I like to bring gifts when I visit. It's polite, I think, and people like little surprises and, as you know, good manners is a bit of a surprise nowadays. I blame all that Women's Lib crap. You ever notice how it's nearly always the really ugly ones, the real *dogs* that are most in favour of it? I'd put the lot of them up against a wall and shoot them. You can't be a gentleman any more, if you ask me, without them looking at you as if you were queer or something – but that's another story. Female eunuchs, my ass: bloody dykes the lot of them.

Anyway, I left the station and stood there on the pavement for a while, blinking in the evening sun, trying to get my bearings. Naturally, I'd never been to that part of London before. To tell the truth I'd always thought of the Old Kent Road as one of those jokey places set aside for tourists, where the Pearly Kings and Queens made the odd appearance to keep the Japs happy. But now, there I was, standing in it, wondering who I could ask for directions. There were a couple of winos sprawled on the pavement, their backs against a railing, but they didn't seem to know the time of day let alone where they were, so I ignored them. And then – and I know this will sound incredible and like something I've made up, but I swear on my life it's true – walking towards me with another girl came Karen. They had a couple of videos and were discussing them, stopping every few strides to read the blurbs.

At first I felt something like panic, and thought about diving back into the Underground. Then I thought, hell, this is chance playing into my hands, so

I walked up to them and deliberately asked Karen's companion where Hatfield Gardens was, being very calm and nonchalant about it all. Oh, she said, you're going the wrong way, and told me to go back the other way and keep straight on until I came to a pub on the left called (what's it called, Karen? The Lion, isn't it?) The Lion, and opposite that, across the road, was a street that led to Hatfield Gardens. I said thank you very much, and smiled at her nicely, giving the tail end of the smile to Karen, and sauntered away from them, taking with me the delicious whiff of perfume. My heart was thumping. I longed to look back, but didn't dare. And when, eventually, I had to cross the road, I did look back, making it seem that I was just checking for traffic, they had both gone.

It's quite funny, but I wasn't upset. I was elated for some reason and, unable to control myself, I let out a great whoop. 'Yes!' I shouted, and elbowed the air like I'd seen footballers do on the telly when they scored a goal.

I was, as they say, the life and soul of the party, cracking jokes and being really witty. Drinking a bit too much as well, but that didn't matter since I wasn't driving.

When it came time to leave – I never like to be the last to leave – there were quite a few publishing types still there freeloading.

'I'm glad you came, Marcus,' Nick said. 'Would have been dull as shit without you.'

'Don't be silly, Nick. It was a great party.'

'Huh.'

'Honestly. I'm really glad I came,' I told him but I didn't, of course, tell him why . . .

I pulled down one of the folding seats in the taxi, and put my feet up. The taxi-driver gave me a bit of a glare in the mirror, but I narrowed my eyes and glared back so he thought better of saying anything. Then I closed my eyes, and began to think. It was time, I decided, to make my first move. I was due a couple of weeks holiday in ten days and I would use that time to find out everything I could about Karen, maybe even meet her – although that would depend on how things went. Yes, unseen and unheard I would – well, I would have to wait and see what exactly I'd do.

Five

Dear Mr Walwyn,

Thank you for your letter acknowledging receipt of the manuscript of my novel, *A Letter from Chile*. I look forward to receiving your comments, and may I say I am particularly pleased it has fallen into your hands?

Yours sincerely,

Helmut Kranze.

Camp Carl brought this letter to me, along with some manuscripts, fortunately only two, on Monday morning. On the face of it there seemed nothing untoward about it, yet the comment about him being particularly pleased it had fallen into *my* hands unsettled me. It could, of course, have simply been a plot to flatter me: authors will go to considerable extremes to have their masterpieces considered. However, I had an uneasy feeling that there was more to it than that. Perhaps the old Germanic devil knew something about me. Perhaps he was psychic. Perhaps he had received extraterrestrial vibes from my brain as I read his novel. All quite ridiculous stuff, I know, yet the disquieting possibility stayed with me. So much so that, for an absurd moment, I wondered if maybe he was about to start stalking me, just as I was about to stalk Karen; had, possibly, already started tailing me. I must admit that when I went out for lunch I did glance over my shoulder a few times to see if I could spot a likely Kranze lurking behind me, even pretending to gaze into a shop window and surreptitiously looking back down the street. There was no such candidate, of course, and by the time I got back to my cubby-hole I had succeeded in dismissing the notion.

By now I had photocopied the manuscript, keeping the original in my desk in the office, and the copy locked in an old oak chest in my bedroom. I had also underlined several passages, ones which, to me at least, were of significance. And now I took the folder from my desk and started reading some of those underlined sentences, dwelling for some time on the one which read, 'Undue haste and failure to plan meticulously are the downfall of every killer. Arrogance, too, is a perilous thing, entertaining the idea that one will never be caught. One should always approach murder with the concept that one will most definitely be apprehended if even the smallest precaution is carelessly overlooked. That is not to say one is forbidden to leave one's stamp of authority on the victim. Indeed, it can add greatly to the excitement if some small mark is left, some small identification of one's handiwork, but it must be such as will baffle the investigators rather than clarify the identity of the perpetrator.'

Why I should have dallied over this advice puzzled me. I had no intention of murdering anyone as far as I knew, yet in some indefinable way I was positive this counsel was meant specifically for me, and it etched itself on my brain. On impulse I decided to reply to Kranze's note, typing it myself, of course, instead of sending it to the secretaries.

Dear Mr Kranze,

Thank you for your note received this morning. I too am pleased it has fallen to me to assess the merits of your work since, although I have only had the opportunity to glance through it, I believe there may be the making of a publishable work here.

I will be away on business for the next few weeks, but on my return I intend to give your novel my undivided attention, and once I have assessed it properly I will be in touch with you again.

Yours faithfully,
Marcus Walwyn,
EDITOR

I wasn't an editor, of course, but I didn't want Kranze to know that. I didn't want him to think he was dealing with some underling. That would never do. For the same reason – to bolster my position, that is – I mentioned I would be absent on business rather than on holiday, leaving him to imagine me as a high-powered executive jetting off to conclude some fantastic deal.

Then, on a similar impulse that made me write the letter, I tore it up. I would let Kranze stew for a while. Temper his ego. I would concentrate on Karen, and see how that fared. Then, maybe, I would write to Kranze.

'It's not like you to stay at home for your holidays,' my mother observed when I told her my plans. 'You said you were going to Greece.'

'That was months ago. Just changed my mind. Tell the truth, I can't be bothered – all that hassle just to be on some island with a lot of Krauts.'

'That's not very nice, dear.'

'*They're* not very nice.'

Mother sighed. 'You know best.'

'Exactly.'

That sounds as if I was cheeky with my mother. I wasn't really. It was just the way we talked. We quite liked sparring. Anyway, I knew the reason she was upset I wasn't going abroad. She'd already started her affair with Harry Rutherford and she'd been looking forward to having the house to herself. And she knew I knew.

'Look,' I told her. 'You won't even know I'm here. I'll slip in and out like a shadow. And I'll eat out most of the time.'

She made a tiny effort to protest, probably that I needn't go to those extremes. 'And I promise I won't make any catty remarks to old Harry if we should bump into each other. How's that?'

'I wish you wouldn't—' my mother began, but then, as usual started getting flustered.

'Wouldn't what? Mention Harry?'

'Well – yes.'

'Come on, Ma. You're like a schoolgirl, for Christ's sake. Go for it, is what I say. Enjoy yourself.'

'You make it sound unnice.'

'*Unnice?* That's a new one. Anyway, as it happens, I think it's great.'

Mother looked surprised. 'You do?'

'Sure I do. Be different if you were laying some right prat, one of those chinless wonders you have cocktails with. But old Harry – he's okay in my book.'

'Thank you, dear,' Mother said, and then frowned, clearly puzzled and trying to figure out why she was thanking me.

'You're welcome.'

I must point out that my mother was really very good about not interfering in my private life, and I did her the courtesy of trying not to meddle in hers. I knew she thought it a bit odd that I never seemed to have any girlfriends, and over the previous Christmas she'd even put out a few little feelers to see if I was queer, like when that dreadful creature Julian Clary

41

came on the telly she'd say something like, 'I think he's *so* witty, don't you?' and eye me, and look disappointed when I didn't answer. On purpose. Once she even got blatant. There was a lot of talk about a Gay Rights march that had ended in violence when a few skinheads got involved. My mother said, 'I think it's quite awful that in this day and age people aren't allowed to be themselves and get on with their lives.' I kept schtum. 'I mean, they're just like us really, aren't they?'

'You think so?'

'Why yes, don't you? I mean if *you* were – well, if you were one of those it wouldn't change my love for you.'

'That's nice to know.'

'I mean—'

'What you mean, Mother dear, is that you want to know if I'm a bloody poof. Well, sorry to disappoint you, but I ain't. Okay?'

And for a moment Mother *did* look a little disappointed. I suppose she'd been reading somewhere, in the hairdresser's probably, how some scatty mothers like their sons to be queer so that they can hang on to them for longer and not have them taken from them by another woman. All down to loneliness, really. And my mother was basically a very lonely woman. That's why she screwed around so much, trying to prove to herself that she was still wanted. That's my theory anyway, for what it's worth. Part of it was my fault. I wasn't exactly what you'd call a doting son. I did love her and everything, but I'm very bad at *showing* my affection. I'm the aloof sort, which often made people think I was arrogant. I really don't believe I am. Don't get me wrong. I'm not given to that humble shit either. I'm very good-looking, and I know it. But when you get to know me I'm a very nice person.

To cheer her up, I said, 'Don't worry, Ma. If I ever do get married you won't be shoved off to some geriatric concentration camp.'

Mother winced at that, and I instantly regretted saying it. But after she'd taken a peep in the mirror and assured herself she was still a very attractive lady, she perked up, and latched on to my mention of marriage.

'You didn't say you had a girlfriend.'

'No. That's right. I didn't. Maybe that's because I don't.'

'Oh.'

'Well, not really.'

'Oh?'

'There *is* someone but you wouldn't call her my girlfriend. Not yet.'

'I *see*.'

'If things develop, you'll meet her.'

'Well, I should certainly hope so.'

I had to smile at that. I could just imagine the scene if my mother and Karen came face to face.

Undue haste and failure to plan meticulously are the

downfall of every killer, was what Kranze said. Well,
I wasn't about to kill anyone but his warning struck
me as being equally applicable to someone about to
do a spot of detective work.

The first time I deliberately set out to learn more
about Karen was three days into my holiday. Those
first three days were spent mostly in my room, quiet
as a mouse, planning meticulously. I even drew some
really silly diagrams about what my movements
would be, and, using a map of London, I traced
Karen's possible routes in red and my own, sneaking
along behind, in green. It took me quite a while,
almost one full morning, to decide which I wanted to
know first: where she worked or where she lived.
Knowing where she worked would certainly make it
easier for me to meet her. I could arrange to bump
into her, accidentally. But I wasn't sure I actually
wanted to meet her yet. Finding out where she lived,
what her background was, what her family was like
and so on would be more difficult, but when I *did*
meet her I would have all this knowledge stored up
unbeknownst to her, giving me a decided advantage.
However, presuming, as I did, that she lived somewhere near the Old Kent Road, I could foresee
enormous difficulties; after all, the Old Kent Road
isn't exactly the sort of place you can loiter without
inviting trouble. So, Plan A became following her
from the Underground and discovering her place of
work.

I dressed carefully (jeans, trainers, blue and grey

tartan shirt, windcheater) so that I would blend in with the other passengers on the Tube and with the majority of those people who seem to spend their days wandering aimlessly about the West End. And I purposely didn't shave that morning although I felt uncomfortable about being so scruffy. As an after-thought I put a baseball cap on backwards. It's amazing how your appearance alters when you hide your hair. It really changes your face, makes it look a lot thinner and older. Luckily my mother didn't see me leave the house or she'd have had a fit. My outfit might have been all right abroad, or maybe even, stretching a point, in the country, but only ruffians and thugs wore jeans in town, in her estimation. Anyway, she was still in bed when I set off.

Karen was on the Tube okay, but she had her friend beside her, the girl I'd seen with her the night of Nick Putty's party. You know, the one I'd asked for directions. For some reason that pissed me off although it was really to my advantage since they spent the whole journey chattering between them-selves and I could watch unnoticed. I felt a real dislike for the other girl. I suppose part of it was me being jealous of the way she was so familiar with Karen, but the biggest part was that she wasn't in my plan. Karen was supposed to be alone, not with that silly little cow in tow. But there was nothing I could do about it. She was there and that was all there was to it, although, looking back, or thinking back, I should say, it might very well have been at that moment the first stirrings of murdering her started. I can't be sure. I *seem* to remember thinking, 'I'll have to get rid of that one,' but maybe I thought that later, or maybe I did think it then but didn't really mean get rid of her in any permanent way. She had a terrible cackle of a laugh and I definitely remember telling myself that if I had to live with someone like that I'd strangle her within five minutes.

Anyway, they left the train together, still nattering like a pair of in-heat chipmunks, and I followed, sauntering, my hands stuck in the pockets of my jeans. They split up outside the station, giving each other half a dozen little waves the way girls do, and Karen made her way down Charing Cross Road. At the Court Theatre she turned left, and went down St Martin's Court and out into St Martin's Lane. She crossed over, walked down the road a bit and then turned left again into another of those little lanes and disappeared into a small, family-run pizza place next door to a bookie's. It was a bit of a dump to be truthful, but it seemed to do a good enough trade as there were quite a few customers in there already (Christ alone knows what time it opened at), mostly men – rough, big-bummed types, construction workers probably, or maybe night-shift workers, or security guards. Not anyone with Holy Orders anyway, although knowing what they're like there could have been a couple of them skulking about.

Imagination is a tricky thing, and mine had certainly

been hoaxing me. You see, I knew, of course, that Karen wasn't any great shakes on the intellectual side. I could tell that from the crap stuff she read on the Underground, and from the silly, giggly way she talked to her friend. So I must have known, too, that whatever job she did wouldn't be all that great, something pretty menial. That's what I must have known, but what I imagined was a different kettle of fish entirely. What I made her out to be in my mind was totally different from what she actually was, if that makes sense. A desired transformation, is what it was and that's a pretty common phenomenon, I hear. In my mind I saw her, sometimes, as a suave personal secretary to some high-powered magnate like the ones you see in the ads on telly for deodorant and sanitary towels that refuse to leak, the ones with mobile phones and convertible Volkswagen Golfs and dim-looking men in Armani suits cluttering about; or sometimes as a milliner, cajoling blousy old bags to buy her creations for Ascot; or sometimes even as a photographer's model – not that cheap page-three stuff – the glossy calendar brigade, shot by Armstrong-Jones, or Bailey, or that cousin of the royals whose name I can't remember. So, although personally I didn't give a damn, my imagination was pretty shattered when I saw her moving in and out of the tables, dressed in a red and white pinafore sort of thing, clearing away dirty plates and cups, and having a banter with the scruffs.

I thought about going in and having a coffee, but

decided against it. Badly dressed though I was by my standards, I'd have stuck out like a prick. She'd definitely have noticed me, and I wasn't ready for that yet. I also thought about hanging around all day and following her home, but I rejected that idea too. I wanted to keep that surprise for another day. You know, string things out a bit. Not have all the fun in one great dollop and be left with nothing to look forward to. So I went to the cinema instead. Went to see *JFK* as a matter of fact. I gave it an iffy verdict – a bit too self-indulgent, I thought; pity, because I'm a great fan of Oliver Stone. Of course I didn't go straight from the pizzeria to the cinema. It was only nine o'clock in the morning, for God's sake. What I did was a bit of window shopping, doing Fortnum's and most of Jermyn Street at my leisure. Well – not only window shopping. I did buy something which I'll tell you about later. And, by the way, Patrick Lichfield is the photographer whose name I couldn't remember.

I got home about seven. Harry Rutherford's Jaguar was parked outside the house, so I went in the back way, hoping to keep my promise to be inconspicuous. Ma's cat, Pissquick (no need to explain why we called it that, is there?), pussyfooted across the kitchen and rubbed its head against my legs, giving a miaow when I took some chicken salad from the fridge. I don't like cats much. I mean, I don't like the *feel* of cats much. I think it's because once you've got through all that camouflage fur you can feel their bones too easily. Always strikes me like you're stroking a bloody carcass. Anyway, just to annoy Pissquick I gave him a lettuce leaf instead of the chicken he was expecting, and I remember having a good old chuckle to myself when he gave me this filthy look, and went off, probably to grass on me to Ma.

Harry and my mother were in the hall when I came out of the kitchen.

'Marcus, dear,' my mother said. 'I didn't hear you come in.'

'Just got in. Hello, Harry.'

'Hello, Marcus,' Harry said, giving my clothes a wry sort of look.

'You look nice,' I told mother. 'Going somewhere special, are you?'

'Just out for a spot of dinner,' Harry said. 'You can join us if you—'

'Thanks, but no thanks. Just eaten as a matter of fact.'

'Ah,' Harry sighed, and sounded relieved.

'Harry's taking me to Le Gavroche,' Mother said.

'*Very* nice. I'd watch it, Ma. He must want something,' I said.

Harry blushed as usual, and I'd have sworn my mother gave me a wink only I know she'd never do anything so vulgar.

'We won't be late,' Mother replied.

'Take your time and enjoy it,' I told her.

'Are you in for the evening?'

'Why's that, Ma?'

'Just—'

'We better make a move,' Harry put in hurriedly. 'The table's booked for eight.'

'Have a nice time.'

That evening I decided to keep a record of my discoveries. Not a stupid diary or anything like that. A proper record, something I could refer to and chart my progress. I locked my bedroom door, and put on Haydn's *Missa in Honorem Sanctae Ursulae* CD, setting the volume pretty high. I like Haydn. Like him better than Mozart which pisses people off, people I know that is, morons who think old Wolfgang is the be all and end all. I happen to think he's overrated, but that's just my opinion.

Okay. Now it's confession time. You know by now that I don't approve of smoking although I'm not fanatical about it. If people want to kill themselves slowly that's up to them is what I say. But I have been known to smoke the odd joint. Like RIP used to have one whisky every evening 'for therapeutic purposes', I liked to have the odd roll-up for the same reason. I always keep a bit of hash in my room. I might not touch it for weeks. But sometimes, like that evening, I'll skin up and relax myself, and I can't see anything wrong in that.

So I rolled my joint and lay back on the bed letting the music sweep over me, feeling really good and contented. I finished it by the time they'd reached the

Sanctus, but I stayed on the bed, my eyes closed, until the Mass was finished. Then I got up and sat at the table in front of the window, and started my Progress Report. For some reason (and to this day I don't honestly know why except that the novel was playing on my mind) I headed it THE CHILE REPORT. Anyway, it had a nice ring to it. It gave nothing away. It was probably to be the only report ever where the title had practically no bearing whatever on the subject. I remember inserting a sheet of paper into my faithful old Olivetti, and staring at it for ages. Then I started to type:

THE CHILE REPORT

Name:	Karen.
Age:	Twenty-plus (plus three, maybe).
Description:	Five-six. Blonde. Slim. Nicely shaped. Small hands, long fingers. Perky breasts. Cute nose. Blue eyes set a bit too close, but bright and clear.
Occupation:	Waitress. Possibly part-time.
Place of work:	Calos Pizzeria, off St Martin's Lane, London.
Home Address:	Unidentified. Possibly near the Old Kent Road, SE14.
Marital Status:	Presumed single.

Family:	Unidentified apart from one niece: Karen Burgess, aged two years approximately.
Relationships:	Only one girlfriend identified.
Remarks:	Appears to be of a friendly, outgoing nature. Easily approachable. Works Monday, Tuesday, Thursday, Friday. Dresses neatly but in cheap clothes. Appears to rotate clothes on a regular basis. Reads trash magazines. Probably hooked on TV. Likes videos. Owns one charm bracelet (broken).

Well, there wasn't a hell of a lot there. I was quite surprised at how little I actually knew since I *felt* I knew a great deal more. I read through it again in case I'd missed something, but couldn't think of anything to add, although I was amused to see I'd typed Calos Pizzeria as her place of work. It should have been *Carlos*, but when I'd been watching her at work I'd noticed that the 'R' had almost been obliterated by rainwater from a leaking gutter above, making it look like Calos, and it was Calos, not Carlos that had been photographed by my mind.

I put the typed page in a blue folder. On the folder,

in thick felt pen, I wrote THE CHILE REPORT, and then, more for fun than anything else, I added, STRICTLY CONFIDENTIAL.

Then, determined to get a move on over the next week or so, I went to bed.

I was still awake when my mother got home. She spent a while in the hall with Harry, probably having a cuddle, and then he left. There was nothing unusual in this. He very seldom stayed overnight. They were afternoon lovers, more like.

Ma never came into my room uninvited. She was very good about that. I quizzed her about it once and she was genuinely surprised that I'd asked. 'Why, I respect your privacy, of course,' she said, and meant it absolutely. But if invited, there was nothing she liked better than to come in and have a little chat, sitting on my bed, relaxing and nattering as if we were pals.

I heard her come up the stairs and pause outside my door. I heard her give a tiny knock – just loud enough for me to hear if I was awake, but not loud enough to wake me if I was asleep. 'I'm awake, Ma,' I said, and she came in, gave me a quick kiss on the forehead, and settled herself on the edge of the bed. 'Had a good time?'

'Very nice, dear.'

'Good. You like old Harry, don't you?'

'Yes. Yes I do. He's very thoughtful. Very kind.' She thought for a minute as if something had just struck her. 'Yes I *do* like him,' she added more positively. 'Do you?'

'Me? Yeah, he's okay.'

'*That's* not being very enthusiastic.'

'Ma, it doesn't matter what I think, does it? You're the one who's – who's going out with him.'

'I know, but . . .' She fell silent.

'You're not thinking of marrying him, are you?'

'Good heavens, no,' Ma said a bit too quickly.

'Well, then, doesn't matter a damn what I think. You just enjoy yourself.' My mother got up from the bed and took a little wander. 'Would it be *so* awful if . . .' she began, toying with the bits and pieces on my mantelpiece.

'If you married him? Of course not. I just happen to think you could do better, that's all. He's pretty dull, isn't he?'

I should have watched her more carefully, but I'd closed my eyes, trying to imagine Harry Rutherford and Ma coming out of the Registry Office to a shower of confetti, so I got a jolt when the next thing she said was, 'And what's this, dear? THE CHILE REPORT?'

I sat up in bed like a shot. She had the folder in her hand, but hadn't opened it yet. 'It's private, Ma.'

'I can see that – "Strictly Confidential". But what is it?'

I gave a little laugh. 'Can't tell you, can I? It's strictly confidential.'

My mother has a habit of jumping to conclusions. I've no objection to that since they're usually the wrong conclusions and that has suited me well on a number of occasions. Like the time I killed the budgie. When I was about eight we had a budgie. I don't know where it came from. Neither Ma nor RIP were likely to have bought it, and if it was a present it must have been someone with a really warped mind who gave it to them. It was kept in its cage in the kitchen, and was the butt of some of RIP's poorer jokes. Like when Ma had this dinner party and served grouse, RIP announced from the head of the table, 'See you got rid of that damn budgie then, dear.' Anyway, come Guy Fawkes' night there was a radio programme telling everyone to cover the cages of their canaries and what have you since the explosions of fireworks could kill them. That intrigued me. So when RIP and Ma had gone to bed I crept down to the kitchen and burst a paper bag next to the budgie cage. And sure enough, down it went to the bottom of the cage with a plop. What I'm getting round to saying is that Ma, of course, concluded that it was the fireworks that had done it. I mean to tell her the truth sometime.

'It's *very* mysterious,' Ma said now.

'Not really. Just something I'm working on.'

Ma latched on to that like a leech. 'You're writing a book, darling. That's it, isn't it? That *is* it. How exciting!'

'Maybe.'

'Can't I have a peep?'

'No, you can't. It's very bad luck to read anything before it's finished. Don't you know that? Brings on writer's block and stuff.'

Ma took me seriously. 'Does it really? Oh, dear. But you will let me read it before—'

'You'll be the very first to read it.'

'Promise?'

'I promise.'

'Oh, it's so *exciting*, dear,' she said again, and put down the folder, almost ran to the bed, and kissed me on the head again.

'Oh, yeah. Very.'

When Ma finally went to bed (only after assuring me that in her opinion I was capable of writing something to rival *War and Peace*) I put the folder in my wooden chest, next to Kranze's manuscript. They looked like bedfellows.

Six

On Monday I followed Karen home.

The weekend had been uneventful unless you want to call having sex with Heather Brazier-Young an event. The first time we ever did it she nearly fainted at the size of my enormous chopper and said, aghast, 'I can't take that,' to which I'd replied, 'It's the only one I have, take it or leave it,' to which she said, 'I'll take it, I'll take it,' so I gave it to her, every foot of it – every inch anyway. But by that weekend we'd done it so often it was no more than a happening, enjoyable enough, better than masturbating which I only rarely go in for. On Saturday I took her to the races at Windsor (Daddy had a super two-year-old running) and then screwed her in the stables when I took her home to Bray. It was as good a place as anywhere to do it, especially as the silly cow kept calling me her precious stallion. Anyway, I needed some compensation for the money I'd lost on Daddy's super two-year-old which ran like a camel and trailed in third-last. In a field of five. Blew up, the trainer told

Heather. Blew up, my arse. If ever there was a damp squib that nag was it, although I have to admit it did, eventually, win a seller in Redcar. When I hadn't backed it, of course.

Sunday I just lazed about, reading the papers, watching a bit of telly, nothing much else. Ma had gone to Scotland for the weekend to see her old school chum, Sue Fortune, at Auchencairn, so I had the house to myself. Myself and Pissquick who did quite well since Ma had left me a steak and kidney casserole, and I detest kidneys although I've never got round to telling her that. Cat must have thought it was Christmas, snarling away to itself as it ate its way through the whole casserole like it was a goddam tiger or something. I settled for an omelette, something I make very well, nice and fluffy. Trick is to put a few spoonfuls of soda water into the eggs before you beat them. I was going to have chips with it but couldn't be bothered peeling potatoes, and Ma, quite rightly, refuses to have those ovenready turds in the house. I'm not going to go into the whole question of fast food, but what I say is if you can't be bothered to take care about what you eat you deserve to be poisoned.

As I said, I followed Karen home on Monday, and sure enough she got off the Underground at New Cross Gate, and set off down the Old Kent Road, just like I'd done when going to Nick Putty's party. In fact, she crossed the road where I'd crossed it (and whooped, if you remember) and walked down the road that led to Hatfield Close, a pretty grotty block of flats which rose high and grey and forbidding into a bruised sky. I guess they must have been habitable enough when they were first erected as an answer to London's slums, when the defects were skimmed with plaster, and the lifts worked, and the stairwells were clean and reasonably well lit, and the rubbish collected regularly. But then, just like it did with high-rises everywhere, the damp and the vandals got to work, and the plaster started peeling off, and the cracks appeared. The lifts only functioned erratically, and the lights in the stairwells got smashed and were never replaced which made the weird grafitti legible only in the daytime, which maybe wasn't a bad thing, but it also made it a good enough place to urinate and there was a choking stink of piss that you could smell yards away. It was the sort of place social workers like to call dangerous just so they don't have to go there too often and make the effort to climb the stairs.

There was, 'tis true, a bit of landscaped ground surrounding the flats. At least, it was supposed to be landscaped, but it was more like wasteland to my way of thinking. Karen told me (I'm just mentioning all this now since it's not all that interesting and I don't really want to have to bring it up again when I'm telling you something of more importance) that nothing had been done with the land for years, and it wasn't until some Mrs Duffy went off her head and chucked her child out of the ninth-floor window that the Council started a sudden drive to improve the environment and make the underprivileged feel they weren't being overlooked by our terrifically caring society. She, Karen that is, told me too that for a while it all looked quite nice. There were rowan and maple trees, and berried shrubs, and big concrete tubs filled with daffodils and wallflowers in the spring, and geraniums and fuchsias in the summer. But in the scorching hot summer of 1987 most of the trees became parched and died, and the shrubs withered under the constant poison of pissing dogs, and the geraniums gave up the ghost and were left there all through the autumn and winter, and were still there the following spring, just brown stalks like wizened fingers reaching from the grave. In 1989 the tubs were taken away, and the trees and shrubs uprooted, and the whole place grassed over. The residents were happy enough with that, and entire families would move out on to the grass and sunbathe, maybe dreaming they were in Benidorm or somewhere. There were a lot of them there doing just that the evening I went there, the evening I followed Karen home, making it a lot easier for me to trail her into the block without her noticing.

It was one of the good days: the lifts were working. I watched and noted that the lift stopped where the little round disc showed 5. I gave it a few minutes and then went up to the fifth floor by the stairs.

There were three doors on the fifth floor, one of which looked like it had been kicked in some time recently and just hammered back into place. There was no way I could learn which one was Karen's, and I didn't want to be caught up there, so I came down again, taking the lift, feeling pretty frustrated as you can imagine. But when I got outside and saw all those people lying about on the grass I decided to join them, and sauntered over to a quiet corner like I belonged in the area, took off my shirt, and lay back with it under my neck, propping my head up nicely so I could keep an eye on the exit from the flats, and pretended to be enjoying the evening sunshine. Nobody gave me a second glance.

I'd been there maybe three quarters of an hour when two motorbikes roared up. They weren't up to much as motorbikes go, no Harley Davidsons, just some Japanese crap all chromed up with the sort of engines you find in a half-decent lawnmower. The men riding them were fake too, all leathered and helmeted like they were London's answer to that dimwit Evil Keneevil. They parked their bikes and went into the flats, and I'd just about forgotten them when they came out – this time with Karen and her mate in tow. That made me sit up, if you like.

Karen had her jeans on and her hair tied back in a ponytail. One of the men – about her age, I guessed, with short, gelled, blond hair combed forward – had his arm about her shoulder, and she was sort of snuggling up to him, like she snuggled up to me in my dreams. They stood by the bikes for quite a while, just laughing and chatting. Then they seemed to come to an agreement, and the lout took another helmet (which I hadn't noticed) from the pillion of his bike and gave it to Karen. The other yob did the same, giving his to Karen's friend, but I didn't give a shit about them. Karen put the helmet on and swung herself on to the bike behind lout number one, putting her arms about his waist, getting herself really close to him, giggling as he settled his backside into her. To be frank, I was fuming. Right, I said to myself. Right. And as I watched them ride off into the sunset, as they say, I knew that the time had come when I'd have to start making things happen, happen as I wanted to have them happen, that is.

When I got home I adjusted my Report. I erased 'Unidentified. Possibly near Old Kent Road, SE14', and put in '5th floor, flats, Hatfield Close, New Cross Gate, Old Kent Road, London SE14'. And I added 'One Yob Boyfriend' under Relationships.

I read somewhere that on the night before they go into action soldiers can make the whole process of war seem the most normal thing in the world, and sleep untrammelled sleep. It must have been something like that with me, because that night I slept like a baby, and woke up completely refreshed, ready for action, and feeling on top of the world. Even Ma (looking pretty refreshed herself after her weekend in Scotland) noticed it. 'Gosh,' she said. 'You're looking very bright-eyed and bushy-tailed. What have *you* been up to while I was away?'

'Oh, just the usual. A couple of orgies. Drunk. Out of my mind on speed. Just the usual.'

She gave one of her tinkly little laughs. 'Of course, dear.'

'Actually, I went out with Heather on Saturday.'

That pleased her. *'Really?'*

'Yes, *really*. Went to the races.'

'She's such a *nice* girl,' Ma said.

'She's okay.'

'Only okay?' Ma sounded disappointed.

'Come on, Ma. Don't push it.'

It was about eleven when I arrived at Calos Pizzeria. I didn't hang about just in case I got cold feet or something. I walked straight in and sat myself down. I purposely didn't look about the place but pretended to be engrossed in the paper I'd taken in with me. And I was a bit rude when Karen came to take my order: I just kept looking at the headlines and said, 'Just coffee,' when she said, 'Good morning. What can I get you?'

I made it up to her when she came back with the coffee though. I gave her a smile and said, 'Thanks very much.'

'You're welcome. Nothing else?'

'No thanks,' I said, and then gave her a puzzled look.

'Something wrong?' she asked.

'Oh, no, nothing's wrong. It's just – just that I've seen you somewhere before, I think.'

Karen gave me an 'oh, yeah, try another one' sort of glance, so I pushed on. 'I know,' I said, smiling like I was really pleased to have thought of it. 'In the

Tube. That's where I've seen you.'

She cocked her head a bit. I pretended to be racking my brains. She stayed there, looking down at me. I knew she was intrigued, and that she was interested in me.

'I use the Tube,' she said finally.

'You had a baby with you,' I told her, speaking hesitantly as if I was only slowly remembering the incident. 'And there was this old biddy beside you who kept playing with the baby's foot.'

Suddenly she laughed. 'That's right! Fancy you remembering that.'

Then some bastard called her, and she had to leave me. But the good thing was that she kept looking back at me, and she'd give small smiles every time she did, and I'd sort of nod back, not being forward or anything, just friendly.

When I finished my coffee she came over to take the money. I said, 'I come up on the Underground every morning. I'll talk to you next time if I see you.'

'Yes,' she said. 'Do that.' And she gave me a shy smile.

'What's your name?'

'Karen. What's yours?'

'Peter,' I lied.

'Well, Peter, you make sure you talk to me next time.'

'I certainly will. Bye for now.'

'Bye.'

And that was how I came to meet her.

Seven

Two things became clear very quickly: the yob on the motorbike was a lot more than just an acquaintance, and if I was going to get anywhere with Karen I was going to have to do something pretty decisive and radical about him. Funnily enough, it was Karen's girlfriend, Sharon, who put me wise. She wasn't being spiteful or nasty or anything, just putting me in the picture so I wouldn't get hurt, she said, which was decent enough of her I thought. Anyway, his name was Darren (which made Karen and Darren and Sharon – the odd one out being Paul, Sharon's boyfriend, and Darren's brother to boot) and he was a mechanic, aged twenty-two, very into the martial arts, and had been going out with Karen for the best part of four years, the same length of time that Sharon had been dating Paul incidentally.

I learned all this one lunch-time in Calos. It was the third-last day of my holidays and I'd been dropping in there regularly. Karen and I had chatted a bit but I'd not really learned anything much about her. I couldn't very well ask her anything outright since I didn't want her to think I was probing, and she seemed just as reluctant to ask me anything about myself. The closest she came to being nosey was when she said, 'Don't you ever work?'

'Of course I work.'

'It must be a great job you have.'

'Why so?'

'Well, you seem to be able to pop in here any time you feel like it.'

'Oh. I'm on holiday.'

'That explains it.'

'Start back again next Monday.'

'Does that mean I won't see you again?'

'Oh, you'll see me all right. Maybe not as often, but you'll see me.'

'Good,' she said, and sounded like she meant it. 'I've been looking out for you on the Tube but—'

'Like I said, I'm on holiday. Don't get the Tube in the mornings.'

'Oh. I see.'

'But it'll be back to the old routine next Monday.'

She brightened, I thought. 'So I'll see you *more* often,' she said with a little laugh.

Anyway, that day, the third-last day of my holidays, I dropped in to Calos as I said. I'd just about finished my coffee and sausage-roll when Sharon came in. Karen was at my table at the time so Sharon came over. 'Not finished yet?' she said to Karen, ignoring me.

'Give me ten minutes,' Karen told her. 'Sit down and I'll bring you a coffee,' she said. 'This is Peter. Peter, Sharon. You can talk to him.'

So, Sharon sat down opposite me, and then looked about the café. 'She'll never be finished in ten minutes,' she said.

I didn't answer.

'And we'll be late,' she added, giving a bit of a pout.

'For what?' I asked.

'We've got an appointment.'

'I guessed that.'

She relaxed a little. 'With our bank manager.'

'Oh?'

'All of us. Our boyfriends too,' she added pointedly.

I was very bland when I answered, 'Hope you get what you want. Just don't let him bully you – the bank manager.'

'We're just going to talk to him.'

'Oh.'

'About mortgages,' she volunteered.

'Oh,' I said again.

Then Karen came back with the coffee she'd promised Sharon, and Sharon said, 'You going to be much longer? The boys'll be hopping.'

Karen was quite testy when she answered. 'I'll be as quick as I can, Sharon. And they can hop as much as they like. We've loads of time.'

'Try and hurry, Karen. You know what Darren's

like when he's kept waiting – especially for something like this.'

'I *am* hurrying, dammit.' Then she leaned down and whispered something in her friend's ear, and Sharon flicked her eyes across my face so I knew it was something about me.

When Karen went off to serve someone else, Sharon asked, 'You known Karen long?'

'Not long. No. Don't really know her at all. Just have a chat when I come in here, that's all. Why?'

'You're wasting your time if you think—' she began, but stopped suddenly and gave me a curious look. I've often wondered about that look. I really think she was for that moment afraid of me. Maybe something had come into my eyes that frightened her. I've been told that my eyes can get really scary if I half close them and let what I'm really thinking show.

'Go on,' I said.

She shook her head and looked down at her cup, and muttered something I couldn't hear.

'Sorry?'

'It's nothing. None of my business.'

'What isn't?'

'You and Karen.'

'What about me and Karen?' I was enjoying this.

And that was when she pushed her coffee cup to one side, and put her elbows on the table and gave me this long spiel about how Karen had a boyfriend called Darren, and how they were madly in love, and how they were going to get married when they'd saved up enough money for a deposit on a house, and how she and Paul hoped to make it a foursome at the church since they were saving up for a deposit on a house too, and how all of them were inseparable and that no one could ever come between them, besides which Darren had a terrible temper and had already beaten the shit out of half a dozen creeps twice his size who'd tried to take Karen away from him, and how she didn't want that to happen to me since I seemed quite a nice bloke, and how – hadn't I seen Karen whispering to her? – well, that was her asking Sharon to warn me off, but not warn me off exactly, just put me in the picture so I wouldn't get hurt.

When she'd finished I gave her my most charming smile, and shook my head. 'You've got it all wrong,' I said. 'Like I told you, I don't even know Karen really. I'm not interested in her that way. I've got a girlfriend of my own and we're getting married this October.' I leaned forward. 'Look. I see Karen on the Underground sometimes. Seen her with you a couple of times. And I drop in here for coffee and we have a few words. That's all there is to it.'

I've never seen anyone so relieved in my life. She gave a great, heaving sigh and said, 'Thank Christ for that.'

I grinned. 'Anyway, I've got to go now. Nice meeting you.'

'Me too.'

'Good luck at the bank.'

'Thanks.'

'Bye, Peter,' Karen called from behind the counter, but I ignored her insofar as I didn't turn round and smile or anything. I just kept walking to the door and raised one hand in the air and gave it a bit of a wave like I'd seen Paul Newman do in some film and thought it pretty cool.

'Ma,' I said, 'is Harry coming round this evening?'

'No, dear.'

'Good. Get your glad rags on. I'm taking you out.'

I'm a bit impulsive at times, and this was one of those times, and as soon as I'd told Ma I was taking her out I regretted it. I didn't want to go out at all. I wanted to go upstairs and brood. But you know how it is: sometimes you get the feeling you should do something even if it's the last thing you want to do. Something tells you, do this, and you do it regardless.

Ma looked up. She was sitting on the settee making lavender bags for some sale of work in aid of the Wildlife Fund which she supported although I don't think she cared a hoot for wildlife. She got sucked into things. Fashionable things. Fashionable things organised by fashionable people. Like I had to live with bloody elephants for months just because the fashionable Joanna Lumley got all het up about them, even selling T-shirts for them in Covent Garden, but getting good publicity for herself into the bargain. Whales, too, were big for a while, and the poor little Nips who hunted them were anathema.

Ma even threatened to throw my Sony Walkman out, but didn't dare, but the Hitachi microwave went to Oxfam and a Zanussi took its place. I told Ma that Zanussi was Japanese-owned (which it very well could be for all I know) and that was about to follow the Hitachi until I told her I was joking. She got quite cross about that. 'You shouldn't joke about such serious matters,' she said in exactly the same tones she'd used when, oh, years earlier, she'd said, 'You shouldn't take the name of the Lord thy God in vain.' Need I mention the Ethiopians? In the name of the Lord my God all of a sudden they were my 'brothers' just because some dimwit – a tinted bloke like them – convinced Ma that we were all brothers despite the colour of our skin. Poor Ma. She'd fall for any crap if the right person said it.

Anyway, she looked up from her lavender bags and asked, 'You're taking me out?'

'Yeah. Why not? I feel like going out with a beautiful woman.'

Ma liked that, and simpered. 'But why me, dear? Why don't you take your Heather?'

'I said a beautiful woman, Ma. Not a bloody horse.'

Ma took her glasses off and peered at all the little empty bags lying beside her. 'Well, it's very kind of you, dear, but—'

'You don't want to go?'

'I do, but—'

'Look, just throw something on, and let's go.'

★ ★ ★

We had a really terrific evening. I'd had a brainwave
while I was shaving. Nick Putty had mentioned this
great pub down near where he lived, The Montague
Arms, so we drove there in the BMW. I had to stop a
couple of times to ask directions, but each time I got
out of the car so Ma wouldn't hear where we were
going. I wasn't being devious or anything. I just
wanted to surprise her.

Ma thought the pub was 'quaint', which was her
way of saying common, but after a bottle of wine and
some scampi (and after she'd knocked back a few
gins while I'd moved on to Coke because I was
driving) she loosened up and started enjoying herself. It was a huge place, The Montague, with all
sorts of maritime gadgetry hanging from the ceiling,
and model ships on the walls. There was a stage, and
on that the owner of the pub played drums and a
blind man played one of those keyboard things that
can be made to make the sound of every goddam
instrument in the orchestra. It was probably Japanese, but I didn't mention that. They were pretty
damn good too. They did requests and the locals got
up and sang. I tried to get Ma up (just fooling) and
we had a right good laugh about that. She's great
company, my mother, especially if you can get her a
bit giddy.

Anyway, everything was swinging along nicely
until I saw this young couple snogging on one of the
benches near the stage. You know how they used to

do it in those old Hollywood films: the hero would be talking to some broad and suddenly she'd change into his old flame, the one that probably died in childbirth or something, or maybe the one he was head over heels in love with before he got amnesia after a car accident? Well, that's how it was with me. A bit like that anyway. I was looking at those two snogging, not really paying them all that much heed, and suddenly they became Karen and that Darren, and I could feel myself stiffen and get really angry. It must have showed too, because Ma said, 'Are you all right, dear?'

I blinked, and Karen and Darren vanished. 'Yeah, I'm fine, why?'

'You looked strange, that's all.'

'What d'you mean – strange?' I really wanted to know.

'White, like you were about to faint.'

I gave a small laugh. 'No, I'm fine, Ma.'

So now you know why I told you about taking Ma out: seeing those two and thinking that they were Karen and the thug, it really confirmed that I had to do something about Darren. Eliminate him, as they say in the best gangster movies. And, in bed that night, I started giving this my most serious attention, and by the time I was ready to fall asleep I had definitely decided to kill him.

You'd think a momentous decision like that would be scary, but it's not. It's the most exciting sensation you can imagine. It gives you this awesome feeling of power. Just *thinking* about killing someone does that, and I couldn't wait to know what actually *doing* it would do to me. In fact, as I was to find out, it's this very sensation of power that can lead to you making mistakes, so you have to be very careful not to let it run away with you and make you rush into anything without giving it proper thought and consideration. Besides, if your killing is just a one-off you have to pay particular attention to detail. It's not exactly the sort of thing you can practise to make it perfect. I was thinking about this over a boiled egg and soldiers when I remembered Kranze had had something to say on that subject, but I waited, teasing myself, until Ma went out (being Saturday, she'd be off to Harrods) before going upstairs and verifying what, precisely, he'd written. Ma seemed to take forever getting ready, and then wanted to discuss what she was going to buy.

'I thought some smoked salmon would be nice, dear.'

'For me or Harry?'

'For you, of course.'

'Be lovely.'

'What about duck?'

'What about it?'

'Would you like me to get some?'

'Fine.'

'Anything else you'd like? Anything special?'

'Uh hùh. I'll leave it all to you.'

'I really enjoyed myself last night, Marcus.'

'Good, I'm glad, Ma. So did I. We must do it again.'

She'd barely closed the taxi door when I was in my room, taking Kranze's manuscript from the chest. I thought the passage I wanted was at the start of Chapter Three, but I was wrong, and it took me what seemed like forever to find it, tucked away in the middle of Chapter Four:

'In practical terms murder requires the same attention as any other serious undertaking, and it struck me that there is something to be said for practising once, or even twice, before performing on the primary victim. However, the subject of any such practice must be selected with considerable care. It must be someone who is easily overcome; someone incapable of putting up time-wasting resistance; someone on whom one will not have to waste too much time in killing so that more time can be allotted to perfecting those elements which can lead to one's downfall. For my part I chose an elderly female cripple, and my practice routine went swimmingly.'

I liked that – Kranze's little joke. Swimmingly, indeed, since he'd drowned the woman in her bath. However, that sort of random selection didn't strike me as all that satisfactory. How much better, I thought, if the practice victim could in some way be utilised, as well as practised upon, to make the murder of the primary victim that much more simple.

I put the manuscript away again, and went to the loo. Sitting there, finished but having a little rest, I thought things through. Okay. Darren was my primary victim, but how was I to get close enough to him without arousing suspicion? I'd have to meet him, even get to know him, so that I could entice him into my web. And then it came to me. What if I practised on Sharon? Get her out of the way and wangle myself into Karen's company by offering my condolences and my shoulder to cry on – in a totally platonic way, of course. I could see her accepting that and letting me walk her home from the Underground. I could see myself having a cup of tea with her mother and saying, yes, wasn't it a terrible thing and what in the name of God was the world coming to. I could see Darren coming in and me saying how sorry I was for poor Paul who must be shattered, and Darren saying, thank you very much, and me saying, when it came time for him to leave, why don't we go and have a beer together and drown our sorrows, and him saying, okay, let's do that, and Karen looking at me and thinking what a nice, kind person I was, and thanking me with her eyes.

I left the loo feeling very pleased with myself. It was an idea, anyway. I'd have to give it a lot more thought, not rush willy-nilly into it. But of one thing I was already certain: Sharon was the one I would practise on whatever followed.

In the event things were to work out quite differently. I mean, the way I came to know Darren was nothing like I'd imagined in the loo, but killing Sharon went nice and smoothly. Swimmingly, in fact, only I didn't drown her.

Eight

I was back at work now so I didn't have that much
time to do anything, but I'd plenty of time to think
about what I was going to do. About Sharon, that is.
I found it interesting that once I'd made up my mind
to kill her she stopped being a person and became –
well, an object, I suppose. I could be really clinical
and objective when I thought about her, a bit like
those scientists who torture animals in their quest for
better cosmetics, I imagine.

So I started getting into work at the crack of dawn.
This meant I didn't see Karen on the Underground
which was very hard, but it was part of the plan: I
wanted to avoid her for the time being, and then
suddenly appear in her life again once Sharon was
disposed of, and be able to console her when she told
me all about it. And from the moment I got into the
office until lunch-time I'd whip through the crappy
manuscripts. My judgment was well respected by
now, and I'd been told if I came across anything truly
awful I could send it back off my own bat and not

bother those frightfully busy editors. Quite a few hopefuls got their masterpieces back during that period. If I didn't like the first three chapters – that was the limit I set – back it went with the little rejection slip. I suppose I might have sent back another *Under the Volcano* without realising it, but I haven't heard that I did. And that left me the afternoons to myself, and like I said, I spent them thinking about what to do. The main problem was getting Sharon on her own, and then getting her to come with me to some place where I could conveniently kill her. By now I knew she lived in the same block of flats as Karen, on the second floor to be exact. Karen let that slip during one of our chats in the café, a couple of days after she'd introduced me to Sharon.

'You seemed to get on very well with Sharon,' Karen said, pretending to be jealous, you know, stressing the 'very' and giving a little pout, teasing me.

'Oh, terrifically,' I said. 'Been talking about me, has she?'

'A bit.'

'I bet. Bet you two share all your secrets.'

'Yes,' she answered. 'No. Not all. Just most. She's my best friend.'

'Dangerous things, best friends.'

'What makes you say that?'

'Just joking.'

'Oh.'

'Known her long then?'

'All my life. Went to school together. She lives in the same flats as me, three floors down.'

'That's handy'.

Handy for them, but not for me. The last thing I wanted was to be seen hanging about those flats. But since Karen was in an expansive mood I decided to prod her a little, and although I knew full well Sharon didn't work in the café, I asked, 'She work here too?'

'Oh no. She works in Leon's – the hairdresser's just around the corner. She's learning.'

'That's why the two of you always look so glamorous, eh?'

'Of course,' Karen said with a giggle, and went off to deal with a fat bloke screaming for attention.

I also had to think about the method I would use. A gun was out of the question since I hadn't got one and hadn't the foggiest where they were obtained. Anyway, shooting struck me as a bit too ordinary, too mundane for something so important. Too removed, too impersonal. Just one little bang and she'd be dead without giving me the chance to enjoy it all. No, I shouldn't say enjoy. Without giving me the chance to *experience* it all, is what I mean. At that stage, the planning stage, I wanted to be able to *feel* her life leaving her. I suppose that's why I settled on stabbing her to death even if it might prove messy.

With that decided, the right place for the killing had to be fixed. Ideally I wanted to do it in my home. Everything there was familiar to me, of course, and that would make cleaning up (if there was any cleaning up to be done) all the easier. But with Ma there I knew it would be impossible. I couldn't very well have Ma walk in just as I was in the middle of things, could I? Easy as it was for me to twist her round my finger, something like a corpse lying in the kitchen would have taken a bit too much explanation.

And then, out of the blue, my old pal, Chance, came to the rescue.

'Darling?'

'Yes, Ma?'

'You remember the Whites?'

'Who?'

'The Whites, dear. John and Margaret.'

'No.'

'Of course you do, dear. Friends of your father's. From Texas. They came to dinner several times.'

'Oh, those. Yeah. I remember them. Why?'

'I had a letter from them.'

'I bet that made your day.'

'They want me to go and stay with them for a while.'

That sounded promising. 'In Texas?'

'Yes.'

'When?'

'They say any time.'

'So when are you off?'

'Oh, I can't possibly go.'

I knew Ma had already made up her mind to go,

but she wanted *me* to insist on her going so she could take off with an easy conscience and not feel in the least guilty about leaving me alone. I think it's because I'm an only child that she's so protective.

'Don't be daft, Ma. Of course you can go.'

'And leave you here all alone by yourself?'

'Ma, for God's sake. I'm a big boy now. You know I'm well able to fend for myself. Anyway, I can always get Heather over to do the cooking.'

Ma shook her head. 'I don't know—'

'I'll never speak to you again if you turn down this chance to see JR country. You've *got* to go.'

After a bit more argy-bargy Ma pretended to give in and decided to visit the Whites – only for a couple of weeks, she said as if a fortnight reinforced her reluctance to leave me.

She telephoned the cowboys that night and arranged to fly out in ten days' time. Ten days and two weeks made twenty-four days altogether, and it was within that time schedule that I would have to deal with Sharon. The very next day I started preparations in earnest.

I set the scene (in my mind), and went over and over what my actions would be, trying to foresee every eventuality. You can't do that, of course; not foresee *every* eventuality. All you can do is pick the most likely ones and make the necessary preparations to cope with those. Anything else has to be dealt with on the spur of the moment, but half the battle is *knowing* that you might be called upon to improvise. Anyway, it all adds to the excitement.

I'd decided on the kitchen, definitely, although I hadn't worked out yet how I would get Sharon there. I was confident I would, but not how. When Ma went to bed I'd go into the kitchen and just sit there, soaking up the atmosphere, taking note of the crockery and stuff that I might have to move in case there was a struggle. I didn't want anything broken or missing when Ma got back from Texas. Everything had to be exactly as it was when she left.

Also in those ten days before Ma took off, I started collecting my equipment. The first thing I ordered (but didn't collect since I would have had trouble explaining it to Ma) was some of that plastic sheeting that pretentious working-class people sometimes put down in the hall so the carpet won't get worn. You can get it in a variety of widths: I only needed two rolls to cover the kitchen floor. At the same time I ordered six (I had to get six since that was the minimum the snotty little assistant would let me have) heavy-duty, industrial waste bags. So now I had the blood-spattering covered and something to cart the body off in. What about myself? I'd probably get blood on me too, so I bought one of those phoney Second World War parachute uniforms from a shop in Tottenham Court Road where they sell all that sort of junk. I bought a pair of boots too, just in case, and a pair of leather gloves. I hadn't yet decided where I was going to dump the body but if it worked out anything like the films it was bound to be a murky, sodden place near a river. That done, all that remained was the weapon – a knife, obviously, but what sort of knife? Certainly nothing distinctive, no jagged edges or anything like that. I also didn't want to run the risk of buying it: shopkeepers are the world's worst when it comes to keeping their mouths shut and I could just see some publicity-seeking git phoning the police and saying, 'Oh, yes, Chief Inspector, I sold a knife like that to a right shady customer,' and, typically, giving a detailed description of me. I thought about using a kris that RIP had picked up in Burma and which was in a drawer in the hall table, but rejected that. In the end, I chose one of the kitchen knives, one of a set of Japanese steel ones someone had given Ma for Christmas years before and which had escaped her anti-Nippon demonstration because she hadn't a clue they were Japanese.

And there I was – ready.

Ma flew off to Texas on the Tuesday evening which suited me perfectly. Karen didn't work on Wednesdays, so I'd a good chance of getting Sharon on her own. I took that day off work, phoning in to say I had this awful bug that was doing the rounds, and spent the morning getting the place ready, concentrating, of course, on the kitchen.

The first thing I did was to put two mugs, the jar of instant coffee, and the sugar bowl beside the electric kettle on the worktop near the cooker. I put two spoons beside them. Then I spread that plastic stuff over the floor, overlapping the strips by about three inches. I put one of the industrial waste bags in the cupboard under the sink so it would be handy when I needed it. I pulled the curtains and went upstairs.

In my room I laid the parachute uniform out on my bed, making sure I could slip into it quickly. I unlaced the boots as far as was necessary to get my feet in, practising a couple of times. I put the knife on the bed beside the uniform, making a small ceremony of it, sort of bowing after I'd placed it there. To be truthful, I was amazed at how cool I was. No jitters at all. I was very excited, of course, but it was a kind of mathematic excitement, maybe like something a scientist gets when he hits upon a formula by accident and can't believe his luck.

When I left the house about midday, and closed the front door behind me, I leaned back against it and took a huge, deep breath, blowing the air out of my lungs in one long whoosh.

I drove up to the West End. I listened to Radio 3: Nigel Kennedy (who'd be good if he wasn't such an arsehole) playing Vivaldi. Inevitably that old saw about music calming the savage breast came into my mind, and for the first time it did dawn on me that what I was about to do was a bit savage, a bit tough on poor Sharon. But by the time I'd parked the car and made my way down to St Martin's Court (that's where Leon's was – upstairs over a jewellery shop) the effects of the music had worn off and I was back to my old self again. It was half past three precisely. I checked. I'd no real idea what time Sharon stopped work. I figured that, as an apprentice, she might work odd hours and could come out at any time. By half past four it crossed my mind that, maybe, she didn't work Wednesdays either. That didn't please me, I can tell you. I decided to wait one more hour, until five-thirty which was the normal time to close, and if she didn't appear by then I'd call it a day and try some other time.

At five past five she came out on to the street. My heart gave a thump that almost knocked the wind out of me. I started to walk towards her, nonchalantly, looking from one side of the street to the other, but manoeuvring myself so that I'd almost certainly come face to face with her. Then I heard her say, 'Hello, Peter.'

I was really delighted with myself the way I acted so taken aback. I gave her this long, hard stare like I sort of knew her but couldn't quite figure out from where. We'd stopped by now, facing each other. 'You are Peter, aren't you?'

I nodded. 'That's right. I'm sorry—'

'Sharon. Karen's friend. We met in—'

'Christ! Of course! Jesus, I'm sorry. I've a lousy memory for faces.'

She was carrying this big box that was sticking out

of the carrier bag, so I could see it was a duvet. 'Been shopping?' I asked.

She looked down at the box. 'Yes.' She giggled unexpectedly. 'It's a duvet.'

'Oh. They're good, those.'

'First one I've had.'

'They're good,' I said again. Then, 'Where are you off to now? Want a coffee?'

'Thanks but no. I've got to get home.'

'Oh. Okay. Well, it was nice seeing you again,' I said, and gave her a winning smile, and made to move off. Then I stopped and turned, and said as if it had just struck me, 'Hey, listen, you live near Karen, don't you?'

'Yes.'

'Well, look, I have to drive out that way. Got this friend who wants a hand decorating. You want a lift?'

She hesitated a moment, and I thought, Shit, she's going to refuse and that'll put paid to everything. You can imagine my relief when I heard her say, 'You sure? That would be great.'

'No problem.'

We didn't speak much as we walked to the car. Couldn't really. Not with all the zombies shoving into us as they made for home.

I put the duvet in the boot and waited until she was comfortably seated in the car (I could see she was pretty impressed with the BMW, looking about it, her eyes glowing) before I told her, 'I just have to nip back to my place on the way to pick up some old clothes to work in. Okay?'

'Where's that?'

'Balham. It's not *that* much out of the way.'

'You won't be long?'

'Two ticks.'

She wasn't thrilled, but she didn't object, and settled back in her seat, gazing at all the poor bastards hurrying for the trains, probably dreaming she was the Queen or something, and I left her to it, not interrupting, just giving her the odd sideways smile from time to time. I think she appreciated that. In fact, I know she did, because we were going over Chelsea Bridge when she said (I think meaning only to say it to herself), 'I feel like a real lady.'

She jumped a little when I answered, 'But you *are* a real lady, Sharon.'

She said, 'Thanks, Peter,' and gave me a really lovely, happy smile, and I thought, nothing like having her die happy.

We didn't speak again until we got to Ritherdon Road, and then she said something like, 'Oops,' as we hit the first hump. There's humps all the way up our road, put there to slow the traffic down to five miles an hour so the middle-class kids don't get run over.

I parked the car right outside the house and switched off the engine.

'This where you live?' Sharon asked, sounding surprised.

'Yep.'

'Very posh.'

'Oh, very.'

'You must have loads of money.'

'Loads,' I told her, and then laughed. 'Just kidding. It's my mother's house actually. I just squat here. Come on in and meet her.'

I could see she was dying to come in – not, I think, so much to meet my mother but to see the inside of the house, but she said, 'Oh, I couldn't.'

'Why not?'

'I just couldn't.'

'She won't eat you. She's really nice. You'll like her, I promise.' She still hesitated.

'Tell you what. You come in and meet her. Have a few words with her while I get my work clothes, and then we'll be off. Okay?'

She nodded, and gave me another smile. 'Okay.'

I don't like boasting but I have to tell you I gave an acting display the likes of which you won't see in a hurry. I closed the front door behind us and called, 'Ma! Ma! Where are you,' and was so convincing I half expected Ma to appear at the top of the stairs. She didn't, of course, being ensconced in Pensacola Court, Dallas, Texas 75211. 'Maybe she's lying down,' I said in a whisper, and ran up the stairs, gave myself a minute or two, and then walked down again. 'No. Sorry about that. She must have gone out.'

'It doesn't matter,' Sharon said, turning back to the door.

'Oh, shit. I've just thought. It's Wednesday, isn't it. Ma's bridge day.'

'It doesn't matter.'

'No, I know it doesn't. But I'd have liked you to meet her. Tell you what. Why don't you go into the kitchen and make us both some coffee while I change?'

'I—'

'Please. I'm gasping.'

Sharon nodded. 'All right, but be quick, will you.'

'Quick as a flash,' I told her with a grin. 'You'll find the coffee – instant, I'm afraid – on the side by the cooker.'

So, this was it. I got a fit of the shakes as I put on the uniform, and my fingers went sort of numb as I tried to do up the laces on the boots. But as soon as I got the knife in my hand, and slipped it into my pocket, a lovely calmness washed over me – if that's not putting it too dramatically. By the time I got down to the kitchen I was in complete control of myself.

Sharon had made the coffee, and as I came in she turned and asked, 'Where's the milk?'

'Oh. Sorry. In the fridge,' I told her.

She made a little face. 'And where's the fridge?'

I grinned. 'Over there,' I said, and made my way towards the corner.

'No. I'll get it,' Sharon said, like she was playing mummy, and moved in front of me.

It was over so quickly I could hardly believe it. I

shoved the knife into her and she sort of fell back into my arms, looking up at me with a quizzical look. Then she sighed, gave a gurgle, and was dead. I let her slide down on to the floor and stood over her for quite a while, just looking at her. She looked quite nice really, all peaceful, and younger in a way. That pleased me, even though I was disappointed that there hadn't been any of the excitement I'd imagined there would be. I mean, I don't think I'm what you'd call cruel, so I hadn't wanted Sharon to suffer, but I had wanted a bit of a thrill. I was even able to watch the blood seep out of her wound on to the plastic floor-covering in a detached way. It was just blood. It could have been water, or milk. I got the rubbish bag out of the cupboard and was about to start stuffing her into it when I noticed the two little lines on her forehead, directly between her eyes, crossing each other in the shape of a perfect crucifix. And then I remembered Kranze writing something about leaving one's mark on the victim, and I cut carefully along those two lines with the knife. Then I put her into the bag. She fitted snugly once I'd bent her double. Then, methodically, I set about tidying up.

I took off the uniform and put it over the pool of blood to soak it up.

I put four of the five extra industrial bags on top of that.

I washed the knife scrupulously and put it back on the rack.

I washed my hands thoroughly, and swabbed down the sink with Ajax.

I washed both the coffee mugs and wiped them dry.

I wiped the coffee jar and the sugar bowl and both spoons to take away any fingerprints.

I wiped down the whole worktop, and the drawer handles just in case she'd been nosing about.

I rolled up the floor-covering, keeping the uniform and the extra bags inside, and put it over in the corner with Sharon.

Only when I was certain that I'd done everything did I go upstairs to my room. I took off the boots and all my clothes and lay on the bed, naked, and fell asleep.

It was just after nine when I woke up, and I had to stay lying there for a while trying to get things into perspective. Although I knew there was a body downstairs I found it really hard to believe that I'd actually murdered someone. Finally, though, I got up, and got dressed. I put on my jeans and a sweatshirt and the boots, and went downstairs. There was no way I was going to get Sharon into the boot of my car without being seen so the only way was to be brazen about it. I just hoisted the bag on to my shoulder and went out to the car, opened the boot, and dumped Sharon in like she was a load of rubbish or something. Then I closed the boot and sauntered back to the house, stopping to smell some of the late climbing roses on the way, just letting anyone who *might* have been watching know that I didn't mind them gawking since I hadn't a care in the world. I used the sixth bag to stuff the rest of the paraphernalia into – the floor-covering, the uniform, the four remaining industrial bags – and took that out to the car too, in the same carefree way. Then, still taking my time, I got into the car and drove off.

I headed out of London towards Windsor which is near Bray where Heather lives. There are plenty of woody places out that way, just waiting for a body to be dumped.

It didn't take me long to find what I was looking for: nicely secluded, but not so secluded the body wouldn't be found. I took the bag out of the car and held it by the corners, letting Sharon topple out. Then I put the bag back in the boot, folding it carefully over and over so that no blood, if there was any, would leak out, and headed up the road to Heather's. At first I was disappointed that there was no one at home: I thought, maybe, I could use her as an alibi if it ever came to that – which I wasn't expecting it to, but one never knew. I drove down to the stables, thinking she might be there, but she wasn't. However, my luck was in. Behind the stables someone had been burning rubbish. It was still smouldering, and I couldn't help thinking there were idiots born every minute: fancy starting a bonfire that close to the stables and then going off without making sure it was out. Then I thought it was another sign of the fickle finger of fate, and I put Sharon's empty bag and the rest of the stuff on it, and then threw a handful of straw on top of that to get it going. All that plastic burned a treat and I only had to give the uniform a bit of a hand, more straw and a good poke, to see that go up too. When it was all burned I gave the ashes a rake with a pitchfork that was lying there, burned a bit of straw, and drove back to London, feeling well and truly chuffed. As a dress rehearsal it had gone perfectly. Not a single hitch. Not a single clue. Brilliant.

I phoned Heather after I got home. Not immediately after I got home. I had a bath first, soaking for ages, and fixed myself something to eat, some prawns which I defrosted in the microwave and then curried mildly. It was around eleven when I phoned Heather.

'And where were you this evening?' I asked, as if peeved.

'Over at the Clarks. Why?'

'Because, madam, I drove all the way out to see you, that's why.'

'You didn't.'

'Yes I did.'

'You should have let me know. I'd have waited for you.'

'Doesn't matter. It was just an impulse. Got bored sitting here all on my own and thought I'd call on my beloved.'

'Piss off, Marcus.'

We went on like that for a while, and arranged a date the following weekend, before I got bored and hung up. Okay, I thought, if anyone did see my car out that way, if some nosey bastard got my number, I was out at Heather's. How else would I have known there was no one home? All right, I could have telephoned, but that wouldn't account for my knowing about the bonfire which I was quite prepared to use if push came to shove. And now you're probably thinking what a half-wit I was: what about all the buttons and zips and things from the uniform? Sorry to disappoint you: there were no buttons and only one zip, on the fly. Everything else was kept closed by that velcro stuff (I told you it was phoney), and I'd taken the zip out of the fire, and brought it home without telling you. I meant to tell you but it slipped my mind. I probably thought you'd realise by now that I was intelligent enough not to have overlooked something as important as that.

It took them four days to find Sharon, and they only found her then because some architect on the way to the Lake District pulled in there so his Labrador could have a piss.

I'd been getting really cheesed off watching the news and hearing nothing. I'd almost taken it for granted that they'd *never* find Sharon when suddenly, on the Six O'clock News, red-haired Nicholas was telling me that the body of a woman had been found in some woodland about a mile from Windsor. He also mentioned that police were treating the death as suspicious, which didn't exactly come as the greatest surprise to me. And, of course, the tabloids were full of it the next morning, although the *Telegraph*, which is what I read, only gave it a paragraph on page three.

That evening Nicholas was back again, saying that the body of the woman found in the woods near Windsor had been identified as that of Miss Sharon Hayes, of New Cross Gate, London, and also telling us that the police were looking for witnesses and information.

I felt better when I went to bed that night. I could now get on with my plans. Four days wasted is a lot when you've got a tight schedule.

I hadn't altogether expected Karen to be working, and was quite surprised to see her when I dropped in to Calos the next lunch-time. She looked awful, all drawn and tired as if she hadn't slept for ages. I ignored all that, of course, and said, 'Hi, there. A coffee and a cheese and ham toasted, please,' all bright and breezy.

She gave me this really sad look, and said, 'You don't know, do you?'

'Know what?'

'Sharon—'

'Who?' I interrupted.

95

'Sharon – you met her in here once—'

'Oh, that friend of yours. Yeah, I remember. What about her?'

'She's been murdered.'

'*What!*' I shouted, so loud that it made everyone else in the café stop talking and turn round to stare at me. I lowered my voice immediately. 'What did you say?' I asked, sounding as near to aghast as I could manage.

'You must have heard about it. The woman found in the woods near Windsor.'

I screwed up my face and gave the matter deep consideration. 'I vaguely remember hearing *something*,' I said. 'But—'

'That was Sharon,' Karen said, and I could see she was about to cry.

'Oh my God,' I said, with feeling. 'Christ, I'm so sorry, Karen.'

She started to sniffle.

'Look, you shouldn't be working. Let me—'

'No,' she interrupted, luckily enough since I'd no idea what I was going to suggest she let me do. 'It's better me working. I don't have time to think about . . .'

I took a hankie from my pocket and handed it to her. She dabbed her eyes and handed it back. I was on the point of telling her to keep it, and then, just in time, I saw that letting her hang on to it would be a grave error. I took it back and put it back in my pocket.

'The least you can let me do is run you home after work.'

She shook her head. 'Thanks all the same. Darren's coming to pick me up.'

'Oh. That's all right then.'

I ate my toasted sandwich and drank my coffee trying to look like someone deeply troubled by the sad news. When it came time to pay I said, 'You take care of yourself now, hear? I'll drop in again tomorrow and see how you are.'

'Thanks, Peter.'

'I don't suppose there's anything I can do?'

She shook her head.

'I didn't think so. Anyway, if you think of anything you only have to ask.'

'Thanks,' she said again, and gave me a little peck on the check.

A nice little downpayment I thought, and went off happier than I'd been for ages.

Nine

I had to play it cool, as the expression goes, so I
didn't go near Karen for a while. My mother came
back from Texas looking tanned and quite youthful
with a new hairstyle that was as close as damned to a
Shirley Temple. For the first few days she affected a
drawl which really got on my nerves, saying things
like, 'ya'll', and 'have a nice day'. And the news on
Sharon had been overtaken by greater world-
shattering events. I supposed the police were still
plodding away trying to find the culprit, or trying to
fit some poor blackie up if they couldn't. Not that it
mattered to me one way or the other. Sharon was a
thing of the past. I'd just about forgotten all about
her; the wretched Darren now occupied my thoughts,
and I knew I could have problems with him. You see,
all that the practice session on Sharon had taught me
was that I *could* do it, but I'd guessed that before-
hand anyway. I hadn't actually learned anything
about the process of killing, and I was still in the dark
as to how I was going to rid myself of Darren –

couldn't very well ask him back for coffee. Probably couldn't use a knife on him either since he looked pretty strong – squat and strong, like a small wrestler, one used to street-fighting.

And then, when I was least expecting it, when I wasn't even thinking about murder, the solution presented itself in a quite spectacular way.

My mother had been to the theatre with some friends – the Aspinalls, I think it was – and I'd driven her to Shaftesbury Avenue and had promised to pick her up again after the show since Balham was well out of the Aspinalls' way, if it was them, but it was well out of the way of whoever it was. They'd gone to see *Five Men Called Mo* – or was it *Six Men Called Mo*? – which didn't run very late. I'd whiled away the time having an Indian meal in a place just off Leicester Square, and watched the buskers for a bit – not your old-time buskers any more, I noted, mostly West Indians as far as I could see, singing reggae and looking menacing if you didn't contribute to their welfare after each number.

Anyway, I was driving Ma home, not really listening to her as she prattled on about how good the show was and how brilliant the actors were, and hadn't those coloured people got just the most fantastic sense of rhythm. I was about halfway down Sloan Street when all of a sudden from this side street a motorcyclist came hurtling out into our path. It owed a lot to God, and a bit to my skill, that we avoided him, and all the bastard did was stick two fingers up in the air at me.

'The stupid brat,' was Ma's reaction. 'He could have been killed.'

And it was the 'he could have been killed' bit that clinched it. *That* was the perfect way to kill Darren. What could be simpler? A nice, tidy, explicable accident. Before I could stop myself, I said, 'Ma, you're terrific!'

'Thank you, dear.'

'I mean it. You're absolutely terrific.'

Naturally, I knew it wasn't going to be all that straightforward. I couldn't just crash into the cretin in my own car. In any case, I couldn't be sure where he'd be so I could eliminate him even supposing I was stupid enough to use the BMW. As the King of Siam was wont to say, 'twas a puzzlement. But I'd already felt the adrenaline starting to bubble again, just as it had when I'd been plotting how to dispose of Sharon. Even more so, I think, because of the extra problems, the extra risks, and most of all because this was the *real* thing, not just some silly rehearsal.

And I didn't have all that much spare time to think about it either. Certainly not at work. It was coming up to Booker Prize time, time for the shortlist to be announced at any rate, and editors all over the country were in their usual flurry, hyping books that were mediocre at best but in the running because they were written by unheard-of ethnics, or old hacks on their last legs but with a 'body' of work behind them, or because they were so god-awfully confusing they could be construed as deeply meaningful and therefore confound the judges. Our publishing house had a runner, hotly tipped by those in the know, an African saga written by a half-caste from Capetown, and everyone was getting sucked into the feverish activity. Even me. You know what they had me do? Look after bloody Kunte Kinte while he was visiting London. They expected me to wet-nurse the black sod. I was livid when they told me but, as it turned out, he was no bother at all. All he wanted to do was get drunk and screw white women. So, I'd make sure any interviews he had to do were timed for the morning. By four in the afternoon I'd have him out of his head on Vodka and Guinness. Then I'd haul him back to his hotel, give the doorman a tenner and a wink, and forget our great black hope. It worked like a dream. He kept telling everyone what a lovely man I was, and I wasn't about to disagree.

I may as well tell you that those in the know were wrong. He never even made the shortlist, so he was packed off back to Africa with his tail between his legs.

Anyway, with the shortlist announced, and none of our publications on it, things returned to normal. True, the place was a bit like a morgue for a while, but it didn't last long. In publishing, you see, there's always next year, always the masterpiece about to come in. Not to my desk, it didn't. I was still getting half a ton of crap every day, and getting depressed by it too. Maybe that's why I decided the time was right to drop Kranze a note.

Dear Mr Kranze,

I apologise for my delay in getting back to you, but I did warn you that the wheels grind slowly in the publishing world.

I have now had the chance to read your novel *A Letter from Chile*, and am delighted to tell you that I consider it a very fine novel indeed, and one which I am confident we will be able to publish. There are one or two points I would like to talk over with you, and I suggest that we meet at your convenience, and in a place that would suit you.

I look forward to hearing from you.

Yours sincerely,

Marcus Walwyn,

EDITOR

I was going to add a postscript asking him what he had meant by saying he was particularly pleased the manuscript had fallen into *my* hands, but I decided to leave that and ask him when we met face to face.

I had a letter back by return, not from Kranze but from his son, Klaus.

Dear Mr Walwyn,

I write to acknowledge your letter concerning my father's novel, *A Letter from Chile*.

Unfortunately my father is in South America at the

moment, and we don't expect him to return until shortly before Christmas. I will be speaking to him this weekend on the telephone and will inform him of your comments. I am sure he will be delighted. It goes without saying that he will contact you immediately on his return.

Yours faithfully,

Klaus Kranze.

A perfectly normal letter on the face of it, but I got the oddest sensation of unease when I read that Kranze Senior was in South America. You won't understand why because I haven't really told you what the novel was about, and I haven't done that because when I tried paraphrasing it in my mind it sounded very glib, very trite, and very staged. But I'm going to tell you now, and you can make up your own mind, as long as you remember I'm just giving you the briefest outline.

It's about this man called Werner Schmidt. He arrives, *in utero*, in England, from Germany, with his mother as you can imagine, just after the Second World War. He's sent to boarding school (just like myself) and loved it (just like me). But from his earliest recollections he feels that he is destined to kill someone, and is fascinated by this and wonders if someone can be born with murder in his genes, if one can inherit the desire to murder.

He's been told that his father was killed fighting for the Fatherland, but not much more about him. He has an uncle in Chile who writes to him every Christmas and birthday. To make a long story short, this uncle turns out to be not only his father but one of the more notorious killers of the Nazi régime to boot.

Now, you're probably thinking I'm out of my mind, and I know the synopsis I've just given you makes the book sound really infantile and dreary. You'll just have to take my word for it and believe me when I say it's an astonishing novel, and if they ever rescue it from my desk drawer and publish it (which they will if they find it) you've got to read it. I promise you won't be disappointed.

So now I can try and explain why I was uneasy when I read that Kranze was in South America. Somehow I knew he was in Chile, maybe checking up on his father (which would make the book more fact than fiction), and if the father bit was true, why not the rest of it? Maybe Kranze had killed off a few people just for the hell of it; maybe one *could* inherit genes that made one murder; maybe I was such a person; maybe Kranze had sensed that (not that I've any idea how) and maybe that was why he had written he was particularly pleased his manuscript had fallen into my hands, maybe he thought we were kindred spirits or something like that. The really strange thing was that, having considered all that I can honestly tell you, I didn't mind what sort of genes I had, but I'd be lying if I didn't admit it was scary nonetheless.

★ ★ ★

I did tell you we were Catholics, didn't I? Not great ones. Sunday ones. And it was coming home from Mass that the car started sounding rough, backfiring and things. 'Due a service,' I told Ma.

'Oh dear,' she sighed. 'That is a nuisance. I hate us not having a car. It's always when you don't have one that you *need* one.'

'It's a car, Ma. Not a policeman.'

'You know exactly what I mean.'

'Just kidding. Only take a couple of days at most.'

'I suppose you could hire one.'

'I suppose. We'll see. I will if it takes more than a couple of days – all right?'

It only took one day as it happens: something in the electrics that they fixed in no time probably, but charged me for a full day. I was happy enough to pay them though, because during that one day when the car was off the road I solved the first obstacle in what I was now thinking of as the Darren Incident: I'd go to one of those used car lots on the outskirts of London and get myself a banger, something I could cheerfully abandon after it had done its job. And that's what I did. I bought a clapped-out A-reg Sierra that had been round the clock fifty times. It sounded like a tank but it went well enough which was all I wanted. I paid cash and didn't haggle since I wanted to get in and out without any fuss, giving the salesman nothing to remember me by. I parked it in the underground carpark near Marble Arch, and took the Tube home.

Now all I had to figure out was some way to lure Darren to a convenient place and run him down.

It was Ma who supplied the answer to that one, too, although, naturally, she wasn't aware of it.

But first I want to tell you about the day my mother met Karen since it was pretty auspicious.

I hadn't spoken to Karen since the day she told me about Sharon being murdered. I'd seen her just about every day, though: not on the Underground because I'd been getting an earlier train like I told you, but at work. Just through the window of the café, just making sure she was all right. I didn't ever go in during those weeks. I figured with the police presumably still investigating, and Karen sure to be questioned, the less she saw of me the less likely she was to mention me, even by chance, casually. I was certain *she* wouldn't connect me with Sharon, but the police might. It would only take her to say my name in passing (even though it would be Peter which was false as you know) and they'd start nosing about, and the last thing I wanted was them arriving on my doorstep just then. I'm not very well up on police matters and I kept thinking they might have all sorts of sophisticated equipment (God alone knows what kind) that would allow them to trace me, even though I knew it was highly unlikely. Maybe I was just torturing myself, a sort of penance maybe, but not likely.

So, I'd just walk past the café and glance in and see her moving about between the tables, and think to myself how sad she looked, and how really beautiful, and how lonely, and how, when she really got to know me, her life would change and she'd be the happiest girl on earth – and me the happiest man, needless to say. It was very hard depriving myself of speaking to her, and maybe getting another little kiss.

Well, one Saturday, the last Saturday in October it was for the record, Ma wanted to go up to Fortnum's, so I drove her in – all that way for a few packets of Fortnum's Breakfast Tea, would you believe. Other things too, things that caught her eye and which she decided would be 'useful to have in the house just in case', but really it was the tea she was after.

I tagged along since I'd nothing better to do, and carried the shopping for her. She bought me a fancy pointed jar of peaches in brandy for being a good boy. She didn't ask me if I *wanted* goddam peaches in brandy, just bought them and then told me they were for me, forgetting there were at least half a dozen more at home – which was the number of times I'd been a good boy, I suppose.

Anyway, we were coming out of Fortnum's, out on to Jermyn Street since our expedition wasn't over and Ma had to get cheese from Jackson's, when we met Karen. I saw her before she saw me, and I know

now that I should have ignored her and let her pass, but I think it was the surprise of seeing her that made me say, 'Hello, Karen,' without thinking.

'Hello—'

'How are you?' I asked quickly just in case she was about to add Peter to her greeting.

'I'm fine,' she said.

'Good. Karen, this is my mother.'

Karen gave a wistful little smile and a nod. My mother nodded too, but she didn't smile I can tell you, and her eyes gave a sniff of disapproval if you know what I mean.

I don't remember what else we said. Nothing world-shattering, that's for sure. When we parted I knew Ma was itching to know all about her, so I didn't explain anything. Finally, after she'd bought her brie and Danish Blue, and we were back on the street, she asked, 'Who was that, dear?'

I acted the fool, looking up and down the street, and up into the sky. 'Who?'

'That girl,' Ma said sharply.

'Oh, Karen?'

'Yes. *Karen*,' Ma said, sort of spitting the name.

'Just a girl I know.'

'She's a rather common little piece, isn't she?'

I just shrugged.

'That accent.'

'I like that accent actually.'

Ma gave me a long hard stare, not stopping walking, just sideways.

'She's really pretty, didn't you think?' I asked.

'No, dear. I certainly did *not* think so.'

'Pity,' I said. 'I might just marry her.'

Ma did stop now. Dead in her tracks like I'd hit her. 'Marry *her*?'

I nodded.

'You wouldn't.'

'I might.'

'Marcus!' Ma said reproachfully, and I could see she was reckoning up how all my expensive education and careful upbringing had gone to waste.

'And then again, I might not.'

For a long time after that Ma used to ask me where I was going when I went out in the evenings, always wondering if I was slipping off to see Karen which, as you and I know, I wasn't. The funny thing is that if Ma hadn't been so inquisitive and so worried that she was going to end up with a 'common little piece' as a daughter-in-law she'd never have said what she did and given me the idea as to how I could get Darren into the open. It was a most innocent remark, one I'm sure she'd made a dozen times before but on those occasions had no significance.

It came about like this: one evening I was feeling really randy and decided to run up and see Heather. I was a bit surprised when Ma looked disappointed when I told her – that I was going to see Heather, not exactly what for – because I thought she'd be pleased. 'Nothing, dear – it's just – well, I'm going over to the Bensons and I was going to ask you to pick me up there later. You know how I dislike taking taxis late at night.'

'No problem. I can do that, sure.'

'Oh, thank you, dear. I don't want to spoil—'

'You're not spoiling anything. I'll be home by ten easily. What time d'you want me to collect you?'

'Would twelve be too late?'

'Be fine. Wimbledon they live, isn't it?'

'Yes, dear. Cedar Avenue. Number eleven.'

'I'll find it.'

Ma said, 'I know it's quite hard to find. I remember the last time I went whoever took me had great trouble finding it.'

'I'll find it.'

It was like as if Ma wasn't listening. 'What I'll do is phone Alice and get exact instructions and I'll leave you a note as to how best to get there. All right?'

'Fine.'

And that was it. It wasn't until late the next morning, after I'd serviced Heather, and collected Ma and taken her home, and was tucked up in my bed, that Ma's words 'I'll leave you a note as to how best to get there' resurrected themselves in my brain. Then it came to me in a flash. I was down at the flats. Darren's motorbike was parked outside. I walked up nonchalantly and slipped a note on to the plastic windscreen, sellotaping it firmly.

The next thing I was out of bed and at my table, composing. When I got the note exactly as I wanted it, I carefully rewrote it as I would normally write a note, in my usual handwriting. Then, keeping that beside me as a reference, I wrote it out again, only this time I altered my writing until it was just about the opposite of the original, so if the police ever did get on to me, and pull me in, as they say, and in their sly way say, 'Mr Walwyn, would you please write the words "I know who killed your brother's bird",' I could oblige with a willing smile and quickly write the words, and watch with some pleasure as they compared the two and see their crestfallen faces.

As you'll have gathered I started the note by stating, 'I know who killed your brother's bird', adding 'Tough shit!' – which I thought was pretty good, the sort of language that an oaf would understand and nothing like the way I would talk, and by revealing the fact that I was aware Sharon was Paul's girlfriend it would, I was sure, make the police think the murderer must be someone local, someone well known to the victim. Then I told him that if *he* wanted to know who it was he would have to meet me in a certain place, on a certain day, at a certain time, and bring a hundred quid, and come alone because he would be watched every inch of the way and if he told the police or was followed I would know and he could just forget it. I know a hundred quid is a paltry sum, but it was a figure I knew he'd have. On the opposite side of the paper I drew him the precise route he was to take to the rendezvous – an old hay shed up a track across the fields from Heather's house. It belonged to

Heather's parents and I knew they never used it. The day I chose was the following Sunday, the time eleven o'clock.

As you can imagine, having committed myself to time and date, I had to get my skates on.

Tuesday: Went down to the flats in the evening and spent about four hours wandering about, returning every ten minutes or so to the flats. Darren, the bastard, never showed. On the way home I remembered Karen didn't work Wednesdays so they were probably out somewhere.

Wednesday: Back to the flats. At seven twenty-five Darren arrived with baby brother Paul in tow, and both of them went inside. At seven thirty I stuck the note on his windscreen. Really wanted to hang about and watch his reaction when he read it. But didn't. By eight thirty I was home, having something light to eat with Ma, feeling pretty chuffed with myself.

113

Friday: Collected the Sierra from the carpark and drove out to Bray. Put the car in the hay shed and walked across the fields to the house. Told Heather the BMW had broken down and had been towed to some garage by the RAC. But she wouldn't mind running me home, would she? Of course she wouldn't, bless her, not after she'd chewed me raw and nearly choked herself on my dick. Made her think it was *her* idea to invite me for dinner the next evening, Saturday.

Saturday: Had dinner at Heather's. Pretended the plonky wine had gone to my head and let Mrs Brazier-Young insist that I stay the night. Had wanted to spend the night thinking about Sunday, but couldn't, not with Heather in my bed as soon as the house fell quiet, gnawing away, and then wanting to make passionate love until

about six when she finally
pissed off.

Sunday: D day.

I got up early, round about seven. I hadn't slept at all
since no sooner had Heather gone back to her own
room than the birds started twittering and the cattle
(Heather's father kept prize Charolais, something to
do with keeping redworm out of the fields where the
horses grazed) began bellowing. Anyway, if you're
used to sleeping through city noise you find the quiet
of the country very distracting and intrusive.

I made myself a cup of coffee and drank some
orange juice. I knew the family wouldn't be up for
hours – the Brazier-Youngs made it a habit of
sleeping late on Sunday and stuck to that routine as
faithfully as my mother did of going to Mass.

I left the house quietly at about half nine and
walked across the fields to the hay shed. I put on my
gloves before I started the Sierra and drove it down
the lane a bit, just as far as the bend. Then I switched
off the engine and just sat there, waiting. It was
twenty-two minutes to eleven. And it was while I was
sitting there waiting that it dawned on me what a
terrible risk I was taking. Suppose, for example,
Darren *had* told the police and a whole posse of them
arrived? What the fuck was I going to do then?
Then I thought, all I'd have to do is nothing. I was
quite entitled to be there. I was, after all, a guest of
the Brazier-Youngs. The Sierra might take some

explaining, but I could always say it was a surprise for Heather – a daft present for her birthday which wasn't due for another month, but she hadn't seen the car yet, had she, which was because I had hidden it in the hay shed. But supposing Darren arrived alone only he *had* told the police and they were waiting at a distance to nab me? Well, the killing could have been an accident, a very sad accident which wouldn't have happened if some toerag hadn't played a wicked hoax on poor Darren. Yes, I thought. I'd be able to swing it – there was still nothing whatever to connect me with Sharon's demise.

Then I heard the sound of a motorbike. I started the Sierra, and put it into gear. I let the engine idle after I'd given it one sharp press of the accelerator. The sound of the motorbike got closer. I took a deep breath, put my foot down and set off round the bend as fast as I could get the old banger to move.

Darren's bike hit me dead centre, and he went sailing over the top of my car. I slammed on the brakes and was out of the car in a flash. He was lying in the track, not dead, but maybe unconscious. Certainly he was well dazed. I jumped back into the car and slammed it into reverse. For a couple of seconds the damn thing wouldn't move, and I thought the gear-box was gone. But the car was only entangled in the wrecked bike, and after a few bits of forwards and backwards it released itself, and I reversed back as fast as I could, making sure one front and one back wheel went over the prostrate Darren. Then I drove forwards over him again. Then back again, and, for luck, once more forwards. Then I got out and checked him again. He was certainly dead now. He'd stopped breathing and there were small trickles of blood oozing from his nose. I raised the visor on his helmet and took a peep at his eyes. Nicely empty, I thought. Nicely dead.

And I went back to the Sierra feeling remarkably calm. I dragged the bike out of the way, and got into the Sierra. Like any suburban Sunday driver I drove to Windsor, and parked the car in the centre of the town. It was about lunch-time when I'd finished all that, so I took a taxi to the Roux restaurant in Bray, sitting quietly in the back, and making no conversation with the driver. I thanked him politely, and paid him, tipping him enough but not extravagantly. When he had driven off I walked back to Heather's house, and strolled into the hall, making some mad comment about how truly wonderful it was to take a walk in all that unpolluted country air, and, my God, I hoped I was invited for lunch.

Heather phoned me that night. 'You're not going to believe this,' she said.

'Well not much point in telling me then, is there?'

'They found a body on our land.'

'You're joking.'

'No, really.'

'Digging in the garden, were you?'

117

'No, silly. A fresh one. Just dead. A motorcyclist. We even had the police here. Ever so exciting.'

'I bet. What did you tell them?'

'Who? The police? Nothing. What could we tell them?'

'Just thought you might have said I'd done him in.'

She laughed merrily at that. 'And have you locked up? Who'd I have to play with then? You weren't even mentioned.'

That was exactly what I wanted to hear. 'Oh, well, it's all happening in Bray, then.'

'It certainly is.'

'Any idea who the poor sod was?'

'No. The police were being very glum about it. No fun at all.'

'They never are.'

'Not like you, my lovebird.'

'Goodnight, Heather,' I said firmly.

She blew a slobbery sort of kiss into the phone and hung up with a snort that was meant to be a laugh, I think.

And that was that. It was over, and I now had a clear path to pursue my interest in Karen. I was, to be truthful, exhausted. I lay there in the cool sheets, my hands behind my head, feeling drained.

It was 14 October. Allowing time for Karen to get over the shock of Darren's unfortunate death, I decided to continue my strategy of being pretty casual towards her for another couple of months.

Christmas, I felt, would be an appropriate time for me to claim her, the time of goodwill towards all men. And with that thought I fell asleep, dreaming only that Karen was standing by my bed, gently stroking my cheek. It was a beautiful dream, just like her fingers were kissing me.

BOOK 2

Ten

Inspector Maurice Birt was a small, thin man in his early fifties, and both his height and age worried him: to compensate for his lack of stature he tended to be excessively abrupt and aggressive, like a small terrier; to overcome the inevitable signs of ageing he dressed in somewhat trendy clothes – lightweight suits in pale shades from Next, his casual wear from continental-sounding manufacturers who upped the price and cunningly got free advertising for their products by embroidering their name on the garments, slip-on shoes from Bally. And sometimes all this worked, and did, indeed, make him appear younger than his years, but more often than not it failed, and he knew he was talked about with the usual jibes of being mutton dressed as lamb. It would have been different, he knew, if Helen had not left him: left him for what she had called a trial separation. But somehow, as they had both suspected it might, that separation had stretched from the agreed-upon three months to what – seven months? Seven and a half to be exact. But, yes, had a reconciliation been negotiated (and a few fruitless attempts had been made over those seven and a half months, all of them doomed to failure because of what Helen described, bitterly, as his neglect of her which, he felt, was unfair, and his obsession with his work, which was true) he would undoubtedly have been more inclined to age gracefully, and would maybe even be wearing the dull-coloured suits, the navy anoraks, the heavy-soled shoes that television had decreed as essential police uniform. But loneliness, and Helen's accusations, had made the ageing process rather more fearful, and although he admitted, if only to himself, that his attempts to hold it at bay by dressing youthfully were both useless and at times absurd, at least it all gave him a spurious identity, something he had found it necessary to develop once his wife's presence and companionship had been withdrawn. What still rankled was something she had said on their last meeting. 'The trouble with you, Maurice, is that you take murder so personally,' she had said. And he had answered, without thinking, 'It *is* personal, Helen,' and he had been amazed when, months later, he had reflected on that pronouncement, and realised that, yes, for some odd reason, no reason in particular, no reason he could put his finger on anyway, he had come to regard the murders of Sharon Hayes and Darren Cornell as a personal affront, to regard the killer of these two young people as a personal enemy, one who was out there, mocking him, laughing at him, enjoying his lack of success.

And now, on what was appropriately the Day of the Dead, he stood by the window of his office, and stared out gloomily. Behind him, Detective Sergeant Ray Wilson leaned his buttocks against his superior's desk, and waited. He was a heavy young man, running to fat already, something which embarrassed and irked him. He envied, but only mildly, the Inspector's natty clothes. He would have liked to dress with such style but with a wife, three young children and a heavy mortgage, it was out of the question. By way of compensation, he had recently allowed himself the luxury of a small moustache of which he was inordinately proud. It would have surprised him to know that Inspector Birt regarded him more as a friend than a work colleague since there had seldom been any indication of that.

He cocked his head and shifted his buttocks, making ready to stand, as the Inspector shook his head and turned from the window, saying, 'There's something staring us in the face, and we're missing it, Ray,' and immediately wishing he had not said it since it smacked of the suave Morse and the grotesque Wexford, both television detectives he loathed.

'We sure are,' Wilson agreed.

Inspector Birt nodded, and sat down heavily behind his desk, picking up a pencil and twiddling it in his fingers like a majorette's baton. He was still nodding when he added, 'After all these months we've got precisely nothing.'

'No suspect. No motive. No clue as to why they both ended up dead on our patch,' Wilson said, counting the depressing information on his fingers. He moved from the desk to a chair and sat down. 'You're still convinced we're just looking for *one* killer?' he asked tentatively.

Inspector Birt nodded again.

'No chance that there's two people involved and that the two murders are *not* connected?'

Inspector Birt would have none of that. 'It's one killer, Ray. And both the killings *are* connected. They've *got* to be. Nothing makes any sense otherwise.'

Sergeant Wilson gave a small laugh. 'Nothing makes sense anyway.'

'No, Ray. It *does* make sense. That's just the point. It does make sense, only we can't see it.'

'So where do we go from here?'

Inspector Birt took his time about answering. He knew where they went all right, but hated having to admit it. Then, suddenly, in a gesture of anger that was uncharacteristic, he slammed his fist on to the desk, and said, 'We start from the top again.'

Wilson sighed. 'I was afraid you'd say that.'

'Any better suggestion?'

'No.'

'Right then. Let's go,' Birt said, jumping to his feet and heading briskly for the door.

As they walked down the corridor to the Incident Room, Inspector Birt started to hum, not any particular tune, just a steady, not very musical purr. It was an ominous sign, Wilson knew. It meant the Inspector was getting thoroughly frustrated. It also meant long hours for both of them which, in turn, meant arguments at home, and Wilson wanted more than anything to avoid this, aware that his marriage, too, was a fragile thing, and the last thing he wanted was for it to collapse and for him to end up like his superior: alone, melancholy and feeling cheated.

Inspector Birt glared about the room, ignoring the lone WPC who typed rapidly in one corner, and growled, 'Doesn't anyone work here except us?' but in such a way it was clear he didn't expect any answer. He shoved his hands in his pockets, spread his legs, and gazed at the blackboard. 'Okay, Ray. Let's make a start. What *have* we got?' But before Wilson could reply he was answering the question himself. 'One dead female – Sharon Hayes. Lived in London, murdered somewhere, dumped here. Right?'

Sergeant Wilson nodded. 'Right.'

'No doubt about that? That she was murdered somewhere else and dumped here?'

'None. According to forensics.'

'Okay. Then we have one dead male. Darren Cornell. Lived in London within spitting distance of the Hayes girl, murdered here.'

'Right.'

'And definitely murder?'

'Definitely. The body had been driven over several times. Backwards and forwards.'

'Okay. So now we have two victims, both from the same area – south-east London. They knew each other. Darren Cornell was dating the dead girl's best friend – Karen Scott. His brother, Paul Cornell, was dating the dead girl herself. Right?'

'And had been for a few years.'

'Quite. And as far as we can ascertain, all four of them got on like a house on fire, went everywhere together, were planning a double wedding. No friction in the relationship at all.'

'None.'

'There's nothing to point to either Paul Cornell or Karen Scott as being our killer?'

'No. Nothing.'

'There doesn't appear to be any ex-boyfriends or ex-girlfriends who might be responsible?'

'None. Scott swears that Cornell – the dead one – was the only boyfriend she ever had,' Wilson said. 'Childhood sweethearts,' he added.

'Quite,' the Inspector said, but sounded cynical. 'And while Paul Cornell admits that he and his brother did have other girlfriends – other than Hayes and Scott – he maintains they were some time ago, prior to meeting Hayes and Scott, and that they were only brief acquaintances.' He took his hands from his pockets and folded them behind his head, stretching his back. 'And neither Scott nor Cornell can think of anyone who might have had a motive, *any* bloody motive, no matter how unlikely.'

'That's about it, sir.'

'There's nothing to link either victim to this part of the country, and the Cornell boy presumably only came here because of the note stuck to his motor-bike.'

'So it's the killer who must have ties here.'

Inspector Birt gave a small, tight grimace, and put his hands back into his trouser pockets. 'We don't know that. He *might* have. On the other hand he might not. He could just have chosen the place at random.'

'Surely he'd have to have had *some* knowledge of the area, sir? That lane where Cornell was killed would take some finding.'

Inspector Birt thought about that for a while, standing motionless, running his tongue back and forth across his teeth. 'The people who own the land through which that lane runs—' he said finally.

'The Brazier-Youngs.'

'The Brazier-Youngs,' the Inspector repeated. 'They saw nothing, heard nothing?'

'Not a thing.'

'No one hanging about in the weeks before Cornell was killed?'

'No. Mind you, they don't seem to be there all that often. He spends most of his time in the City, and she seems to travel a lot.'

'The daughter?'

'Never saw a thing, she says. Probably wouldn't if it didn't have four legs.'

Inspector Birt sighed and ran one hand through his hair. 'All right. Let's suppose he – or she – has *some* knowledge of the area, are we looking for someone local, or someone who comes here from time to time, or someone who came across the lane by chance and decided to use it?'

Sergeant Wilson shrugged. 'I'd go for someone who came here from time to time. A traveller. A sales rep, maybe.'

'Maybe. And then there's the car. Or van. We know Cornell was run over several times, and some transport was used for Hayes. Surely to God someone saw a car or a van?'

'No feedback on that at all, sir.'

Inspector Birt gave an exasperated whistle through his teeth. 'And then there's motive. What possible motive *could* there be, Ray? What links Cornell and Hayes?'

'The only common links are Karen Scott and Paul Cornell.'

'I know that,' the Inspector said testily.

'Just answering your question, sir.'

'Thank you.'

'As to motive – there just doesn't seem to be one.'

'There's always a motive. Always. We just have to find it. It's there, believe you me. It's there.'

'What about Paul Cornell? Could he have got tired

of Hayes and wanted the Scott girl and got rid of his brother?'

Inspector Birt turned slowly and gave him a sceptical look.

'I know, I know,' Wilson said. 'He didn't strike me that way either.'

'So, we've got nothing?'

'Looks that way, sir. If you like I'll take someone and question Cornell and Scott again.'

Inspector Birt turned and faced the Sergeant. His face was grim. 'You'll take me, Ray. And we'll question the whole lot of them again. Every bloody one of them.'

'Right.'

'And we'll start this evening,' Inspector Birt said.

'Ah. Em . . .'

'A problem with that?'

'I was supposed to be taking Jean and the kids over to her mother.'

'Well, you'll just have to postpone that pleasure.'

'I already have – twice.'

'Do it a third time.'

'We're here, sir,' Sergeant Wilson said, swinging the car into a line of rush-hour traffic and getting a wicked pleasure in rousing the Inspector.

Inspector Birt awoke with a start, gazing sleepily about him before uttering a grunt. 'Huh?'

'We're here,' Wilson repeated. 'This is Walworth. Thurlow Street's just over there on the left.'

'Oh,' Inspector Birt said, and glanced at his watch. He had slept all the way down to London. He hadn't wanted to sleep: he had hoped to use the journey to go over yet again their plan of action. But he had slept, just as he always slept in cars when someone else was driving, just as he always slept in trains and buses and planes. As soon as whatever transport he was using started to move, he collapsed into sleep. There was nothing he could do about it.

Wilson turned into Thurlow Street and drove slowly between the massive blocks of flats that gave the whole area an air of impending doom. It was drizzling, and the huge grey buildings wept. Pedestrians scuttled about like animals of the night caught unawares in the headlights of the car. A group of young men stood by one of the entrances, smoking, drinking lager from cans, eyeing the strange car with hostility. A large, flat-bottomed black woman dragged two children along, swinging them off their feet from time to time. A couple of stray dogs circled each other, each sizing up the opposition, their hackles raised.

'This is it,' Wilson said. 'Wendover Flats.'

Inspector Birt gave him a baleful look. 'I remember it, Ray.'

'Number 445 we want,' Wilson told him.

'I know.' The Inspector leaned forward and peered out of the window. 'What a wretched place to live,' he said, mostly to himself. 'How in God's name people *can* live here is beyond me.'

'Got to, don't they? Nowhere else for them.'

'But they shouldn't have to.'

'There's others a lot worse off.'

'That's not the point.'

Sergeant Wilson stopped the car, pulling in beside a rubbish skip. He wasn't about to argue. What he wanted was a cigarette, and was relieved when the Inspector showed no inclination to pursue the subject of rotten housing and the effect it had on the underprivileged, one of his pet topics. He rolled down the window, and almost guiltily produced his cigarettes.

'Go on,' Birt said. 'Kill yourself.'

Wilson lit his cigarette and drew deeply on the smoke, exhaling slowly and blowing the smoke out of the open window. He had managed to cut down to ten a day: it was this restriction that was killing him, he thought wryly.

The Inspector let him smoke half his cigarette before saying, 'I'll question Cornell, Ray. I want you to listen carefully to everything he says. See if you sense anything wrong.'

'You don't really suspect him, do you?'

'No. It's not that. Just sometimes there's – there's a hesitation that usually means they have something in their minds that they can't quite figure out. I mean, something they say reminds them of something else but they can't put their finger on it. If that happens, interrupt, for heaven's sake.'

'Right.'

'Ready?'
'Ready.'
'Let's go then.'

Inspector Birt yawned as the lift rattled its way up to the fourth floor of the Wendover Flats, and stopped with a shudder. The doors shuddered awhile before opening, and the two men stepped out, almost colliding with a youngster on a skateboard. 'Watch it,' Wilson said, and the child gave him an impudent look, and took off again, scooting down the concrete verandah that ran the length of the building. 'Good clip on the ear is what that brat needs,' Wilson remarked.

'Solves everything, does it – a good clip on the ear?' Inspector Birt asked.

'Teaches them manners.'

'I see. Manners, of course, would be so very important around here.'

'Wouldn't do them any harm to have some.'

'Wouldn't do them any good either, Ray. That's the trouble. Try and be decent in a place like this and you're a poof or fodder for the bullies.'

Cornell's flat was three doors down, and the two men took their time walking to it. Inspector Birt hesitated for several moments before pressing the bell: it echoed harshly within the flat. A sudden gust of wind sent rain spitting on to the verandah making him shiver. He had just started thinking that no one was at home when the door opened a couple of inches and a woman peeped out, squinting inquisitively before recognising him, and saying, 'Oh, it's you again.'

'Yes, Mrs Cornell. Me again. And DS Wilson too.'

'What is it now?'

'Is Paul in, Mrs Cornell?'

'Why?'

'We want a word with him.'

'You've already—'

'Another word, Mrs Cornell. It won't take long.'

Mrs Cornell opened the door wide, and stood back. She was a thin, gaunt woman with puffy eyes, and straggly unkempt hair. She had the look of someone who had been ill all her life but was probably as fit as a fiddle and tough into the bargain. 'Better come in then,' she said, adding, 'in there like before.'

'Thank you,' Inspector Birt said, making his way into the sitting-room.

'I'll get Paul. He's in the bath,' Mrs Cornell said pointedly, as if cleanliness was one of her priorities despite what people might say.

'Thank you,' Birt said again, and stared about the sitting-room. Spotlessly clean and tidy, it still had a musty smell to it as if, at some time in the past, it had been flooded. Behind the television some shelves had been erected, and on them was a collection of framed photographs: over one of these a black ribbon had been draped. Birt moved across and stared at it, pointing it out to Wilson with an inclination of his head. Wilson nodded back, but stayed where he was, waiting for Birt to turn back to the picture before sitting down in one of the two armchairs. Even without the black ribbon, Birt thought, even without knowing the young man on the motorbike had been murdered, you could have told that the smiling, happy face belonged to someone already dead. It was as though some light had faded from the eyes in the photograph the moment Darren Cornell had died, as though the photograph didn't just represent an image of the dead man, but mirrored him in some obscure way, fading and disintegrating as he died. Maybe, Birt reflected, that was why some Indian tribes in South America were so terrified of being photographed, believing the camera stole part of their life, part of their spirit at least. And perhaps they were right.

He turned slowly from the photographs as the door opened behind him. 'Ah, Paul. Close the door, will you?'

Paul Cornell closed the door, and came into the room. He flopped down on to the settee, looking from Birt to Wilson and back to the Inspector again. He wore only a pair of jeans. His hair was wet, and he had cut himself shaving: a small square of tissue was stuck to a cut on his jaw.

'You remember DS Wilson?'

Cornell nodded.

'Look, I'm sorry about this,' Birt said reasonably. 'But I need to ask you—'

'I've already told you everything I know,' Paul said, his voice quiet, strangely high-pitched, emotionless.

Birt nodded, and spread his hands, palms upwards in a curious gesture of supplication. 'Yes, I know that. But to be honest with you, Paul, we're getting nowhere. We don't have a suspect. We don't have a motive. And the longer this drags on the less likely we are to catch whoever it was killed your brother and your girlfriend. I'd sort of hoped you might have thought of something since we last spoke – something that you hadn't already told us?'

Paul Cornell shook his head.

Inspector Birt grimaced. 'Nothing?'

Cornell shook his head again. 'Nothing.'

Birt moved from the shelves, and settled himself into the other armchair, crossing his legs. He leaned back and made a steeple of his fingers, resting his chin on the tip of the spire. 'You see, Paul, there's *got* to be something more. I'm not saying you're withholding anything. But there sim-ply *has* to be something more. Something that's been overlooked. Something not mentioned because it doesn't seem important. Something that's simply been forgotten.' He paused, waiting for his words to take effect. 'Was there anyone at all – anyone – who might have had a grudge against Darren and you?'

'Not that I can think of.'

'Nobody you fell out with?'

'No.'

'No friends who might have felt—'

'Didn't have any friends, did we?'

'No friends at all?' Inspector Birt asked, sounding incredulous although he remembered this information from the first interview.

'No,' Cornell told him, looking surprised at the Inspector's tone. 'Didn't need any. There was Darren and me, and Sharon and Karen. That was it. We just cared about each other. Working most of the time, doing overtime – me and Darren anyway – so we could get the money together to get the houses we wanted. Get out of this fucking place. Get married. Have families of our own.'

'But before you and Darren met the girls . . .?'

Paul Cornell shrugged. 'Yeah, we had one or two girlfriends. Not even girlfriends. Just birds we'd meet at a disco or something. Nothing serious. But once Darren met Karen and fixed me up with Sharon, that was it.'

'And pals? What about pals before you met Karen and Sharon?'

'Yeah. We had pals. From the flats here, mostly. Knocked about with them like you do. Drinking and stuff. But like I said, once the four of us got together there was no one else.'

Inspector Birt glanced across at Sergeant Wilson, who merely nodded unhelpfully. 'All right, Paul,' the Inspector continued. 'What about Sharon?'

'What about her?'

'Was there anyone who might have – did *she* have—'

'Any enemies?'

'Yes.'

'Don't know that for sure, do I?' He rubbed a small tattoo on his left arm as if it had suddenly started to itch. He looked down at it, and kept staring at it as he said, 'Not as far as I know. Like I told you already, I met her about the same time Darren met Karen and we'd been going steady ever since.'

'And she never said anything to you that would make you think—'

'Never said anything about anyone wanting to kill her, if that's what you're getting at.'

'And you saw her the evening before she died?'

'Yeah.'

'And she was all right? Not nervous or anything?'

'No.'

'Nothing out of the ordinary?'

'Just the same as ever. We'd started buying stuff for when we got married. Collecting stuff for the house. We were all over at Karen's talking about that most of the evening. She—'

Paul Cornell stopped suddenly, and frowned. He put his hands to his head, one either side, and appeared to squeeze.

'She what, Paul?'

'It's nothing.'

'Tell me.'

'She was going to buy a duvet the next day in her

lunch hour. She'd seen them reduced in some shop near the hairdresser's and she was going to get one. I told her she was daft 'cause we hadn't got a bed yet, but she said we had to start somewhere, and that she was going to get this duvet whether I liked it or not.'

'You don't know if she did actually buy the duvet, I suppose?'

Paul Cornell shook his head. 'Never saw her again after that night.' He leaned forward and put his head in his hands.

'Okay, Paul. That's fine. That's something we can look into. See what I mean? That duvet – that's information we didn't have before. Now, is there anything else?'

'No,' Paul Cornell said, quietly through his fingers.

Inspector Birt closed his eyes for a moment, feeling genuinely sorry for the young man, giving him time. Then he asked, 'What about you, Paul? I know you said neither you nor your brother had what you'd call *real* enemies. But would you think about yourself specifically for a minute. If you can think of no one who would want to harm Darren or Sharon, was there someone who might have it in for you?'

'Me?' Paul Cornell sounded totally surprised.

For the first time in the interview Sergeant Wilson spoke. 'What the Inspector means, Paul, is that it was *your* brother and *your* girlfriend who were killed . . .'

'I fucking know that—'

'. . . so it is very likely someone was trying to—'

'Look, so not everyone loved me and Darren but, like, we didn't have enemies,' Paul Cornell said. He got to his feet and went to the window, staring out and down and about him, perhaps trying to cull from the darkness the spectre of some outrageous foe. 'Not those sort of enemies, anyway. Not fucking psychos. You try living in a shithole like this and you're bound to have people who don't like you, but they're not going to fuck about killing you.'

'All right, Paul. All right,' Inspector Birt put in. 'We know all this is very hard for you.'

'Too bloody right it is. Jesus Christ, if you ever catch the bastard I'll kill him.'

Inspector Birt ignored the threat, and said, 'We have to catch him first.'

Paul Cornell swung away from the window. 'You really don't think you will get the bastard, do you?'

'We'll get him, Paul. We'll get him. I promise you that.'

'And you expect me to believe that?'

'You better, Paul. You better. We're the only hope you've got.'

Paul Cornell gave a small snort and returned to the settee, sitting on the arm, swinging one leg.

'That leaves Karen Scott,' Sergeant Wilson said.

'What d'you mean – that leaves Karen?'

'You've just told us there was no one who had any grudge against you or your brother, and that as far as you know Sharon hadn't a care in the world. That leaves Karen Scott. Who hated her enough to kill *her* fiancé and *her* best friend?'

Paul Cornell hung his head, and shook it. He took to scratching his tattoo again. 'Like I told you,' he said quietly after a while, 'it was just the four of us.'

Sergeant Wilson looked as if he was about to ask something further, but Inspector Birt suddenly got to his feet. 'Right, Paul, thanks for your help. That's it for now. If you do think of anything else – *anything* else, mind – you'll let us know, okay?'

Paul Cornell nodded. 'You're not going to get him, are you?'

'I'll get him,' Inspector Birt said with uncharacteristic vehemence. 'I'll get him.'

'What do you think?' Birt wanted to know.

They were back in the car, sitting in the dark. Wilson had lit another cigarette and was trying to blow smoke rings, unsuccessfully. He abandoned the attempt and blew a mouthful of smoke out of the window. 'I'd say he was telling the truth.'

Inspector Birt nodded. 'So would I. Unfortunately. Leaves us precisely where we were.'

'Except for the duvet.'

'Except for the duvet. Now, that really *is* a help!'

Sergeant Wilson ignored the sarcasm and started the car. 'Scott?' he asked.

The Inspector nodded his head slowly.

'Right,' Wilson said.

'We'll reverse the procedure, Ray. You question Karen Scott.'

'All right by me.'

Already the Inspector could feel his eyelids getting heavy. He managed to say, 'Glad you approve,' before falling into a gentle doze.

There was something remarkably like desperation in Sergeant Wilson's voice when he asked, 'And what about at work, Karen? In the café?' He had already spent the best part of an hour and a half under the watchful, silent gaze of Inspector Birt, questioning Karen Scott, covering the same ground that Birt had covered with Paul Cornell. And the results had been equally unrewarding. There seemed to be no link between the four young people and the mysterious person who had killed two of them. And Karen's mother, a large, fat woman with heavily bandaged varicose veins and toothless on the top gum, hadn't helped, wheezing in and out of the front room, offering tea but keeping an eye on her daughter's well-being at the same time. In truth, Wilson's reference to Karen's workplace was a last-ditch effort. 'You're a very attractive young lady,' he continued. 'There must have been customers who—'

'Made passes at me?' Karen asked, then hung her head shyly. 'Some. But nothing to talk about. Just the usual. Jokey, sort of.'

'Did you ever go out with anyone from the café?'

Karen bridled. 'No. I told you that. The only person I ever went out with was Darren.'

'Yes. I'm sorry,' Wilson heard himself apologise,

and glanced at the Inspector who raised his eyebrows in an arch way. 'All I'm trying to do, Karen, is find someone who knew you, and knew either Sharon or Darren, or both. Did Darren ever come to the café?'

Karen was adamant. 'No. He didn't like me working there really. Said I was too good to be doing that sort of work. He never came near the place. He said it made him furious to see me serving people.'

'And what about Sharon? Did she ever come to the café?'

'Sometimes. Not very often though. Only when we were going on somewhere together. She'd come and pick me up then.'

'Going somewhere?'

'You know – shopping or something. Somewhere the boys wouldn't want to go. Or if we were going on to a party and didn't have time to go home and change.'

'Just you and Sharon?'

'What do you mean?'

'Just you and Sharon went to parties sometimes?'

Karen Scott still didn't seem to get the drift of Wilson's question. She looked blankly at him for a while. Then, slowly, it dawned on her and there was an angry touch to her voice when she answered. 'No. Not just the two of us. Darren and Paul always came too. I keep telling you: we wouldn't go anywhere like a party or a disco without Darren and Paul.'

'But you did it quite often, did you – go to parties?'

'No. Not often at all really. Only when someone –

maybe someone from Sharon's place, the hair-dresser's, was having a birthday or something. I can't remember when the last one we went to was. I can't—' Suddenly Karen stiffened a little. She looked away, letting her long, blonde hair fall over her face and taking her time before drawing it back with the fingers of one hand. Inspector Birt leaned forward. Outside, the lift door rattled open, a child screamed, a woman shouted, a door slammed, and then all was quiet again. 'Let's go back to the café, Karen,' Inspector Birt said gently.

Karen jerked her head towards him, as though startled. 'What?' she demanded.

'You've just thought of something, haven't you, Karen?' he asked, still keeping his voice low and gentle.

Karen Scott shook her head. 'It's nothing.'

'Tell me.'

'It's nothing. Really.'

'Let me decide that. Just tell me.'

'Just – there was this lad who came in sometimes,' Karen said, shrugging her shoulders.

'And?'

'And nothing. He just came in sometimes. I told you it was nothing.'

'So why mention it?'

'I don't know. Look, maybe it was your asking me about – I don't know. I just remembered that the last time Sharon came to collect me this lad was there. All of us – Sharon and Darren and Paul and me – we had to go and see the bank manager to talk about getting mortgages. You know, to see if we could get them – to see if what we'd saved was enough to get them – and Sharon came to pick me up and he was there.'

Inspector Birt and Sergeant Wilson eyed each other. Both men felt a small tingle of excitement. The Inspector nodded to Wilson, and leaned back in his chair.

'Tell us about him, Karen,' Sergeant Wilson said. 'Take your time, and tell us everything you can remember about him.'

Karen Scott gave a small embarrassed laugh. 'There's really nothing to tell. He was just a bloke. A customer. That's all.'

'But you specifically remembered him. Why's that?'

Karen Scott shrugged. 'He was nice, I suppose.'

'Came on to you, did he? Ask you for a date?'

'No, no. Nothing like that. He was just nice. Polite. Said please and thank you. Not like the other yobs we get in there sometimes. Treated me nice. With respect.'

'A regular, was he?'

'Fairly regular.'

'How regular?'

'I don't know. Not every day. Maybe once a week. Maybe a bit less than that.'

'Describe him to me.'

Karen Scott screwed up her face in concentration.

'Well, twenty-something. Twenty-two, twenty-three
– something around that, I'd guess. Quite tall. Taller
than me. A bit smaller than you. Thinner than you,
too. Dark-haired. Nice-looking. Quite posh, I'd say.'

Sergeant Wilson's voice sounded strained as he
asked, 'Does he have a name by any chance?'

'Yes. Peter.'

'Just Peter?' Wilson asked and was surprised at the
disappointment in his tone.

'Yes. Just Peter. I didn't *know* him. Just a customer, like I said. I know lots of the customers by
their first name. It's like that in there. Friendly. They
call me Karen and when I've known them for a while
I get to know their names and use them.'

'And this Peter was there one day when Sharon
came to collect you?'

'I told you he was.'

'Did he speak to Sharon?'

'For a bit. Not for long.'

'How did that come about? Did he go up to Sharon
and—'

'No. I wasn't ready when Sharon came so I introduced her to him, and they sat at the same table, just
chatting, I guess, waiting for me to finish. But he left
before I was ready to go.'

'He had left and Sharon was still there?'

'Yes.'

'And that's the only place you've ever seen him –
in the café?'

Karen hesitated. 'Well . . . no.'

Inspector Birt was leaning forward again, his hands joined as if in prayer, his elbows resting on his knees. 'Go on, Karen,' he said in a low, encouraging voice.

'It was quite funny really. Before that . . . before the day Sharon and him met in the café – weeks before, I think – we, Sharon and me, had been coming home after getting a couple of videos, and he – Peter – stopped us and asked us the way to somewhere. He—'

'Just a minute, Karen. Coming home from getting videos, you said. So that was where?'

'Near home. The Old Kent Road. Near the Underground. I think maybe he'd just got off the Tube.'

'And he stopped you and asked the way to somewhere?'

'Yes.'

'You don't remember where he wanted exactly?'

'Hatfield Gardens, I think.'

'He asked the way to Hatfield Gardens?'

'I *think* that's where he wanted.'

'That's very close to here, isn't it?'

Karen nodded. 'Just round the corner. Houses, they are there. Not flats.'

'Now, think carefully – did he ask you or Sharon the way to Hatfield Gardens?'

Karen Scott thought carefully. 'Both of us, I think. Maybe a bit more Sharon than me.'

The Inspector nodded. 'Go on.'

'There's nothing more. When we told him where to go, he thanked us and walked away.'

'Do you remember – had he ever been to the café *before* he met you and Sharon on the Old Kent Road?'

'I don't think so. If he was I never noticed him anyway.'

'Do you think you *would* have noticed him?'

Karen gave a shy smile. 'Probably. Unless we were very – I mean *very* busy.'

'All right. The next time you saw him – after he'd stopped you to ask directions on the Old Kent Road – the next time he came to the café you introduced him to Sharon, right?'

'Oh, no. No. He'd been in several times before he met Sharon.'

'How many times, would you say, Karen?'

'I don't know. Three. Maybe four.'

'And you spoke to him on those occasions?'

Karen nodded. 'Just chat. Just like to the other customers.'

'Just chat?' the Inspector probed.

'Yes . . . except once—' Again Karen Scott paused and looked embarrassed.

'Go on, Karen. You're doing really well.'

'It was just funny. He said he'd seen me on the Tube. He said he'd seen me the day I'd taken my niece up to town.'

'Did you see him on the Tube?'

'I said he saw me. I never saw him. In fact, I remember saying to him, fancy you remembering that.'

'And what did he say to that?'

'Nothing. Someone called me and I left him.'

'And nothing more was said before he went?'

'Nothing.'

'But you've seen him since – since the day he met Sharon?'

'Yes.'

'In the café?'

'Yes.'

'When was that?'

'A while after Sharon was found dead.'

'How long after?'

'I don't remember. Look, this is all nothing. He was really shocked when I told him about Sharon. He's got nothing to do with all this. I'm sure he hasn't.'

Sergeant Wilson pressed on. 'You told him Sharon had been murdered?'

'Yes. He asked me if anything was the matter, and I told him about Sharon.'

'Why did he ask you if anything was the matter?'

'I don't know. I suppose he saw I was upset.'

'And when you told him about Sharon – how did he react?'

'Like I told you, he was shocked. He couldn't believe it. He was really kind about it, said if he could do anything for me just to ask him. I mean, I know he probably didn't *mean* it or anything, but it was really nice of him to say it the way he did.'

'And you haven't seen him since?'

'No.'

'That's a bit odd, isn't it, if he was such a regular before?'

'He wasn't a regular. I told you that already. He just came in from time to time. Once every few weeks, that's all.'

'And you've no idea where he lives or where he works?'

'No. Like I said, I didn't *know* him.'

'You can't tell us *anything* more about him?'

'No.'

'Not even what sort of person he is?'

Karen Scott gave him a quizzical look.

'You know – you can tell things about people from the way they dress, the way they talk.'

'He dressed ordinary. Jeans, I think, and a jacket. He spoke nice though. Not dirty or anything. Always very polite.'

'An educated man?'

'I suppose so. Spoke a bit like Prince Charles.'

'I get you. Now, do you think he ever met Darren?'

'Oh, no. I'm sure he didn't.'

'Why so sure, Karen?'

Karen shrugged. 'He wasn't the type to know Darren, if you know what I mean. Too different. Darren would have hated him. Called him a stuck-up dickhead or something.'

'I see.'

'I suppose, though, he might have met Darren at work.'

'At work?'

'Yes. Well, if Peter had a car and brought it into the garage where Darren worked, I suppose they might have met that way.'

'So Peter has a car?'

'I don't *know* if he had a car. I just said *if* he had a car and brought it into the garage they might have met.'

'Okay. I understand. Let's go back to Sharon for a minute. As far as you know the only times this Peter met Sharon were on the street when he asked you both for directions, and on that one occasion in the café when you introduced them?'

'That's right. I'm sure they never met outside of those two times. Sharon would have told me. We never kept any secrets from each other, and she'd definitely have told me. We . . .' Once again Karen Scott paused and looked away shyly.

'What is it, Karen?'

'Nothing.'

'You were going to add something.'

'Just – well, he's very good-looking and we both sort of fancied him a bit. Just fooling really. Like, we talked about him once or twice. Kidding. That's why I *know* she'd have told me if she'd ever met him again.'

Sergeant Wilson glanced towards Inspector Birt who inclined his head in the direction of the door.

'Right, Karen. That's fine. Thanks very much. You've done really well.'

Inspector Birt stood up, and Wilson followed his example. 'All I would ask you, Karen,' he went on, 'if you *do* happen to think of something else, anything at all, please get in touch with us. Will you do that?'

'Yes. But, honestly, there's nothing else.'

'Just one other thing, Karen,' Inspector Birt said, opening the sitting-room door and turning. 'We'll want you to help us get an artist's impression of this man Peter as soon as possible.'

'Yes. All right.'

'Tomorrow?'

'Yes. I don't work on Wednesdays.'

'Fine. I'll have someone down with you tomorrow morning.'

'All right.'

'And thank you again for your help.'

The drizzle had turned to heavy rain by the time the two men reached the car. It bounced off the windscreen like pebbles hurled by angry gods.

'Christ!' Wilson swore. He reversed out of the parking bay, and swung out towards the main road, thumping the steering wheel as he waited for a gap in the traffic. He reached the first set of traffic lights before saying, 'Well, we got a name.'

'A name,' Inspector Birt agreed, nodding.

'Better than a bloody duvet.'

Inspector Birt gave a thin smile. 'Only a little better,' he said, staring straight ahead as though mesmerised by the flip-flop of the windscreen wipers. Then, out of the blue, in a tight angry voice, he said, 'It's him, you know, Ray.'

'Sorry?'

'It's him. This Peter character. He's our man.'

Sergeant Wilson gave the Inspector a sideways glance. 'How do you make that out?'

'I *feel* it.'

'Oh. I see. That'll look good on the report.'

Birt fiddled with the catch under his seat and let the back down. He lay back with a sigh, and closed his eyes. 'Tomorrow I want as many men as we can spare to get out with photographs of Hayes, and I don't want them back until they've found that shop with the duvets on sale.'

'If she ever got round to buying one.'

Briefly Inspector Birt opened his eyes. 'Yes. *If* she ever got round to buying one. And I want that artist's impression on my desk by tomorrow afternoon.'

'Right,' Sergeant Wilson said, and gave a small smile as he heard the light snore from the seat beside him.

Eleven

For Inspector Maurice Birt, mornings were worst. That was when loneliness descended upon him with all its vigour. Evenings – well, evenings you could go out, visit friends if you had any, get drunk even. But mornings were there to deliberately make you see what a fool you were, how unreasonable you'd been, how inconsiderate you'd been. There was nothing, Birt thought now as he waited for the toaster to deliver, nothing more irrevocably lonely than a man sitting down to breakfast by himself, especially a man who had once known the cosy satisfaction of a woman who had looked after his every need. What he should do, of course, now that his marriage was irredeemable, was to get a clean, decent, civilised divorce, and move to a small flat. Eradicate Helen from his mind. Exorcise her. And yet . . . and yet, there was always that impish idea that something would happen to get them back together again.

He poured himself a mug of black coffee and cursed quietly as some slopped on to the worktop.

He couldn't see a cloth, couldn't be bothered to hunt for one, and used his handkerchief to wipe up the mess, tossing the soiled handkerchief into the empty vegetable basket.

Sitting at the table – a small pine affair with matching chairs that Helen had picked up for a song at an auction, and restored with inordinate pride – munching on his buttered toast, he gazed idly about him, seeing everywhere other touches that Helen had brought to the place. Her stamp was in every room in the house, but particularly here, in the kitchen, her domain, as she had once put it sulkily after he had made the mistake of jokingly saying a woman's place was in the kitchen: the huge urn (another auction bargain) of dried flowers by the door, the bowl of remarkably realistic artificial fruit strategically placed on the windowsill, the modest collection of willow-pattern plates in the dresser, the old-fashioned milk dispenser filled with wooden cooking spoons – one of which she had waved at him threateningly when he had made his chauvinistic remark. All hers. The place would be bare if she took everything. In fact, she had taken nothing except her clothes, moving to her mother's and, no doubt, listening to the old bat as she berated him *in absentia*.

He finished his coffee, tilting his head back to drink the last drop. Then he noticed the stack of dirty plates in the sink, and let out a low, despairing growl. He had meant to attack them last evening, but had forgotten. They would be there when he got home tonight, stickier and greasier. Suddenly he smiled. They would probably be there tomorrow night as well. And the night after. That would certainly have driven Helen to distraction. Always wash up directly after use, had been her motto, and there had been something touchingly romantic on the odd occasion he had helped her with that loathsome chore: she washing, he drying. Sublime domesticity. That was what he missed. Domesticity.

He stood up and walked to the sink, adding his coffee mug and plate to the pile. It would have been different had there been children. How they had wanted a family! But after three pregnancies and three heart-breaking miscarriages . . . Inspector Birt turned abruptly from the sink and left the kitchen.

When Sergeant Wilson pulled up outside the house, Inspector Birt was ready. He walked quickly down the short path, hunching his shoulders against the bitter wind. When he reached the gate he noted that his neighbours on either side had put their rubbish out, and thought about returning to the house to collect his. But he discarded the idea, leaving the rubbish, like the dirty plates, to wait a while.

'Morning, sir.' Wilson sounded cheery enough.

'Morning, Ray,' Birt answered.

And those, as usual, were the only words spoken on the drive to the station. But Inspector Birt didn't doze off that morning which was surprising, the more so since he had slept little during the night. To begin

with he had tossed and turned, the faces of Paul
Cornell and Karen Scott flicking through his consciousness, sometimes distorted into profiles of great
anguish, and as he waited for sleep to come Birt had
felt considerable sorrow for those two young people
whose lives had been shattered, lives that had not
held out much in the way of success in the first place.
And when, finally, sleep did come, it was fretful, and
he woke several times, each time with another face
looming into mind, that of the man Peter. So clear
was he that Inspector Birt felt he could identify him
without the aid of any artist's impression. Even more
disturbing was the fact that, as he shaved, for one
brief and frightening moment it seemed to be his
vision of Peter who stared back at him from the
mirror. So shocked was Birt by the incredibly life-like
image that he felt an urge to shatter the glass, to
remove that hint of mocking laughter from the
phantom face. Instead, as his own face returned, he
muttered a quiet promise to himself.

'I've had a thought,' Sergeant Wilson said, and
Inspector Birt gave him a shaded look as though
suggesting such indulgence at this hour of the day was
dangerous, or tricky at the very least.

They were in the Inspector's office. Wilson had
just returned from getting sandwiches and two plastic
mugs of indifferent coffee which was their lunch, and
Maurice Birt was probing the contents of his sandwich with the tip of a pencil as though about to

perform surgery on it. 'What is this?' he asked.

'Tuna – they said.'

The Inspector took a tentative nibble, and grimaced. 'Tuna, they said,' he repeated. 'And lied,' he added, nonetheless taking a bite and chewing for several seconds before swallowing. Then he carefully removed the lid from his coffee mug, and drank, swilling the liquid about like a mouthwash. 'You said you had a thought.'

Wilson looked as though he now regretted mentioning that. He made a great show of pretending his mouth was too full to talk for the moment, giving himself a little more time. Finally, under the Inspector's relentless if mildly humorous gaze, he swallowed. 'I was thinking,' he began, taking a pad from his desk and studying it.

'For God's sake, Ray, say what you have to say,' Inspector Birt said.

'Well, I think it's the Scott girl who holds the clue to all this,' he blurted out.

'Indeed?'

'Sharon Hayes was *her* best friend, and Darren Cornell was *her* boyfriend.'

'That had occurred to me, Ray, but go on.'

'What if . . .' Again he hesitated.

Inspector Birt gave an exaggerated sigh. He assumed a long-suffering face. 'Please, Ray, just tell me, will you?'

'Okay. What if – let's say this Peter character is our man – what if Peter is eliminating the opposition, so

to speak, in order to have a clear way to get Karen?'
Wilson suggested. It was as though speaking his
thoughts had made him realise how outlandish they
were, and he added hastily, 'It was just a thought,'
and went back to studying his pad. To his surprise the
Inspector made no reply, and when he looked
towards his superior he saw that he was nodding
quietly, his eyes half-closed. Encouraged, he said,
'It's the only thing I can think of that would give us a
motive.'

'You're suggesting a pretty strange obsession,
Ray.'

'I know. But they happen – these obsessions.'

'Indeed they do,' Birt agreed, as if he personally
knew about such things. 'But . . .' It was the Inspector's turn to pause. 'But,' he went on eventually, 'the
murders apart, his actions aren't those of someone
exactly obsessed, are they? I mean, he hasn't been
throwing himself at her, has he? Never made a pass.
Never asked her out. Hardly ever saw her, if what
Scott says is true.'

'Maybe just being crafty.'

'Oh, he's crafty all right, Ray.'

'Anyway, just thought I'd pass on what I was
thinking.'

Inspector Birt gave him a warm smile. Then as his
face became serious once more, he changed tack. 'No
word on that duvet, I suppose?'

'Not yet. Clark, Simpson and Mather are out now
hunting for the shop. Should have something later

this afternoon. Should have that artist's impression too.' He looked at his watch. 'Shelley should be finished with Scott by now.'

'Good.'

'Andrews and McKenzie are having another word with the café owner, just to see if he can maybe corroborate Scott's story. Don't hold out much hope there, though. Spends most of his time behind the counter cooking. Doesn't seem to see anything but the money coming in.'

'Good,' the Inspector said again.

'Also . . .' Sergeant Wilson started to flick through a small notebook, not one he carried, one he kept on his desk. 'Also I asked Clark to check in the hair-dresser's again to see if Hayes made any mention there of buying a duvet or if, by any chance, she had one when she went *in* to work.'

'Good,' the Inspector said for the third time. He got up from behind his desk and started to pace up and down, measuring his strides, his head bowed.

'Also,' Sergeant Wilson looked up and grinned. 'Also, Jennings and Campbell went out to the Brazier-Young house. Found some old codger there who said Mister and Missus were away – Cyprus – and the daughter was at some gymkhana – wouldn't be back until late this evening.'

'The old codger?' Inspector Birt asked.

'Part-time gardener. Old as Methuselah. Saw noth-ing, heard nothing. Can't remember if he was even there on the day. *Could* have been, he said. Didn't seem to know what time of day it was.'

Inspector Birt stopped pacing, coming to a halt in front of Wilson. 'When's the next *Crimewatch* due to go out?'

'No idea.'

'Find out, will you?'

'You going to appear?' Wilson asked, his eyes smirking.

'Just find out when it's on,' Birt snapped, and left the office in a hurry.

But he wasn't gone long, and he seemed in a better mood when he returned.

'No more tuna sandwiches – ever,' he said.

'Fish is good for you, sir. Keeps the bowels moving.'

'So I found out. What about—?'

'Next Thursday.'

'Tomorrow?'

'No. Sorry. A week tomorrow.'

'Right. Now listen. I want an appeal put out *immediately*, right this minute, for this Peter to contact us. Just say we want to eliminate him from our enquiries. The usual guff.'

'He's not going to contact us,' Wilson said.

'If he doesn't, then I want the artist's impression of him on *Crimewatch*.'

'You don't really believe he will contact us?'

'If he's innocent, he will.'

'In that case I hope to hell he doesn't. He's the only lead we've got.'

'And while you're at it, book a slot on *Crimewatch* for us. Make it optional. Tell them we might *not* use it.'

'Will they do that? You know these TV people.'

'Just make them.'

'Yes, sir,' Wilson said, and gave a mock salute.

Inspector Birt was on his way back to his seat when the telephone on Wilson's desk rang. Wilson grabbed it. 'Yes? . . . Oh . . .' He cupped his hand over the mouthpiece, and whispered, 'Clark,' to the Inspector. 'Right, I'm listening. Yes . . . Yes . . . Spell that . . . Yes . . . How come he's so sure? . . . Okay. Good . . . Good . . . Yes . . . Oh . . . Nothing? . . . Okay. Thanks, Joe.' He replaced the receiver and leaned back in his chair. 'They found the shop. A Mister . . .' he peered at the pad he'd been writing on, '. . . Parvese Patel runs it. He's definite that Sharon Hayes *did* buy a duvet there. He remembers her because she wanted a special cover for it and made him open a pile of packets and then ended up buying none.'

'There's no doubt whatever that it was Sharon Hayes?'

'Not according to Patel,' replied Wilson. 'Clark also went to the café. But like we thought, he got nothing.'

'Shit,' the Inspector swore quietly. Then, he gave a low, bitter chuckle. 'So after all that all we have is one missing duvet.'

'We know, at least, that Paul Cornell's story is true.'

'That part of it.'

'And we've more chance of someone having seen Hayes carrying a duvet than if she was just another girl in the crowd.'

'A very small chance, by the look of things.'

'A chance, though.'

Inspector Birt nodded, albeit reluctantly.

'You never know. She might have bumped into someone, or dropped the damn thing. I mean, they're awkward things to carry. Bulky. If you do go on *Crimewatch*, it's worth a shot.'

'Anything's worth a shot at this stage, Ray.'

'That's what I meant.'

It was just before five when Shelley returned with the artist's impression. 'The girl thinks it's a very good likeness,' he said. 'She really remembered a lot about him.'

'Too much?' Inspector Birt asked.

'No. Not under the circumstances.'

'What does that mean?'

'Well, he's very good-looking and she fancied him. If he'd been an ugly bastard who she didn't fancy she wouldn't have remembered half as much. Seen it a million times. Not only with people. I mean, you get someone who likes, say, a particular make of car – if that make of car is involved they'll tell you every detail about it. If it's another make, they're blank.'

Inspector Birt and Sergeant Wilson leaned over the drawing on the desk, and peered closely at it.

'Thanks, Shelley,' Inspector Birt said without looking up, and he waited until the door had closed before asking, 'Is that him, d'you think, Ray? Is that our killer?'

'Don't know about that, but you can see why the girls would go for him. Regular bloody Chippendale, he is.'

'Soft,' Inspector Birt said. 'A soft face.'

'You sound disappointed.'

'No,' Birt snapped rather too quickly. He certainly wasn't about to admit that, yes, he was a bit disappointed, but only because the face in no way resembled the one which had stared at him from his mirror that morning. 'I merely said it was a soft face, Ray.'

Wilson peered closer. 'I suppose you could say that.'

'Always the worst. The most dangerous. Men with soft faces . . . Anyway, at least now we know what he looks like. You've organised that appeal for him to come forward?'

'All taken care of. Be in all the papers and on all the news programmes.'

'Then we just wait.' Birt handed the drawing to the Sergeant. 'Get that copied in case we have to issue it. But I want the original back here before I go home.'

'Right. But . . . never mind.'

'But what, Ray?'

'Well, why not issue it right away and see what it brings in?'

'Because.' For a moment it seemed that the

Inspector was about to leave it at that. Then, with a strange undertone in his voice that Wilson had not heard before, he continued, 'Because I don't want *him* to know that *we* know what he looks like. Not yet. Not yet.' He looked at his watch. 'I'll treat you to a beer.'

'You're on.'

'Ah, before we go, get hold of Clark again. Tell him to chase up the Brazier-Young girl this evening. Just see if she happens to know someone called Peter.'

'Is he to show her this?' Wilson asked, waving the drawing.

Birt shook his head. 'Uh huh. That's *our* secret. I want him to think he's absolutely got away with it. We're going to have to nail him, Ray. Not just catch him. Nail him. And something tells me that to do that we're going to have to watch him every God-given hour of the day without him knowing it.'

'And suppose this Peter didn't do it?'

'Then you better tell that pretty wife of yours that she won't be seeing much of you for the indefinite future.'

'She'll love that.'

Birt grinned wickedly. 'She just might, you know. Come on, let's get us that drink.'

It was WPC Williamson who stopped them, chasing them down the corridor, her face beaming, calling, 'Sir! Sir! Sir!'

Inspector Birt wasn't all that keen on police-women, particularly not ones who chased him down corridors screaming 'Sir!'. He pulled a sour face, and turned. 'What is it now?' he demanded.

'They think they've found the car, sir. The one that was used to kill the Cornell boy.'

'Oh, really,' Inspector Birt said, keeping his voice bland, and feeling pleased with himself when he saw the WPC's enthusiasm deflate.

'Yes, sir. They're bringing it in now.'

'Thank you,' he replied, relenting a little.

'I thought you'd want to know,' WPC Williamson said, sounding disappointed.

'Thank you,' Inspector Birt said again, and watched as she retreated. Then he turned and grinned at Wilson. 'We were about to have a drink, I think?'

'What about . . .'

'Oh, they won't want us down there just now. It'll keep till the morning. Give us something to look forward to, eh?'

'If you say so.'

'And something for us to celebrate now.'

'Why not?' Wilson said, opening the door and standing to one side.

'Why not indeed.'

Twelve

Ray Wilson lay on the settee, his legs hanging over
the end, his head cradled in his arms. One slipper had
fallen off and the other dangled precariously from his
big toe. The television was on, but he wasn't watching it: the comedy programme didn't interest him,
but he was too lazy, too tired to make the effort to
change it. Upstairs he could hear his wife threatening
their eldest son with strangulation if he didn't get into
his bed straightaway and stop acting the fool. 'Aw,
Mum,' wailed its way down the stairs.

'Never mind the aw Mum. Into bed, my lad, and
be quick about it.'

'Do what you're told,' Ray Wilson shouted, but
half-heartedly, and swung his feet on to the floor,
rose and stretched, yawning loudly. Kids, he
thought, and wandered into the kitchen. He took a
can of lager from the fridge, and snapped it open. He
carried it back to the sitting-room and sat down
again, sipping his drink. He leaned back and
stretched out one arm, taking his wife's hand as she

came towards him, pulling her down beside him. 'All done?'

'Well, they're all in bed, if that's what you mean,' Jenny Wilson said, taking her husband's beer, and drinking. She handed back the can, and looked at him curiously. 'What's the matter, pet?'

She was a small, plump woman, with blonde hair going prematurely grey, green eyes that smiled most of the time, and a wide, friendly mouth. Some people had accused her from time to time of being pushy, and perhaps she was, but it was well intentioned and based on kindness. She was generous with her time and in her consideration of others, and if ever anyone was needed to organise some charity for a struggling cause, Jenny Wilson's name came top of the list. Although strict with them, she loved her children dearly. She loved her husband too, and worried about him; not so much that he might be injured or, indeed, even killed in the line of duty (such thoughts were consciously excluded from her mind) but that he was working too hard, being *made* to work too hard by that miserable Inspector Birt, a man she had met twice and liked even less the second time. A smug little twit, she called him.

'Just tired,' Ray answered, putting his arm about her, cuddling her close as if hoping some of his fatigue would be absorbed by her warmth.

'You're *always* tired,' Jenny pointed out.

'And worried.'

'About what?'

Ray Wilson laid his head on his wife's shoulder and gave a low groan. He snuggled closer, and ignored her question.

'It's that case, isn't it?' Jenny persisted. 'Those two young people who were killed?'

'Hmmmm.'

'You want to talk about it?'

'Uh huh.'

'Why not?'

Wilson sat up and put the empty can on the floor. He rubbed his eyes.

'Because it's not the case itself that I'm worried about.'

Jenny Wilson got to her feet. 'I'm going to make myself a mug of hot chocolate. Want one?'

'Please.'

In the kitchen Jenny put spoonfuls of chocolate powder into mugs, and placed the milk on the stove. 'So, if it's not the case itself, what is it?' she called through. It was a deception she had discovered. If something was on her husband's mind, something he wasn't all that keen on discussing, the thing to do was to go into another room and question him from there. Why this worked, she had no idea. Maybe he thought it was like talking to himself. But the reason it worked didn't matter. It *did* work: that was what counted.

And as though to prove it, her husband called back. 'It's Birt, if you must know.'

'Oh, *him*.'

'Yes. Him.'

'What's the matter with him?'

'That's what worries me – I don't know. He's just – just being very peculiar.'

'He *is* very peculiar, dear.'

Ray Wilson chuckled.

'What's so different about him now?' Jenny asked, snatching the pot from the stove as the milk started to rise. 'You want sugar in yours, I suppose?'

'Please. It's just that he's dealing with this investigation – well, not like he usually does.'

'So?'

Ray Wilson sighed, and switched off the television with what the household knew as 'the gizmo'. He walked to the kitchen door, and leaned against the jamb, folding his arms. 'So it's just not like him to – thanks,' he said as Jenny handed him his mug of chocolate, and followed her back to the sitting-room. 'It's a lot of things. We have this person who *might* be a suspect. Only might, mind you, but I think Birt is convinced he's the chap who committed both murders.'

'Does that matter? I mean . . .'

'But – it's like he's going to play with him. I can't explain it, Jenny. He won't let us circulate his description. I tried to get him to tell me why and all he said was we've got to nail him. Not just catch him. *Nail* him.'

'That seems reasonable enough.'

'I suppose. Oh, I don't know. There's just something that's not right. It's a bit like as if he's taking the whole thing personally, and that's really not like him. Always very detached, he's been. That's why he's so damn good. But on this one – oh, bugger him. Come on. Let's take these upstairs and go to bed.'

'Best offer I've had all evening,' Jenny told him, laughing coyly, but letting him go up the stairs first, and frowning to herself when she was sure he couldn't see her.

None of Wilson's worries were in evidence the next morning as he and Inspector Birt studied the report on the car that had been brought in the evening before. It was Wilson who was reading while the Inspector sat at his desk, his hands folded across his stomach, looking as benign as a bishop. 'Just give me the relevant points, Ray,' he had said before adopting his episcopal pose. 'Spare me the jargon – *please*.'

So, Sergeant Wilson was saying, 'A-reg Sierra. Registered to Whitehall Motors, Wandsworth. Indentations on front bumper and front wing consistent with damage that could have been caused by striking the Cornell motorbike.'

'Could have been,' Inspector Birt interrupted.

'That's what it says – could have been.'

'Go on.'

'Tyre tread consistent with those found at the scene, and with those on the victim's clothes.'

'Where was it found?'

'Oh . . .' Wilson turned back a couple of pages. 'In the tourist carpark. The Castle carpark. Some woman – Mrs Cynthia McBane – reported it. Only because she thought it was an eyesore, apparently. She thought someone had just dumped it.'

'She was right.'

'Yes, but you know what I mean. She thought someone had abandoned it since it was such a banger.'

'Fingerprints?'

'Hundreds. They're trying to match them up now, but it isn't too hopeful, sir. Door catches, steering wheel, gear shift – all wiped clean.'

To Wilson's surprise, Inspector Birt said, 'Good. That's what I wanted to hear.'

'Good?'

'It means, Ray, that we can be ninety-nine point nine per cent certain this *is* the car we've been looking for.'

'Oh. Yes. I suppose.'

'More than suppose, Ray. More than suppose.'

Inspector Birt opened the centre drawer of his desk and took out the artist's impression of Peter. He placed it carefully on his desk, only nodding without looking up when Wilson asked, 'Oh, you got it back then?'

Still staring at the drawing, he responded with a question of his own. 'Clark get anything from the Brazier-Young girl?'

'I'll go and see.'

Alone, Inspector Birt used his finger to trace along the jawline of the face staring up at him. It was a curious gesture. Very gentle, it was like a caress. A few strands of hair, delicately drawn, hung down over the forehead, and inexplicably the Inspector tried to push them back as he might have done with a beautiful woman as he was about to kiss her. He touched the lips, the full, perfectly formed lips, pursing his own. What was astonishing about his actions was that they were in total contrast to the hatred he felt building up inside him. Slowly he sensed a desire to grab the drawing and crumple it up, to wring that handsome face in his hands, to crush the life out of it. He was shaking when he returned the drawing to the drawer, and had only just recovered his composure when Wilson hurried into the room looking very pleased with himself. 'We've another name,' he announced.

The Inspector didn't look so thrilled about that. He looked puzzled for a moment. 'Tell me.'

'The daughter – Heather Brazier-Young – has a boyfriend. Marcus Walwyn. He was staying with them the weekend Cornell was killed.'

'Do we have an address?'

'We do.'

'For Christ's sake, Ray!'

Sergeant Wilson jumped. 'Sorry, sir. Ritherdon Road, Balham.'

'Why wasn't he mentioned when we first questioned her?'

'Says she forgot. Didn't think about it at all.'

'Did Clark believe her?'

'Says he did. She's a bit of a nutter as you know.'

Inspector Birt swung his chair round and gazed out of the window. 'Does he have a car?' he asked quietly.

'Walwyn? Yes. A BMW.'

'Did he have it with him that weekend?'

'Well – I don't know.'

'Well, find out, for God's sake. Better still, get Clark in here.'

Alone again, Inspector Birt opened the drawer in his desk and looked at the drawing once more. He didn't take it out this time, just left it lying there and stared at it. 'Marcus Walwyn,' he said almost to himself, and nodded. 'The name fits you, my lad. The name fits you.' He shut the drawer quickly as Clark and Wilson returned.

'Sir,' Clark said, and nodded.

Inspector Birt returned the nod. 'Wilson says you believed the girl, is that true?'

'Yes, I believed her, sir. She's not the sort to lie, if you know what I mean. Too open. Has everything. The sort who probably never had to lie in her life.'

'Unlike the rest of us,' Inspector Birt said, and allowed himself a thin smile. 'You're certain it was the weekend that Cornell was killed that Marcus Walwyn was there?'

'Yes, sir. She was positive about that. She says her parents will confirm it when they get back from Cyprus.'

'He goes there often?'

'Quite often, it seems.'

'And he has a car?'

'A BMW, sir. Black. He inherited from his father, I understand. By the way, the father committed suicide some years ago. Walwyn lives with his mother. Pretty comfortably off. He works for a publishing firm in the West End – the name of it is on my report.' He leaned forward and put the typed pages in front of the Inspector.

Inspector Birt ignored them. 'The weekend he was there – did he drive his BMW?'

Clark looked puzzled. 'I don't know, sir.'

For several seconds Inspector Birt eyed Clark coldly, and then, in an icy voice he said, almost in a whisper, 'There's a telephone there. Would you kindly see if you can find out?'

As Clark moved to Wilson's desk Wilson bent over to the Inspector, and asked, 'Why?'

'Because you can't drive two cars at the one time,' Inspector Birt said, his voice still frozen. Then he leaned sideways and peered round Wilson's body. 'What are you doing now, Clark?'

'I don't have the phone number, sir.'

Inspector Birt sighed. 'Jesus, Wilson, give him a phonebook, will you, like a good man?'

'Top drawer on the left,' Wilson said.

They waited in silence while Clark found the number and dialled. Inspector Birt doodled; Wilson watched him doodle and tried to make some sense out of the erratic scribbling. When Clark started to speak, keeping his voice unnecessarily low, Birt looked up at the Sergeant and raised his eyebrows in a gesture of hopelessness. They were still raised when Clark hung up and, still seated by Wilson's desk, said, 'Yes, sir. He did. He drove up on the Saturday for dinner. He was supposed to go home again that evening but drank too much, and Mrs Brazier-Young insisted that he stay overnight. He left again just after lunch on the Sunday.'

'Damn,' the Inspector said, and got quickly to his feet, sending his chair scudding backwards into a filing cabinet. 'All right, Clark. Thank you.'

'Thank you, sir.'

'So, where does that leave us?' Wilson asked after Clark had left.

Inspector Birt was flicking through the report Clark had given him. He wasn't reading, just turning from page to page in a random, hopeless kind of way. 'I don't know, Ray. I just don't know,' he said. Then he stood up, tossing the report to one side. 'What I do know is that you better not have anything planned for the next few days.'

'Nothing special.'

'Good. Come on,' the Inspector said, heading for the door.

'Where are we going now?'

'Out to the Brazier-Young place. I want to look at that lane again.'

Wilson grabbed his overcoat from behind the door and followed Birt out. They were halfway down the hallway when the Inspector stopped. 'Hang on a minute,' and spun round, making his way briskly back to the office. When he reappeared he was carrying the drawing of Peter. 'I want to take our friend with us,' he said matter-of-factly.

Sergeant Wilson drove the car slowly up the narrow lane, braking when he came to the spot where Darren Cornell had been found. 'You want me to stop here?' he asked.

'No. Just keep driving.'

Wilson put the car into second gear, and did as he was told, cursing quietly as the car shook and juddered, pitching into potholes, the wheels getting stuck in ruts, making driving difficult.

Inspector Birt seemed not to notice his companion's problems. The hedgerows on either side were bare of leaves, and through them, across the fields on the left, he could just make out the roof of the main house, smoke rising from two chimneys. Further on, round yet another bend, the stable block came into view, and in the fields surrounding it horses grazed, protected from the cold by New Zealand rugs. As the car drove past, two of them, blades of grass still sticking from their mouths, galloped across the field to take a closer look, and cantered alongside the car, their breath steaming from their wide nostrils.

'What are we looking for?' Wilson asked.

Inspector Birt wished he could answer that. He gave a morose snort. 'I wish I knew,' he said.

'Oh.'

Just at that moment the car rounded a sharp turn to the right, at a point where four gates opened from the fields on to the lane. 'For that,' Inspector Birt said suddenly, pointing to a sad-looking, dilapidated barn standing some way back from the laneway with a small, overgrown, partially cobbled yard in front of it.

Wilson drove into the yard, and stopped the car. Before he had time to switch off the engine, the Inspector was out of the car, striding towards the barn. By the time Wilson reached him, he had the doors wide open, and was crouched down on his hunkers, peering at the earthen floor. He looked up as Wilson approached. 'We . . . are . . . so . . . fucking . . . *stupid*,' he announced, standing upright. 'Jesus *Christ*! . . . Ray, see if you can get someone from forensics out here. Tell them to come now. Tell them I want casts made. I want them here *now*.' Then he stooped down again, his hands clasped behind his back, looking oddly Oriental as he took to muttering to himself as Wilson went to radio from the car; muttering still when he returned. 'Well?'

'Twenty minutes.'

'The keys in the car?'

'Yes.'

'You stay here. I'll pick you up later.'

Inspector Birt was making for the car, almost trotting. At first he didn't appear to hear Wilson calling him. When he did, he turned, and barked, 'What *is* it, Ray?'

'What do you want casts made of?'

'The bloody tyre marks. The bloody tyre marks, of course.'

'The bloody tyre marks. The bloody tyre marks,' Wilson mimicked to himself as he watched Birt drive out of the yard. He turned up the collar of his coat, and hunched his shoulders. 'The bloody tyre marks,' he said once more to himself, just for the hell of it.

Heather Brazier-Young was in the stable-yard, checking the horse she had ridden in the gymkhana the day before, when Inspector Birt drove up. She raised one hand and shielded her eyes: it was a curious, automatic gesture she had, doing it, as now, even when there was no sun. 'I thought you'd be back,' she said.

'Oh? Why is that now?'

Heather shrugged. 'Just thought you would.'

'Well, you were right.'

'So I see.'

Inspector Birt raised a tentative hand to pat the horse that stuck its head over the stable door and gazed into the distance. 'A handsome animal,' he ventured.

'He'd be pleased you think so, I'm sure, but I doubt you came here to admire the horses.'

'No. You're quite right. I came to talk to you about a Mr Marcus Walwyn.'

'I knew it. I bloody knew it,' Heather said. 'I knew I shouldn't have told that idiot anything about him.' She was clearly very angry.

'DS Clark is many things, but he's no idiot,' Inspector Birt told her. 'And the fact remains that you did tell him about Mr Walwyn.'

'And I suppose you're going to hound the poor sod now.'

Inspector Birt looked hurt. 'Certainly not,' he said, trying to look appalled. 'We don't hound people. In fact, all I want to do is eliminate him from our investigations.'

Looking only partially pacified, Heather put her hand on the horse's nose and pushed it back into the stable, shutting the top half of the door which she secured with a sliding lock. 'Anyway, I told your precious DS Whatever-his-name-is everything I know, so you're wasting your time.'

'Fortunately I have the time to waste,' Inspector Birt told her, and for some reason that made her laugh.

'All right. What is it you want to know?' she asked, but before he could answer she added, 'I have to check one of the mares in the copse field. We can talk as we walk.'

The last thing Inspector Birt wanted was to go tramping off across wet fields, but he agreed so to do with good enough grace. When he caught up with Heather, he asked, 'That shed at the top of the lane – over that way – don't you use it?'

For a moment Heather looked perplexed. 'Over where?' she asked, and then following the Inspector's somewhat wavering wave, she said, 'Oh, that. The old barn. No. Not really. Not since we had the new barn built next to the stables.' She gave a small titter. 'Daddy wanted to have it pulled down actually, but they wouldn't let him. It's listed or something. He was furious. Kept on for ages about man's right to do what he liked with his own property.'

Inspector Birt gave a little smile of understanding. 'So no one goes near it?'

'Oh, sometimes. Sometimes we shove a tractor in there overnight. A couple of years ago we used it for hay, but that was only because we got really super stuff and thought it wise to buy plenty. Apart from that – it's quite silly really. It's going to collapse anyway, so you can see Daddy's point of view.'

'Oh, indeed,' the Inspector agreed although he was already beginning to dislike the banker, just as he disliked anyone who went about stripping the country of what he rather pompously thought of as its heritage. It dawned on him that he disliked the conservationists too, but they were the lesser of the two evils. 'Would Mr Walwyn ever have gone over there, to the barn?' he asked suddenly.

'Oh, I shouldn't think so. Not exactly agriculturally inclined is dear Marcus.' She put her hand on the top bar of a gate and vaulted over it.

Inspector Birt eyed the gate askance, in his

mind's eye seeing himself attempting to hurdle it, and landing flat on his face. To his relief Heather gave him a pathetic look, and unfastened the chain which held the gate shut, and opened it for him. 'Thank you,' he said, waiting for her to rechain the gate before asking, 'Can we go back to that weekend again, the weekend when the young man was found dead on the lane? There was just yourself and your parents and Mr Walwyn here, right?'

'Yes, that's right.'

'And Mr Walwyn came here in his own car – the BMW?'

'Yes, of course.'

'And he left in his own car?'

'Naturally. Really, Inspector—'

'Yes, I'm sorry. I know how it must sound. Now, previous to that weekend – how long was it since Mr Walwyn had visited you?'

'A week maybe. Why?'

'Oh, he came here *that* often?'

'There's really no need to be *that* surprised. Marcus and I are very good friends, and my parents have known Emily – Mrs Walwyn, Marcus's mother – for donkey's years.' She giggled again. 'They're all hoping Marcus and I will get married.'

'And will you?'

'Probably not,' Heather answered frankly. 'We – well, we *enjoy* each other, if you know what I mean, but we'd possibly drive each other mad if we had to *live* together.'

'Of course,' the Inspector said, as if he understood perfectly, feeling uneasy as he saw another gate coming up.

He beamed excessively when Heather said, 'That's the mare I want to check. Just hang on here a tick. Won't be a sec,' and made another perfect vault.

Inspector Birt watched her walk across the field, one hand outstretched, calling to the horse. He had started to feel sorry for her, but then, as he watched, his sadness waned. She was clearly a resilient young woman, clearly, also, more at home with her horses than with humans, and would probably grieve more over the loss of a pony than over a lover. She was smiling when she returned and looked – well, not beautiful, but like someone *about* to be beautiful. 'She's fine,' Heather said, and jumped back over the gate. 'In foal to Ozymandias,' she added.

'Indeed.'

'Might just as well have said Elvis Presley, mightn't I?'

'I'm afraid so.'

Heather laughed delightedly, and the laughter was still in her eyes when she said, 'You were asking me about—'

'Yes. About the previous time Mr Walwyn visited – a week or so before the unfortunate weekend. Did he drive up on that occasion too?'

'Inspector, he *always* drove up.'

'In the BMW.'

'It's the only car he has. He was really lost without it.

Like a big cuddly baby. I thought he was going to cry.'

'I'm sorry?'

'It broke down on the way up. In Windsor. He had it towed to a garage. I had to run him home.'

Inspector Birt stopped in his tracks. His mouth was open slightly, and he put one hand over it, stroking his jaw with his fingers. When he took his hand away, he exhaled as though winded. 'Let me get this straight, Miss Brazier—'

'Oh Heather, for God's sake.'

'Heather. Yes. You say he drove up. His car broke down near Windsor. He had it towed to a garage. You drove him home?'

'Yes.'

'So *you* never saw his car on that occasion?'

'No, Inspector, I didn't.'

Inspector Birt grabbed Heather's hand and pumped it like a maniac. 'Thank you, Heather. Thank you.'

'What have I said?'

But the Inspector was already striding away. He never even faltered as he came to the gate. He climbed it, swinging his legs jauntily over the top. Safely on the other side, he turned and waved.

The forensic team were just packing up when Inspector Birt got back to the old barn. One of them, a dour, gaunt man with rimless spectacles on the end of his nose, strolled across. 'You owe me one large, one very large malt, Maurice.'

'A bottle, Charlie, if you come up with what I want.'

'And what's that?'

'You've got the casts?'

'Of the tyre treads? Yes.'

'Clear ones?'

'I've taken worse.'

'Match them to the ones you took down the lane and from the markings on the Cornell boy's clothing and there's a bottle in it for you.'

'Macallan?'

'Yes.'

'Twenty-year-old?'

'Yes.'

Charlie gave an open-mouthed leer. 'I'll match them to anything you want for that.'

'Today?'

'Today.'

'You're a good man, Charlie Hilton.'

'The very best.'

Inspector Birt gave Hilton a friendly jab on the arm, and moved away towards Sergeant Wilson. He was feeling better than he had for a long time. Even Wilson seemed to notice. 'You're looking very pleased with yourself, sir.'

'You know something, Ray? I am. I damn well am. Let's get back to the Incident Room. I'll tell you all about it in the car.'

'You mean you're going to stay awake, sir?'

'Wide awake.'

Thirteen

Inspector Birt's buoyant humour had carried over to the morning. He didn't say much as Wilson drove them down to Wandsworth, but he didn't sleep either, didn't even close his eyes, which was something of a miracle. He had the drawing of Peter, now encased in a folder of clear plastic, on his lap, and from time to time he looked down at it, and smiled. Once, when he was certain Wilson couldn't see him, he appeared to wink mischievously at it.

'You see the appeal on the telly this morning, sir?' Wilson asked, more to break the monotony than anything else.

'I *heard* it,' the Inspector told him. 'On the radio,' he added in a tone that suggested he disapproved of watching television in the morning.

'It's in the paper too.'

'Good.'

'And PR have a slot for you on *Crimewatch* if you need it. Very good about it they were, apparently.'

'Remind me to send them some flowers.'

Sergeant Wilson ignored the sarcasm. He waited until they were nearing Wandsworth before saying, 'It's a Solly Whiteman we need.'

Inspector Birt turned his head, and looked at Wilson as if he didn't comprehend. 'Sorry?'

'Solly Whiteman. Owns and runs Whitehall Motors.'

'Oh, *that* Solly Whiteman,' Inspector Birt said with a comical smile.

'Yes, sir, *that* Solly Whiteman,' Sergeant Wilson said, returning the smile.

'Just let's hope our Solly, whoever he is, has a good memory.'

'And that he keeps decent records.'

'Ha,' the Inspector snorted. 'Fat chance. Bound to be on the fiddle. More than likely sold the car for cash and syphoned that off.'

'Oh, probably,' Wilson agreed. 'They're all at it.'

'Isn't everybody?' the Inspector asked cynically.

'I'm not,' Wilson said, in a manner that suggested he wished he was.

'But you're the Law, Ray.'

'Tell me about it.'

Sergeant Wilson drove slowly along the street, peering to either side of him. 'God almighty,' he said. 'Every banger in the country must end up here . . . Hang on – that's it. Over there. On the corner.' He indicated, and turned into the forecourt.

It was a ramshackle place. About twenty cars were lined up on the broken tarmac, their prices, pasted to the windscreens, were hard to decipher since grime and rain had almost obliterated them. A small shed made of unplastered concrete blocks, with just one metal-framed window covered on the inside by wire mesh, stood in the corner. Solly Whiteman came out of the door and eyed them, perhaps sizing up with his cunning eye which decrepit vehicle he could persuade them to buy. 'Gentlemen, gentlemen,' he was saying as he walked to meet them, smiling with yellow teeth, a smile which wiped itself away in an instant when Inspector Birt asked, 'Mr Whiteman?'

Instantly Solly was suspicious. He didn't answer, but allowed his balding head to bob a little.

'Inspector Birt, Thames Valley CID. DS Wilson.'

Solly gave a nervous smile. 'I never did it.'

'I'm sure you didn't,' Inspector Birt reassured him. 'Just a question or two about a car registered to Whitehall Motors that you sold.'

'Look – I give no guarantees—'

'Just shut up, Solly, and listen,' Sergeant Wilson said.

'A Sierra,' Inspector Birt said. 'Registration – Ray?'

'A74 RSW.'

Solly Whiteman gave the number his full concentration. 'A74 RSW,' he repeated. His face brightened. 'I remember it.'

'Terrific,' Wilson said.

'Bought it at auction.'

'Of course.'

'Honest.'

'And lost money when you sold it, right?'

Solly gave them another wily smile. 'Maybe not a loss. Not a total loss. A shilling or two for the Building Society.'

'Remember who you sold it to?'

Solly shook his head. 'Never did get a name. Cash. I mean cash. Walked in. Looked at the car. Handed over his lovely money. Drove away with my blessing.'

'So you remember what he looked like?'

'A young schmuck. Scruffy. Hadn't shaved.'

Inspector Birt produced the drawing from under his topcoat, and handed it to Solly without saying anything.

Solly took his time about studying the drawing, pulling faces. 'S'pose.'

'Suppose what, Solly?'

'S'pose it *could* be him. If he'd cleaned himself up a bit,' Solly told them. Then he shook his head. 'Naw. Not him.' He held the drawing at arm's length, and scratched his temple. 'Maybe it's him,' he conceded. 'Don't think so, though.'

Sergeant Wilson looked as if he wanted to strike Solly Whiteman dead. He took the drawing from him and, with both hands, held it under the motor-dealer's nose. 'Is it him, or is it not him?' he demanded.

Solly looked affronted. 'You want me to swear? Okay, I swear it's not him. You want me to say what

I think? Okay, I think it might be him. What more can I tell you?'

'God, Solly, you're a great help.'

Solly spread his hands. 'I try.'

'Sweet Jesus,' Sergeant Wilson said. 'If they're all like that it's no wonder they needed someone to lead them out of Israel.'

'Into,' Inspector Birt corrected. 'Into Israel.'

'Whatever.'

They had, of course, hit the rush-hour traffic; traffic that was worse than average since it was the weekend and people were rushing to get home or get away. 'What do you think, sir?' Wilson asked as he braked near the roundabout, then shot forward again, making the Inspector wince as he asked, 'About?'

Wilson took one hand off the wheel, and jabbed a finger towards the drawing on Birt's lap. 'Did he buy the car?'

'Oh yes.'

'You're very sure, sir.'

'I have been all along, Ray.' He sounded smug.

Wilson glanced at him. 'You're really *enjoying* this, aren't you, sir?'

'Yes. Yes, I am,' the Inspector told him, and closed his eyes.

Wilson swung the car on to the M4 and headed for home. He switched to the outside lane, and pressed his foot down hard on the accelerator. Suddenly he was feeling angry. He was, he felt, being excluded from the investigation, not being made privy to some vital information which Birt possessed and was unwilling to share for whatever reason. After about ten minutes he surreptitiously took a cigarette from his pocket and lit it from the lighter on the dashboard. He lowered his window half an inch, and blew the smoke towards the gap from the corner of his mouth. But even the nicotine didn't help. Indeed, by the time they reached Slough, everything seemed to be conspiring against him: he was starving, thirsty, and dying for a pee. He was, therefore, surprised when, as though reading his mind, the Inspector opened an eye and said, 'I'm famished, dying for a drink, and I need a pee.'

Wilson was forced to smile. 'Join the club.'

'You'll be rushing off home, I suppose?'

'No. No rush this evening. Jenny's got her Children in Need meeting. That goes on till the small hours. The kids are with their Gran.'

The Inspector sat up. 'Well now, it so happens that I have what promises to be a very excellent steak and kidney pie in the fridge. Perhaps . . .'

'Can't think of a better offer. Thank you, sir.'

'And I think there's a bottle of something.'

'Gets even better. Didn't know you were into cooking, sir?'

'Me? Indeed I'm not, Ray. I can boil an egg if you like it solid. No. My neighbour. The excellent Mrs Cassidy. Worries about me. Keeps saying I'm losing weight. Looking peeky. Brings in "little goodies". The pie is one of those.'

'Maybe she fancies you, sir,' Wilson said, and gave a laugh.

'Probably,' the Inspector said. 'I can be very attractive to women, you know, Ray. And by the way, don't feel I'm cutting you out of the investigation. I'm not.'

Sergeant Wilson could feel the unease spreading through him. It was almost as if Birt *had* read his mind. And not for the first time. 'There are things I think you've kept from me, sir.'

'Not really. Wait till we get something inside us and I'll try and explain everything to you.'

'Fair enough.'

Almost the first thing the Inspector did was apologise. They were in the kitchen and he eyed the pile of plates in the sink balefully. 'They just seem to accumulate,' he said, sounding genuinely bewildered. 'I'll—'

'No,' Wilson interrupted. 'I'll do them. If you're cooking, I'll do these,' he said, taking off his jacket and rolling up his shirt-sleeves. 'Any washing-up liquid?'

'Try under the sink.'

'Got it.'

'You'll be used to this, of course?'

'Yep. All of us have to pull our weight in our house. Jenny sees to that.'

'Ah . . . I've got some frozen beans.'

'Fine.'

'Or broccoli.'

'Beans, thanks.'

'Bring slightly salted water to the boil . . .' the Inspector was saying.

'You want me to do it?'

'I can manage.'

With the pie in the oven and the water for the beans coming to the boil, Inspector Birt opened a bottle of Barolo. He poured two glasses, holding Wilson's for him until he had dried his hands. 'Cheers, sir.'

'Cheers.'

They sat down at the kitchen table.

'Smoke, Ray, if you want.'

'Ah, thanks.'

'There should be an ashtray somewhere.' Birt got to his feet and rummaged in the cupboards. As he passed the stove he put the beans into the boiling water, and returned to the table with a saucer, and watched the Sergeant as he lit his cigarette.

An hour later, the meal finished, he watched Wilson light another cigarette. Perhaps it was the wine, or perhaps it was because loneliness was again soon to return, he suddenly felt a great affection for Wilson, and he said, meaning only to think it, 'You're a good man, Ray.'

Sergeant Wilson looked embarrassed. His cheeks

reddened, and he looked away with a shy smile. 'Thank you, sir.'

'No. I mean a *good* man.'

'Like Solly, I try.'

Inspector Birt himself, now, looked embarrassed, like someone who had divulged a secret he had promised to keep to himself. He got up and ambled over to the tall cupboard beside the fridge, coming back with another bottle of wine. 'No more Barolo, I'm afraid,' he said, holding the bottle to the light and squinting at the label. 'Château Senilhac,' he read, and made a wry face. 'Means nothing to me. Helen was the wine expert.' He gave a snort. 'Helen was *the* expert. In everything.' He opened the bottle and went to pour some into Wilson's glass. Wilson placed his hand over the glass. 'I don't think I should, sir. Driving.'

Birt looked disappointed. He filled his own glass. 'You could stay in the spare room,' he suggested, again aiming the bottle at Wilson's glass.

'I better get home, sir.'

The Inspector nodded. 'I understand,' he said. Then he gave a conspiratorial grin. 'You could get a taxi?'

Sergeant Wilson didn't really want any more wine. Beer was his drink. Already he could feel his head getting slightly muzzy. But so pleading were the Inspector's eyes, so childlike almost, that he relented, and said, 'I could, couldn't I? Just one more glass then, thank you, sir.'

And, indeed like a child who had just got his own way, the Inspector beamed with delight, and filled the glass. '*In vino veritas*,' he said, mostly to himself, and sat down again.

For some moments the two men sat in silence. It was a comfortable, unstrained silence: the silence of two people who suddenly, for the first time despite a long acquaintance, found they are at ease with each other. And perhaps it was this relaxed atmosphere that encouraged the Sergeant to say, 'Can I ask you something, sir?'

'Ask away.'

Yet now, with permission granted, Sergeant Wilson floundered. 'It's just – well, I've worked with you for the best part of five years now, sir. I know *how* you work. But – but on this case you're . . . you're acting differently. It's like you're playing some sort of game. Some game for which you've made the rules. Shit, I don't know what I mean. You're . . . well, look, for instance . . . we've *got* a prime suspect in Marcus Walwyn, but you've done nothing to . . . you haven't even shown an *inclination* to haul him in and question him. You . . . it's just not your way, sir. Christ! Normally you'd have had him in here without letting his feet touch the ground. You—'

'Ray, Ray.' Inspector Birt held up his hand. He stared at his glass and then, taking it by the stem, turned it round and round as though rinsing it with the remaining wine. But before he could say anything more, Wilson started again.

'We haven't even established that Walwyn and the Peter character who visited Scott in the café are one and the same, simply because you've been hanging on to that artist's impression and refusing to let us show it around. I just don't know what we're *supposed* to be doing any more.'

Inspector Birt gave the Sergeant a long, slow, penetrating stare. 'You're right, of course,' he conceded finally. 'All right. We don't know if Walwyn and Peter are the same person. That's my fault. I accept that. But I have a reason which I'll try and explain in a moment. But let's say they are the same person. What does that give us by way of evidence against him? Nothing, if you think about it. He goes to a café and has coffee. Never steps out of line, behaves himself like a thorough gentleman. Speaks to the victim Hayes only because he's introduced to her. Never met – as far as we know – the other victim, Cornell. Certainly, he's been close to the scene where Cornell was found, but he's *entitled* to be there. The girl his mother wants him to marry lives there, for God's sake. And the one person I *do* show the drawing to, Solly Whiteman, can't absolutely identify him as the man who bought the car. And, Ray, tying him to the car is the only real evidence we have that could make us really suspect him. Try going to court with that. I can just see the defence running rings around Solly.' He gave a morose chuckle. 'I told you some time ago, Ray, we've got to nail this man, not just catch him.'

'That doesn't explain why you won't let us bring him in for routine questioning, sir.'

The Inspector poured them both another glass of wine. He put the bottle back on the table with exaggerated care and exhaled in a long sigh. 'Let me tell you a story.'

It was very curious. There was suddenly an aspect of Inspector Birt revealed that Wilson had never before seen. His voice was gentle and, yes, paternal. Sitting there in the homeliness of the kitchen with only an occasional noise from outside the house to disturb the tranquillity, Wilson was reminded of his own father – a gruff, unyielding man as hard as the coal he mined – and of one evening in particular when, drunk, he had uncharacteristically taken the young Raymond on his knee and told him a fantastical tale of monsters that dwelt underground, terrifying him. It was only years later, long after his father had died, choking on his own vomit, that Wilson realised that had been the point of the story: to scare the living daylights out of him, to toughen the little bugger up, as his father had said on that, and several subsequent occasions. And Sergeant Wilson wondered if Inspector Birt was about to try and perform the same unpleasant trickery. Certainly the manner he now adopted had a sinister edge to it, and his voice assumed a hollow ring, sepulchral almost.

'. . . back twenty-five years,' he was saying. 'The very first murder case I ever worked on. Under Chief Inspector Simmons.' He shook his head as though the mere thought of Simmons filled him with awe. 'Long before people spoke about serial killers.' He now fiddled with the salt cellar, and asked it, 'I suppose three is a serial?' He became more abrupt. 'Anyway, three it was. Mind you, it was less problematic than this case, Ray. All three murders were identical in a number of ways. All drownings, and in each case the killer left – a signature, I guess you could call it that: four intersecting lines cut into the sole of the left foot, like noughts and crosses, so we knew we were after just one murderer.' He gave a pitying, thin smile. 'The Stalker, the papers called him. Not for any good reason, mind. Well, he did admit he followed his victims over a period of time, but *stalk* them – a bit too dramatic. Anyway, he became known as the Stalker, even to us.'

The Inspector was talking more slowly now, his eyes half closed as though seeing what he spoke of in his mind's eye. 'We suspected quite early on who our man was, but Simmons would never go for him, and I was just like you, Ray.' He gave a knowing glance, before adding, 'Impatient.' He took a sip of wine, and then topped up both glasses.

'So we waited and waited and waited, watching him all the time – stalking *him*, if you like. And then, finally, he made the mistake we were waiting for – and we *got* him.' He leaned back and heaved a great sigh of relief. Then, almost immediately, he leaned forward again, a new sense of urgency creeping into his tone. 'He was an – an *amazing* man, Ray. He was,

I think, the only person I've ever met, until now anyway, who was completely *conscienceless*.' The Inspector appeared to give a small shudder. 'Dispassionate,' he added. Then he gave a sardonic laugh. 'He would sit and lecture us, I remember. Of course, it wasn't like it is now, don't forget – no recordings made. Pity, come to think of it. I'd have liked you to have heard what he had to say. He was so – well, so *practical* about everything he said. So totally matter-of-fact. When Simmons asked him if he *had* committed the murders, he said, "Oh, yes," just like he was admitting to – like he'd been offered a cup of tea. Strange. And once . . .' the Inspector started shaking his head as he could barely believe the thoughts now coming to his mind, '. . . once, when we were alone – I forget where Simmons had gone – he said something to me that has stuck with me all my working life. He said that if Simmons had brought him in for questioning, if he had *not* waited and waited, we'd never have proved a thing against him. And, you know what, Ray? He was absolutely right. I went back over everything, and if Simmons had had him in for questioning like I had wanted, he'd have walked free as the breeze.'

Inspector Birt looked across the table as though expecting a comment from the other man. But Sergeant Wilson sat perfectly still, gazing back at the Inspector, his eyebrows slightly raised as if questioning the point of all this. 'Now, what I want to tell you is this, Ray. When I saw that small cross cut into the

Hayes girl's forehead, I had – well, a premonition, if you like. I felt myself thinking, dear God, not again. Don't ask me why, but I honestly thought Zanker – that was his name, Hubert Zanker – was at it again. Quite unreasonable, I know, but it was such an *overwhelming* feeling.' The Inspector shook his head in disbelief. 'For some inexplicable reason I had always assumed Zanker was dead. Maybe wishful thinking,' he added, looking mildly shamefaced. 'So I checked. He's alive all right. Served twenty years.' Birt allowed himself a wry smile. 'I checked his record and, of course – I wouldn't have expected anything else – he was a model prisoner. Got out four years ago. Lives in Cricklewood. Still married to the same woman. A grown-up son, even,' Birt explained, sounding a little surprised. 'Cricklewood,' he repeated. Then he gave another huge sigh. 'I didn't tell you all this, Ray, because . . . well, if you want the truth, because I was – not ashamed – embarrassed, I think.'

'I can't see why, sir.'

'Neither can I – now. There's just one more thing. I saw Zanker after he was sentenced. Just before they shipped him off to Dartmoor. It was as if he was going to Butlins. Smiling. Cheerful. Like it had all been a huge and enjoyable game. He said, "I nearly got away with it, didn't I?", and I said, "Nearly." That's when he waggled a finger at me and said, "One day. One day." Then they took him away. I got the feeling then that he was going to spend his entire sentence plotting. To get even with me. To commit a crime and get away with it. The perfect murder, maybe. One day.'

The Inspector stood up, staring at the ceiling. It was clearly an absentminded movement since he sat down again almost immediately. 'Anyway – and this is what is important, Ray – having had Zanker in mind, I started looking at these murders in the same light. I remembered something else Zanker had said. He explained that the very first of his killings – he drowned a crippled old woman in her bath – was a practice run. That's exactly what he called it, Ray. A practice run. And that's what I think we *might* have here. You don't think so?' he asked suddenly, noticing the face Sergeant Wilson pulled.

'A bit far-fetched, isn't it, sir?'

'Can we just think about it for a moment? It would explain why we haven't been able to come up with a common link. Look – suppose – just suppose that the Hayes girl was Walwyn's trial run. Right?'

Wilson nodded, albeit reluctantly. 'And that Cornell was his main target?'

Slowly the Inspector now nodded, yet his nod was also hesitant, more as if he was trying to shake his thoughts into an acceptable pattern than as if he was agreeing.

'But what was his motive for killing Cornell, sir? We're no closer—'

'Unless . . . unless, Ray, there's to be a third.'

Sergeant Wilson gave the impression of a man now

thoroughly confused. He leaned forward, and pointed out, 'If there's to be a third murder, why kill Cornell?'

The Inspector pursed his lips, and shook his head. 'That, I don't know. I thought at first it might be *two* trial runs, but I don't think that now. It wouldn't fit the *pattern*, you see. You know what I *do* think, though? I think it's Karen Scott who is his main objective.'

'Wait a minute. Wait a minute, sir. I'm getting – look, we don't even know if the Peter character Karen Scott talks about and Marcus Walwyn are the same person.'

'We will tomorrow, Ray. We will tomorrow.'

Alone, Inspector Birt leaned his back against the closed front door, and listened as the taxi taking Sergeant Wilson home hummed off into the distance. Then he went back to the kitchen and looked about. He thought about tidying up, about washing the glasses he had refused to let Wilson wash. But he only thought about it. Then he took the drawing of Peter from the dresser, and left the kitchen, carefully switching out the lights.

In his bedroom he pinned the drawing to the wall at the foot of his bed. There was an angle-poise lamp on the bedside table: he manoeuvred it so that the beam shone directly on to the handsome face. Then he undressed and got into bed. He folded his arms behind his head, and stared at the drawing. It was more than an hour before he fell asleep.

Fourteen

Neither Inspector Birt nor Sergeant Wilson made any reference to the conversation of the night before, but there was an air of unusual tension in the office. Wilson had felt it before, each time a case was close to being solved, but never to quite such a keen degree. For his part, Inspector Birt was particularly business-like, curt and aggressive as was his wont. His instructions that every garage within a radius of five miles of the Brazier-Young house was to be questioned about repairing Marcus Walwyn's BMW were brusque and left no room for doubt that none of the team had better return until either the garage had been located or that it could be reasonably established that no such incident had taken place. By lunch-time he was satisfied that the latter was the case, and didn't seem in the least surprised. On the contrary, he planted a smug smile on his face when Wilson passed on the information. But the smile was whipped away when he said, 'Right. Are you ready, Ray?'

'Ready.'

'Let's go then,' the Inspector said, and shoved his arms through the sleeves of his overcoat and took the top copy from the pile of artist's impressions in one economical movement.

Even the traffic, Wilson thought, seemed to share the sense of urgency. It flowed evenly and rapidly as drivers used Saturday to go in to central London to shop, to beat the Christmas rush, to raid the shops and purchase toys they could not afford to appease children who would tire of them before the holiday was even over, to buy over-priced perfumes and jewellery for wives who would probably prefer something more practical, for girlfriends who wouldn't be their girlfriends by the New Year.

Oddly enough, Inspector Birt had Christmas on his mind too. Perhaps it was the decorations in the shop windows that made him think of it. But his thoughts were morose. He thought of himself, spending the holiday alone, and for a moment he had a grim vision of himself hunched over a turkey of gigantic proportions, condemned to consume it alone when the very sight of it nauseated him. Then he thought of Karen Scott, and wondered if she would be alive by Christmas. He *knew* he was right, *knew* that she was the next victim, yet there was that awful nagging doubt that he was wrong. Perhaps, as Wilson had said at one stage, perhaps it was all too far-fetched. Perhaps he simply *wanted* it to be the way it seemed to him. Perhaps . . .

They had reached Balham High Street. Wilson drove past the entrance to the Underground and under the bridge. 'Ritherdon Road is just up here on the left, sir,' he said.

The Inspector nodded.

Wilson turned into Ritherdon Road, and slowed as he came to the first of the speed-restricting bumps. 'Slowly,' Inspector Birt said.

'I'm—' Wilson started to say.

'Slower,' the Inspector told him.

Wilson slowed to a crawl.

'The house will be on your side, Ray. Uneven numbers your side.'

'Seventy-seven, seventy-nine, eighty-one,' Wilson counted aloud.

Inspector Birt was counting ahead of him. He could already make out which house number ninety-nine was, and flicked his tongue over his lips. The car heaved itself over another bump. The Inspector felt suddenly ill, and was relieved when Wilson stopped momentarily to let a car pull away from the footpath on his left. 'Go in there,' the Inspector said quickly.

'But—'

'In *there*,' Birt snapped.

Obediently, Wilson parked the car in the vacated space. He was almost surly when he pointed out, 'The house is up *there*, sir.'

Inspector Birt nodded. He had a clear view of the house. Like many others in the road it had been smartly renovated. Ninety-nine was painted a very dark blue-grey, the woodwork of the windows a sparkling white. Climbers grew up over the door although it was impossible to tell what they were; roses probably, or clematis, maybe wistaria – only spring and summer would tell. In the tiny, pocket-sized garden, creosoted tubs had been placed, three in all, and a miniature conifer thrived in each.

Sergeant Wilson switched off the engine, and made to open his door. Immediately, Inspector Birt laid a restraining hand on his arm. It was as though this was too much for Wilson. His voice was cold with suppressed anger when he said too quietly, 'For God's sake, sir!'

If he noticed the Sergeant's anger, Inspector Birt gave no sign. His tone was reasonable. 'Too soon, Ray.'

'What in Christ's name did we come here for?'

'To watch, Ray. To see if Walwyn matches this,' – he patted the photocopy of the drawing he had taken with him from the office – 'and to watch.'

'Sir—'

The Inspector sucked his lips, and put a single finger to them, somehow conveying that it was not so much silence he wanted, but no argument. 'Trust me, Ray. Have a cigarette, and trust me.'

There was no sign of the BMW. Indeed, there were none of that make of car in the road as far as the Inspector could see. Peugeots, Volkswagen Passats, a couple of Mercedes. Plenty of Japanese makes, but no BMWs. Even as he remarked on this to himself, a car went slowly past them. A man drove, a woman, her head down as if she was looking for something on her lap, beside him. It stopped outside number ninety-nine and the woman got out, walked to the hall door and let herself in. Immediately, Inspector Birt tensed, and Wilson slowly returned the lighter to the dashboard leaving the cigarette dangling from his lips unlit. 'It's a BMW. It's *him*, sir,' he said, with a kind of awe.

'Yes,' the Inspector said.

The car drew slowly away from the house, went to the top of the road, turned, and came back down again, rising and dipping over the bumps like a ketch in a fairweather sea. 'Talk to me,' Inspector Birt said urgently.

'Eh?'

'Turn to me and talk to me. Quickly, Ray.'

Sergeant Wilson turned to the Inspector and started to jabber. 'Ladybird, ladybird fly away home. Pack your bags and get a move on. The flight to Los Angeles has been cancelled due to bad weather.'

The Inspector nodded gravely.

The BMW glided past them.

Inspector Birt readjusted the rearview mirror and watched. 'He's looking for parking. Damn!'

Across the road a woman, young and pretty, and carrying a briefcase, came out of number eighty-seven, and hurried to a Volkswagen Golf. She got into the car, and pulled out.

'You want me to go after him and tell him?' Wilson

asked, thinking it quite funny.

Inspector Birt shook his head, clearly missing the joke, his eyes glued to the mirror.

Wilson took the cigarette from his mouth, and shoved it into his top pocket, making a wry face as he felt the other broken cigarettes already there. He leaned sideways and peered into the side mirror. The reverse lights on the BMW shone clear and white, and the car came back towards them, and was parked with considerable deftness in the space left by the Golf. A young man stepped out. Wilson stared at him. Then he took a quick glance down at the artist's impression. 'Jesus,' he said. 'It *is* him.'

'Yes, Ray, it's him,' the Inspector confirmed, giving a beatific smile and exhaling slowly.

The young man locked the car and then, swinging the keys in his hand, walked to number ninety-nine and went in, just pushing the front door open.

'What now, sir?'

'Now, Ray, we wait. We wait and watch. We wait and wait and wait—'

'And watch and watch and watch,' Wilson concluded.

The Inspector gave him a benevolent smile. 'Precisely'.

And they didn't have long to watch, not for another glimpse of Marcus Walwyn at any rate. He came out of the house again, and trotted back to the car. He had taken off his overcoat, and looked thinner, more wiry, somehow more formidable because of it. He opened the back door of the car and took out several pale green Fortnum and Mason plastic bags. Then he locked the car again, and returned to the house.

'Been shopping with Mummy,' Wilson observed.

And so, the waiting and the watching began.

3.45 p.m.	Lights in the downstairs front room of number ninety-nine go on.
3.50 p.m.	Light outside front door of number ninety-nine goes on.
6.59 p.m.	Maroon Jaguar, J3 LPZ, arrives. Elderly man, carrying flowers, goes to front door of number ninety-nine, and is admitted.
11.25 p.m.	Downstairs front room light goes out.
11.27 p.m.	Light outside front door goes out.
11.31 p.m.	Light in front upstairs room goes on. Curtains are drawn, from the left by woman, from right by man with flowers.
11.53 p.m.	Upstairs light goes out.

Inspector Birt gave a satisfied sighing purr. 'Right, Ray, let's head for home.'

'Thank Christ for that!'

'Get used to it. There'll be plenty more.'

To take his mind off the pangs of hunger and his nagging bladder, Wilson said, 'So, Mummy has a boyfriend.'

Birt nodded. 'So it seems.'

'I'll check the registration of the Jag in the morning.'

'Yes,' Inspector Birt agreed, but he sounded distracted.

'You all right, sir?'

The Inspector looked slightly startled. 'Me? Yes, I'm fine, Ray. Just thinking.'

'Oh.'

'From now on I want a round-the-clock stake-out team on the Scott girl.'

'On Scott?' Wilson sounded surprised.

'On Scott. I also want twenty-four-hour surveillance placed on Marcus Walwyn. You organise teams. We'll be one.'

'I'll see to it first thing.'

'Tonight, Ray. Deal with it tonight.'

'It'll be the early hours of Sunday morning when we get back, sir. *Sunday*.'

'So?'

'I just thought—'

'As soon as we get back, Ray.'

'Yes, sir,' Wilson said resignedly.

'I don't want Walwyn to so much as fart without my knowing about it. If anyone fucks up—'

'I'll tell them, sir.'

'I mean it, Ray. Everything he does – *everything* – I want to know about it. Everywhere he goes, every-one he meets—'

'I've got it, sir.'

'And for God's sake, tell them to be discreet,' the Inspector said wearily.

'Right . . . You'll clear it with the Super?'

'I'll clear it with the Super,' Inspector Birt promised.

'Not tonight, though?' Wilson asked with a wicked grin.

'In the morning.'

'And you'll be discreet, won't you, sir.'

Suddenly the two men started to laugh as though what Wilson had just said was the funniest thing in the whole wide world.

Fifteen

Sergeant Wilson looked desperately tired. His eyes were bloodshot, and had dark smudges under them. It was late Tuesday afternoon, and he stood by the Inspector's desk, a sheaf of papers in his hand.

Inspector Birt, by contrast, looked remarkably chipper. He had his overcoat on, and looked like someone who had been stopped in his tracks when preparing to leave the office in a hurry. That was not the case, however. True, both he and Wilson were due to leave the office, but not for over an hour. Perhaps he had just forgotten to take his overcoat off.

Wilson began turning the pages. 'Well, sir, nothing exciting to report from yesterday. The Scott girl – you want me to begin with her?'

The Inspector nodded.

'She went to work. Took the Tube. Came home on the Tube. Never went out. No one visited the flat.' He turned another page. 'The barrister – Rutherford – the one with the Jaguar—'

'I know, I know.'

'—took Mrs Walwyn out. Picked her up at seven thirty. Went to a restaurant – Casa Vulpino in Wendover Street. Brought her home just after eleven. Went in with her. Stayed half an hour.' He paused and looked up at the Inspector.

'Go on.'

'Right. Marcus Walwyn. 8.30: left the house. Took a taxi to work. Arrived at work shortly after nine. 1.07: came out. Went to a pub. Had half a lager and some sort of roll. 1.55: back to work. 5.37: left work again. Took the Underground home. Met no one, spoke to no one. 6.58: arrived home. Didn't come out again.'

'And nothing extraordinary has come in for today?'

Sergeant Wilson shook his head. 'Just checked.' He looked up at the clock on the wall. 'He should still be at work.'

'Okay, Ray. That's fine. What time are we on at?'

'We relieve Clark and Paterson at six thirty.'

'Time for a pint?'

'If you don't mind, sir – goes through me. I'll be—'

The Inspector smiled. 'Quite right, Ray.'

'A coffee though?'

'A *decent* one. Not—'

'Oh, I forgot. The TV want to know if you want that slot on *Crimewatch*. They need to know today.'

The Inspector frowned. 'I suppose,' he began, but stopped when someone knocked on the door. 'Yes?' he called.

A WPC put her head round the door. 'Sorry, sir,' she said. 'There's someone downstairs who wants to see you. Says his name is Marcus Walwyn.' Inspector Birt seemed to freeze, and it was some seconds before he said, 'Thank you, Meeker. I'll be down directly.'

'Well, now, that's a turn-up,' Wilson said.

But to Wilson's surprise the Inspector shook his head. 'It's perfect,' he said, and gave a tight smile. 'Just what he *would* do, Ray.' He took off his overcoat. 'Organise someone to take our shift,' he said. 'Tell Clark to stay until they arrive.'

'Right.'

'Then, Ray, come down and join us.'

'Wouldn't miss that for the world.'

'I'll wait for you, then.'

'Thank you, sir.'

BOOK 3

BOOK 4

Sixteen

I wish you could have been there to see their faces when they came into the interview room where I'd been put. Of course, they tried to look ever so nonchalant about it all, but I knew I'd caught them on the hop. The older one, a little ferret-like chap, was making great attempts to be – well, pukka's the best word, I think, like nothing bar an earthquake would rock him. He looked a right prat in his trendy suit (trendy if he was thirty years younger, that is) and dainty shoes. And the other one, built like a brick shit-house, was trying to give the impression of being your good solid copper, for God's sake, hovering in the background with a face that suggested he'd been on the booze all night.

To tell the truth, I'd been planning to drop in and see them for several days: ever since good old Heather had phoned me and told me they'd been sniffing about, and that she'd seen 'lots of activity' down at the old barn. But I kept putting it off. I wasn't afraid of them or anything, don't think that. I just wanted to let them stew for a bit. Mind you, it was a bit scary when Heather got round to mentioning they'd been asking about my car, and quizzing her about when I'd been to the house, and specifically about my actions the weekend they'd found Evil Cornell, so I thought I better make my call. The fact that I'd noticed them in Ritherdon Road, watching *my* house, had nothing to do with it. That just gave me an extra thrill. And I really enjoyed having the two morons follow me to work. I'd have given a year's pay just to be able to watch them as I got into my car and drove all the way to their own stupid police station. Quite a laugh *that* gave me, I can tell you.

Anyway, there I was, sitting in that interview room with my legs crossed, putting on an expression that said I didn't have a care in the world, when these two came in. 'Mr Walwyn?' the older one asked.

I didn't stand up. 'That's right,' I told him. 'Marcus Walwyn.' I gave my Christian name on purpose. It's a trick I've learned: if ever you come face to face with someone who could be on the belligerent side, get your Christian name in there quick. It's surprising how it throws them. As though it's impossible for them to be angry with you if you're on first-name terms.

He nodded. 'I'm Inspector Birt. This is Detective Sergeant Wilson. You asked to see me?'

'Yes, well, I hear you're looking for me.'

He pretended to be perplexed, raising his eyebrows, and then frowning like he didn't have a clue what I was talking about. Well, that was fine by me. I'd be playing that game too. 'Your appeal for Peter to come forward – the mysterious Peter who visited the Carlos café from time to time?' I spoke nice and slowly, the way you do to someone who's a bit impaired mentally.

He didn't like that. 'Oh,' he said.

'Well, I'm Peter.'

He was off frowning again. 'I thought you said Marcus Walwyn?'

'I did.'

'Then?'

'I lied.'

'About?'

'Lied in the café about my name being Peter.'

'And why should you do that?'

I gave him a really nice disarming smile. 'You know how it is,' I told him, like we were all men of the world.

'I don't believe I do.'

I gave a great big sigh. 'You meet a girl, don't know who she is, don't know what she's after, don't want to get caught up in anything you can't handle, so you say your name is – Tom, Dick or Harry.'

'Or Peter,' the bullock of a sergeant said.

I gave him a smile too, just so he wouldn't feel left out. 'That's it.'

'I thought Miss Brazier-Young was your girl-friend?'

'Oh, only allowed one, am I?' I asked, giving him a cheeky look. 'But you're right,' I went on. 'She is. But a bit on the side never hurt anyone, did it?'

The Inspector was looking as if he didn't approve, whether it was with me or his side-kick, I don't know. He pulled up another chair and sat down opposite me, putting his hands on the table and folding them. 'Mr Walwyn,' he said, and I knew he was going to try the 'I'm being reasonable' tactic. 'We are investigating two murders, and—'

'*Two*?' I interrupted, loading that little word with incredulity.

'Two,' he said sombrely, but his eyes gave a small twitch too which told me I'd evaded one of his silly traps.

'I know about Sharon, but who's the—'

'Mr Cornell.'

I really should take up acting professionally. You'd have been proud of me if you could have seen the utter bewilderment I managed to get on to my face. 'Cornell?' I asked. 'Who's he?'

'Darren Cornell.'

I shook my head. 'Never heard of him.'

'Miss Scott's fiancé.'

I kept shaking my head. 'Look, Inspector, I don't want to seem stupid or anything, but you really have me confused. Who's Miss Scott?'

'Miss Karen Scott. From the café.'

'Oh, *Karen*. Didn't know her name was Scott. Didn't know she was engaged either. And her fiancé

226

was killed too? Jesus, that's really terrible.'

'You mean you didn't know?'

'How would I know?'

'It was in all the papers. On the TV,' Wilson put in.

I acted like I was giving that serious consideration. 'Yeah, now that you mention it, I *do* remember something about it, but I didn't connect – I mean, I didn't realise the man you found was Karen's fiancé. That's awful. She must be *shattered*.'

'You never met him?' It was the Inspector again.

'No. I'd *heard* of him,' I volunteered. 'I mean, I knew Karen had a boyfriend. Sharon told me that. But I didn't know his name or anything. Didn't even know they were engaged, like I told you.'

'You did know Sharon then?'

'Inspector,' I said, trying to sound reasonable myself, 'I *met* her. Once. I didn't *know* her. I don't *know* Karen either.'

'How did you meet her?'

'Who? Karen?'

'Sharon.'

'Met her in the café. She came in one time to collect Karen. Come to think of it, it was Karen who introduced us. Just spoke to her for a few minutes while Karen was finishing off.'

'And in that few minutes she told you Karen had a boyfriend?' He tried to make that sound highly unlikely.

'That's right. Look, she was just sort of warning me off.'

'I'm sorry?'

'Telling me I was wasting my time if I was interested in Karen.'

'Why should she think you were interested in Karen?'

'How do I know?'

'She must have had some reason.'

I thought it was time to get a bit testy. 'Look, I fancied Karen, okay? Wouldn't have minded having her. Maybe that showed. Maybe Sharon saw something in the way I looked at her. I don't know. Women spot things like that.'

'Indeed they do,' the Inspector said, giving a small smile as if that would pacify me, knock me off guard too, probably. 'And that was the only time you met Sharon Hayes?'

'That her name? Hayes? . . . No, I'd met her once before, apparently.'

'Oh?' The Inspector made as if that was news to him.

'Yes. Funny really. Met her on the street – with Karen incidentally – and asked her for directions.'

'Oh? To where?'

'A friend's house. He was having a party.'

'Does he have a name, this friend?' It was Wilson again.

'No. You just whistle and he comes,' I answered. He was really getting up my nose.

'A name, Mr Walwyn,' the Inspector said.

'Nick Putty.'

'And an address?'

I told him Nick's address and was expecting him to tell me they'd check on it, but he didn't. Wilson did though. 'We'll check that,' he told me like, wow, I better watch my step.

'Really?' I asked, and gave him a pretty fair approximation of a cringe. Then I leered at him. 'Lucky I told you the truth, then, isn't it?'

'No more than we expect, Mr Walwyn,' the Inspector said, calming things down. 'No more than we expect,' he said again, and I was to discover he had a habit of that – repeating himself.

'I've no reason to lie.'

'You lied about your name,' Wilson said, determined to niggle me, maybe to get me so angry I'd slip up on something.

'Yes. I did. But that was to Karen. Not to the Inspector,' I told him, putting him in his place.

'Mr Walwyn is being very co-operative,' the Inspector said.

'I'm trying to be,' I said.

'Perhaps you'd do one more thing for us?'

'Sure. Anything if it will help.'

'I'd like you to write something for us.'

Well, I'd been waiting for this. Looking forward to it really, as you can imagine, and it was all I could do to keep a grin off my face. 'Not a cheque, I hope,' I said wittily.

Inspector Birt gave me his favourite supercilious look, and turned his head. Wilson bent down (as if he'd been specially trained for this, like it was a party trick) and they had a little whispering session. Then Wilson lumbered out of the room, leaving me and the Inspector alone. Cosy.

And now it was time for the Inspector to lull me into that famous sense of false security. 'It really is good of you to come forward, Mr Walwyn,' he said.

'My pleasure.'

'Not everyone would – in your position.'

'And what's my position, Inspector?' I asked. That rattled him. I wasn't supposed to ask that, you see. I was supposed to get all het up and nervous, and start worrying like hell.

I don't know about you, but when I'm having an argument and put my foot in it, I find the best way to get out of it is to put on an enigmatic smile, and look sort of pityingly at my opponent, like he was really stupid for not understanding my point of view. There's nothing like a superior glare to make them wilt. Well, that's what the Inspector tried now, giving himself a breather and time to make something up. I wasn't about to let him off that lightly, though. 'You mean I'm a suspect?' I asked, getting just the right touch of astonished indignation into my voice.

'Should you be, Mr Walwyn?'

That was pretty clever, I thought. Better than I expected him to come up with anyway. 'Well,' I told him. 'If I was heading the investigation, and was getting nowhere, and everyone was saying what a fool I was, I'd make *everyone* a suspect until they proved themselves otherwise.'

I felt almost sorry for old Birt. Of course, he wanted to tell me that everyone *was* a suspect, but he couldn't now: if he did he'd be agreeing with the rest of what I said, that he was getting nowhere and everyone was calling him a fool. And I'd just settled back to enjoy his discomfort when Wilson ruined it by coming back into the room, carrying a pad. He put the pad in front of me, and took a ballpoint from his pocket, putting that beside the pad. Then he handed a slip of paper to the Inspector. It was all I could do not to laugh. I looked down at the pad and straightened it, keeping my eyes down for a while so they wouldn't show my glee – wouldn't show that I recognised the slip of paper as the note I'd put on Darren's motorbike either. When I'd composed myself, and put on an appropriately serious and obliging face, I looked up and raised my eyebrows.

The Inspector cleared his throat. 'Would you write "I know who killed your brother's bird. Tough shit".'

I made a face as if I found the words pretty vulgar and distasteful, but I wrote them down without hesitation, and pushed the pad across the table to the Inspector. To give him his due, he didn't show his disappointment when he compared the two and saw they were totally different. 'All right?' I asked.

He just nodded, and passed both to Wilson.

'Someone send you that then?' I asked.

The Inspector just stared at me.

'Pretty vulgar language,' I said. 'Don't approve of calling girls birds myself.'

'Oh?'

'Pretty demeaning, don't you think. You wouldn't, would you?' I asked, and then, only because I couldn't resist it, I added, 'The Sergeant there might, but you wouldn't.'

Wilson got all red in the face, and looked the proverbial daggers at me, but the Inspector couldn't help laughing with his eyes. 'Why do you say that?' he asked.

I shrugged. 'Question of class, isn't it? Whoever wrote that is really working class. Even I can tell that.'

The Inspector stood up. 'Well, thank you, Mr Walwyn,' he said.

'That's it?'

'For the moment.'

I stood up too. 'I can go now?'

The Inspector inclined his head.

'Right.'

'You won't mind if we talk to you again?'

'Lord, no. Any time, Inspector,' I told him and walked towards the door.

'Oh, just one more thing—'

I turned. 'Yes?'

'You have a car?'

'Of course.'

'What make is it?'

'BMW. My dad left it to me in his will. No, sorry.

He left it to my mother but since she doesn't drive it's sort of come to me.'

'And it's just the one car you have?'

I decided to look puzzled for a moment. 'Well, yes – why would I want two?'

'Some people have more than one.'

'Not me, Inspector. One's plenty. Besides, I couldn't afford two. Just a working boy, you know.'

Wilson had to get in on the act. 'You've never owned a Ford Sierra?' he asked, and I could see the Inspector give an irritable little look.

'Ford Sierra?' I asked, making the *Ford* sound really common. 'Good God, no. Sooner walk than drive one of those heaps.' I had my hand on the door knob, and was about to leave it at that and walk out, but I couldn't stop myself. 'That what you drive, Sergeant – a *Ford Sierra*?' I asked, like I was truly sorry for anyone reduced to having a load of crap like that.

'Thank you, Mr Walwyn,' the Inspector cut in, trying to sound stern, but clearly enjoying my digs at the Sergeant.

'Thank *you*, Inspector,' I said pointedly.

Even now I don't know if the Inspector was genuine about having just remembered something else he wanted to ask me, or if this was his way of playing cat and mouse, but I'd no sooner opened the door and put one foot into the corridor than he said, 'I am sorry, Mr Walwyn. There's just *one* more thing.'

I came back into the room, and shut the door behind me. I marched back to where I'd been sitting, and sat down again, crossing my legs, trying to assume the exact position I'd had. Then I looked up at him, and said, 'Yes, Inspector?' making it obvious I was getting pretty fed up with all his questions.

'You don't happen to know a Mr Zanker?'

'Zanker?'

'Hubert Zanker?'

To tell the truth I was quite worried about that question. I didn't, of course, know any Mr Hubert Zanker, but there was something about the way Birt said his name, and something about the silence that followed which made it all sound ominous. 'Never heard of him,' I said, and waited, feeling a bit uneasy under the Inspector's gaze.

'You're quite certain?'

'Absolutely. Not a name I'd forget, I don't think.'

The Inspector nodded slowly, looking very serious. Then he brightened, and said, 'Very well. That *is* all, Mr Walwyn,' and he went to the door and opened it for me.

'You're quite sure?' I asked.

'Oh, quite sure.'

'Jolly good.'

I stood up and pushed the chair neatly in under the table. I had to have one more dig, and thought about it as I made my way across the room to the door. They'd slipped up by not asking me for my address, so when I got to the door, I turned, and said, 'Well, you know where to find me if you want me . . .' then I paused. '*Don't* you?' I added significantly, and sauntered off down the corridor.

'I'll bloody crucify him,' Wilson said.

The Inspector chuckled. 'Got to you, didn't he?'

'You can say that again.'

'Just as he wanted to. He's really very clever, you know, Ray,' the Inspector said, and then seemed to recall something, and fell quiet, all trace of merriment disappearing from his face.

After several minutes, Wilson said, 'Sir?'

'Hmm? Oh, sorry, Ray. Just – never mind. Look, get those down to . . . what's his name?'

'Loring?'

'Yes. Get them down to him and see what he can come up with.'

Sergeant Wilson studied the note found on Cornell's motorbike and Walwyn's copy. 'They look very different to me,' he said mournfully.

'They *are* different,' Inspector Birt told him. 'But just get Loring to examine them, will you?'

'You still think he's the one?'

'Oh, yes,' the Inspector said firmly. 'More than ever I'm convinced.'

Wilson waited a moment. 'But you're not going to tell me why?'

'Not for the moment,' the Inspector said quietly. Then he shook himself. He gave another small chuckle. 'To be honest, Ray, I don't honestly know *why* I'm so convinced. I just am. Oh, and get someone to check out that Nick Putty, will you? See if there was a party and if Walwyn was there.'

'Sure.'

'Not that it matters. I'll lay you a hundred quid to a penny it all checks out.'

I strolled out of the police station feeling pretty pleased with the way things had gone. Mind you, I'd been quite impressed with Inspector Birt. A shrewd enough chap. I'd have to watch myself with him.

Seventeen

I knew it was part of his plan to unnerve me (the
Inspector keeping a couple of his clowns following
me wherever I went, and having the house watched
day and night) and if I'd been your average miscreant
I guess he might have succeeded. Even so, I found it
an irritation, not to mention a challenge. The important thing was I had to behave normally. But it's
really difficult to do that when you *know* you're
doing it. You have to sort of act all the time. I think
everyone's the same – you behave normally when
you're *not* thinking about it; once you *have* to think
about it all your actions seem to become staged and,
well, yes, *ab*normal. So, before I did anything I had
to sit down and think seriously about it, contemplate
the ramifications, make sure I wasn't about to hand
the Inspector my head on a plate. I'm referring, of
course, to my dealings with Karen. With regard to
my homelife and work I had no such problems.
Everything at home was the same as ever. As you can
imagine I didn't tell Ma anything about the goings

on. Didn't want to upset the old girl – and that's exactly what I planned to tell Birt if he ever got round to asking me why I hadn't mentioned it to her. At work, nothing out of the ordinary was happening. I was still ploughing my way through the fake Jilly Coopers and Jeffrey Archer soundalikes, and writing my witty condemnations of them, getting well and truly bored out of my skull. There'd been a rumour going about that I was going to be made a junior editor (whatever that's supposed to be) but I hadn't heard anything definite and was beginning to think it was some arsehole playing tricks on me. They do that a lot in publishing: build your hopes up and then dash them, just to keep you in your place, as they like to think of it.

Then, two days after I'd been to see Inspector Birt, I had a note from Kranze telling me he had arrived home, and wondering when it would be convenient for us to meet. I thought about phoning him, but decided, no, I'd write back. I just didn't want to speak to him until we were face to face. There was no reason I could put my finger on for that. It just seemed the right thing to do. So, write back I did, suggesting the following Friday, giving myself some-thing to look forward to. The next morning (the Royal Mail having gone mad and actually delivered a first-class letter within twenty-four hours) his son phoned me to say, yes, Friday would suit ideally, and how about nine thirty? Fine, I told him – I'd be at the house in Cricklewood at nine thirty the following

Friday. Now all I had to do was work out some strategy that would give my shifty friends from the police the slip. Not as easy as it sounds. I wanted to get away from them without it looking as if it was intentional – make them feel they'd fallen down on the job rather than that I had deliberately set out to lose them. All part of my behaving naturally.

I'd been thinking, too, that it would seem very odd if I didn't go to the café and see Karen after hearing the terrible news about the death of her beloved fiancé. I mean, I'd have been a pretty heartless character if I didn't go and offer my sympathy: Birt would expect me to do that anyway.

I chose Tuesday afternoon, leaving it quite late so that there wouldn't be all that many people in the café; also so that Karen would be about to finish work and have more time to talk to me should the need arise. So, I left a note on my office door saying I had to go to the dentist, and that I might not be back, and off I went.

I walked all the way (sometimes I'd taken a taxi) since I wanted to make it easy for Rosenkrantz and Guildenstern to follow me, and I amused myself *en route* by stopping along the way to gaze into shop windows and watch the lads duck and dive into doorways, just like G-men, or Keystone cops more like. I also had fun thinking of them reporting back with bated breath that I'd been to the café, believing they were really on to something.

As I'd hoped, the café was nearly empty, just a

couple of old ladies having shepherd's pie, and three of your labouring types stuffing their faces with cheese and chutney rolls.

Karen's reaction when she saw me come in was quite interesting. I could see she wanted to come straight over to me, and maybe fall into my arms for comfort. In fact, she made a couple of steps towards me, and then stopped. She gave me a sad little look, and then her eyes flicked away like she was feeling guilty about something. I just gave her a friendly wave and sat down at the nearest table, one close to the window so I could see out and keep an eye on the Unlikely Lads. That way, she *had* to come to me, if only to ask what I wanted. And that's what she did.

'Hi, Karen,' I said, with my very best smile.

'Hello, Peter,' she said.

'How are you?' I asked, sounding really concerned.

'Coping,' she said.

'Good. I'll just have a coffee, please.'

Karen wanted to say something. I could easily tell that. She lingered by the table, her pretty little mouth open a bit, her eyes searching my face. But in the end all she did was smile, and nod, and walk slowly off to get the coffee. She did keep throwing sideways glances at me, though, as she waited for Carlos to make the espresso. I pretended not to notice, and took to gazing out of the window, smirking to myself as the lads walked past a couple of times, and looked in. I was tempted to invite them for a cup of something but thought that really would be a bit cheeky. Besides, it was amusing to see them out there in the cold, freezing their stupid balls off.

Karen took me by surprise when she put the coffee on the table in front of me. 'There you are, Peter,' she said in a very low voice.

'Oh. Thanks, Karen.'

Again she stood by the table, not wanting to leave. It was difficult for me not to ask her what was the matter, but I behaved as if I didn't notice anything. I was trying to think of something to say, something quite insignificant and chatty, when she said, 'Peter, I've got to talk to you.'

'Sure,' I said, and waved her to a chair opposite.

'Not here. Look, I'll be finished in about ten minutes. Can you wait?'

'No bother. Is something the matter?' I asked, frowning nicely with concern.

'I'll tell you all about it when – I must go.'

I couldn't see why she had to go. There didn't seem to be anyone in need of her services, and the boss was reading the paper, marking something with a pen – horses probably. But I just nodded, and smiled some more, understandingly.

The coffee was cold as usual, and I'd finished it when she came back. She was wearing a sheepskin coat, not a good one, just imitation that really looked like imitation, and I thought to myself I'd have to get her a proper one when we knew each other better. 'You look like you could use a drink,' I told her.

'Peter—'

'I know this little pub. Nice and quiet. Let's go there and you can tell me what the problem is. Okay?'

She nodded, and smiled up at me. I held out my arm, and she linked it, and we walked away from the café.

'Well, you were right, sir. It all checks out. Nick Putty used to work as an editor in the same place Walwyn works. He *did* have a party and Walwyn was there. It was also the *first* time he had been there so it fits that he might have to ask directions.'

Inspector Birt nodded.

'As to the two notes – both quite different.'

Inspector Birt sighed.

'But Loring did say something interesting.'

Inspector Birt brightened.

'He said they were *too* different. Does that make sense to you?'

Inspector Birt rounded on the Sergeant in a flash. 'You spoke to Loring? I mean, *you* spoke to him?'

'Yes.'

'And he said they were too different?'

'Yes.' The Sergeant sounded puzzled.

'Now, think, Ray. Try and remember exactly what Loring said.'

'I just told you, sir. He said the two sets of writing were quite different. And then he added, too different.'

'He didn't say you were to tell *me* they were too different?'

The Sergeant looked uneasy. 'Well, yes, as a matter of fact. He said the two sets were quite different. Then he said, tell Birt they're too different.'

The Inspector sucked his teeth. 'I *knew* I was right,' he said to himself. He started slapping his fist into the open palm of his other hand. 'But how – that's the thing. How?'

'Sir?'

'It's Zanker all over again, Ray.'

'I'm sorry?'

'He did the same thing. Told us all about it. Exactly how he did it.'

'I'm lost, sir.'

Inspector Birt relaxed and went to the chair behind his desk, and sat down. 'You remember I told you about Hubert Zanker?'

'Yes, I remember that, but—'

'Well, he did the same thing – lured his second victim to the canal with a note. We examined that note and compared it against his writing. Mind you, we didn't have any great technology in those days. He wrote the note quickly in his own writing and then copied it again, altering his writing completely. Loring was on that case too. And he said then that something was bothering him. He actually said that the writing was *too* different. And that's what he means now. Somehow – Christ alone knows how –

Walwyn is copying Zanker to the letter.'

'Old newspaper cuttings?' Wilson suggested without much enthusiasm.

The Inspector shook his head. 'The bit about the notes never got into the papers.'

'Been any books written about Zanker?'

Birt shook his head again. 'Not that I know of. I would have known. I'd have known that for sure.'

'Maybe I better check on it just in case?'

'Yes. And, Ray, see if you can find the files on the Zanker case, will you?'

'They'll take some finding, sir. Probably been destroyed by now. Or lost.'

'Just see if you can find them, Ray,' the Inspector said, sounding tetchy.

'Now?'

'Now.'

The Sergeant moved to the door, and almost collided with WPC Williamson who was coming in. She gave Wilson an apologetic grin, and said, 'Sir, a report's just come in. Walwyn and the girl Scott have left the café and gone to a pub together.'

Surprisingly, the Inspector didn't seem that concerned. 'Just keep them under observation,' he said. 'You still here, Ray?'

'Just going.'

It was really nice and cosy. Under other circumstances I suppose you'd have called it romantic. I got myself a large Jack Daniels, and a Bailey's Irish

Cream for Karen, and we sat in this little cubicle, side by side, close. I can't remember exactly, but I don't think we said anything until I'd got the drinks: if we did it was boring inconsequential stuff, chit-chat about nothing. When she'd taken a couple of sips of that crap she'd wanted, Karen said, 'Peter, I feel awful.'

I pretended I thought she meant she was going to puke, so I half stood up.

'Oh, no,' she said. 'I mean I might have got you into trouble.'

I sat down again. 'Me? Trouble? How could you do that, Karen?' God, my voice was tender.

'I told the police . . .' she began, and then started to sniffle, and tears came into her eyes. I had a clean handkerchief in my top pocket, and gave it to her. Then I held her hand, just to encourage and pacify her, mind. 'Just you tell me all about it,' I said gently.

Well, then she started pouring the whole thing out. All about Sharon (again), and about how Darren had been murdered too (at which I gasped in utter horror) and how the police had questioned her a couple of times (I nodding understandingly) and how she'd told the police about me but only because they had insisted on knowing about anyone who had known her and Sharon (there's me smiling my 'don't you worry your pretty head about a thing') and that the police were probably looking for me now.

I put my arm around her, and pressed her head gently on to my shoulder. Then I put my cheek on her hair. I could feel her heart pounding. I could feel something of my own pounding too, but it certainly wasn't my heart. She was sobbing again, and I really wanted to put her out of her misery, but I didn't want to spoil the moment of closeness. Eventually, though, I did. I gave her a little cuddle, and said, 'There's nothing to worry about, Karen. I've already been to see the police and told them everything I know.'

She sat up, and gazed into my eyes. 'You have?' she asked, with a wispy little smile.

I nodded. 'They put out an appeal for—'

'I know,' she said.

'So I went and saw them.'

'And everything's all right?'

'Everything's fine,' I said, and gave her a reassuring peck on the forehead.

I thought this would be a good time to tell her my name wasn't Peter. 'Anyway, I've a confession to make too. My name—' I began.

'Isn't Peter,' she finished off for me. She ran a finger down my cheek. 'I know that.'

'Oh,' I said, thinking the police must have told her.

'I think I knew the minute you told me.'

'Oh?' I knew I was sounding pretty stupid with all my ohs, but I couldn't really think what else to say.

'You want to tell me your real name?'

'It's Marcus. Marcus Walwyn.'

'That's really nice,' she said, and repeated the

name quietly to herself. 'Marcus. I like that much better than Peter.'

'Good,' I said. 'I'm sorry about lying, Karen. I—'

'Shush,' she whispered.

So I shushed.

We sat there like a couple of lovebirds for about twenty minutes, saying nothing, just comfortable and content. I could have stayed like that all afternoon, holding her, smelling her Impulse, feeling her breath on my neck. But as always happens when you're enjoying yourself something disrupts it. In this case it was a crowd of office workers coming in for a pre-Christmas do of some kind. Loud-mouthed bastards the lot of them, the men; tarty and flirty, the women.

'I suppose we better go,' Karen said, like she was just waking up.

I sighed. 'Suppose so. Hey, Karen – look, this mightn't be the right time, but I'd really like to see you again. Maybe go out to dinner or something. A play maybe.'

'I've never been to a play.'

'Well, we could do that. Whenever you feel—'

'I'd like that – *Marcus*,' Karen said, and gave a sweet little laugh as she stressed my real name.

'Really?'

'Yes. Really.'

'Maybe this weekend?'

I was helping her on with her coat, and couldn't see her expression. When she didn't answer I thought I'd pushed things too hard. But then she turned and said. 'Saturday?'

I beamed at her. 'Great.'

Outside we walked down to Piccadilly, and I started looking for a taxi. I wasn't about to let any girl of mine go home in a Tube. Eventually one came along. 'Here you go,' I said.

She looked surprised. 'For me? Oh – no, Marcus. I'll take the Tube.'

'No you won't,' I told her firmly, but with a charming smile, and opened the door for her. I gave the driver twenty quid and told him Karen's address. She had the window down, and was looking out. I kissed her on the lips. 'Till Saturday,' I said, and stood back.

Karen started to giggle. 'Where, Marcus? What time?'

I came over to the taxi again. 'Sorry. Let's think. What time would suit you?'

'Anytime.'

'Let's say six, then, will we? Let's meet at the café at six – okay?'

She nodded. Then she kissed two fingers and pressed them to my lips. As you can guess, I was over the moon when the taxi took off.

It wasn't until I got back home that I realised my mistake. I wasn't supposed to know where Karen lived, yet I'd told the taxi-driver where to go. Bloody stupid, that was. Still, there was nothing I could do about it now. I'd have to worm my way out of it somehow if it ever became an issue. But I'd have to be more careful in future. A lot more careful.

Sergeant Wilson answered the phone. He gave a couple of grunts, and then cupped his hand over the mouthpiece. 'They've arrived, sir. They're downstairs.'

The Inspector raised his eyebrows.

'The files on Zanker. They've sent them over by car.'

'Oh. Right.'

'Want them sent up?'

The Inspector shook his head. 'No. Say I'll collect them on the way home.'

Sergeant Wilson gave the message and hung up. He leaned back in his chair, and stared at the Inspector. 'You're taking them home, sir?'

'Yes.'

'Does that mean I'm—'

'No, Ray, it doesn't. I want to go through them by myself. You can go home and enjoy the simple pleasures of married life.'

'Thank you, sir.'

The Inspector gave Wilson a hostile glare as if he had detected sarcasm in his voice. But the Sergeant was looking blandly back, and Birt relented. 'I just want to be by myself when I read them.'

'I don't mind giving a hand if you want me to,' Wilson said.

'Still feeling left out in the cold, eh?'

'No, sir. That's not what I meant.'

'Do you *want* to come back with me and read them?'

'Yes, sir. As a matter of fact I do.'

'All right, then, Ray. We'll do it together.'

But later, much later, in the early hours of the following morning, Sergeant Wilson was beginning to regret his enthusiasm. He and Birt sat at the Inspector's kitchen table, the files spread out before them. There were two empty glasses, and two mugs, one with pale coffee congealing in it. The Inspector had taken off his jacket and tie, and rolled up his sleeves. His hair was tousled from constant meditative scratching. Beside him, a foolscap pad was covered in notations, many underlined, some with stars after them. Sergeant Wilson, too, had a pad, but there was less writing on it. He was, now, smoking a cigarette, blinking, and studying a page the Inspector had just passed him. It was Loring's report on Zanker's handwriting.

'I see what you mean,' he said finally. His voice was hoarse, and he coughed before adding, 'But I still don't see how Walwyn could know—' He stopped abruptly as the Inspector held up one hand, demanding silence, turning back a page and reading the final part of it once again, mouthing the words. Then he made a short note on his pad, tossed his pen on to the table and sat back looking, if not satisfied, at least quite pleased.

He looked at his watch. 'Is that the time?' he

asked, sounding astonished.

'Flies when you're enjoying yourself, doesn't it, sir?' Wilson asked.

The Inspector ignored the remark, and stood up. 'More coffee?' he asked, and without waiting for an answer gathered up the mugs and went to the work-top, switching on the kettle, and rinsing one of the mugs.

'I take it you found what you wanted, sir?' Wilson called.

The Inspector spooned instant coffee and sugar into the mugs. He made no immediate reply. He frowned to himself, looking mildly confused as though the question, put to him so baldly, had shattered some small confidence he had achieved. The kettle boiled and he poured water into the mugs, adding milk from a carton to Wilson's. Then he returned to the table, and sat down, pushing one mug towards the Sergeant. For some moments he just sat there in silence, holding his coffee mug in both hands as though warming them, and sipped noisily, his eyes darting over the papers strewn across the table. 'Reading all that,' he said finally, pleasantly enough, 'reading all that it's amazing how it all comes back. Like it was yesterday. Not twenty-odd years ago.'

'Yes,' the Sergeant agreed, just for something to say. 'Did you find what you wanted though?' he asked again.

The Inspector gave a weary smile. 'I don't honestly know, Ray. I mean, it's *there*, but I don't know if I've

– what's the word? – *extracted* it.' He made a small gesture towards the notes he had made on his pad.

'Oh,' Sergeant Wilson said.

'What I'm going to do is give myself a day or two. Go over these . . .' he indicated the notes again, '. . . and see what I come up with.' He sighed. 'It's there,' he repeated. 'All I have to do is *recognise* it.'

'And then?'

'Then, Ray, you and I are going to pay Mr Hubert Zanker a visit.'

Eighteen

I was up bright and early on Friday morning. I had showered and shaved, and was dressed in my second-best suit by seven o'clock. I made a pot of tea and some toast for Ma and took it up to her. 'Goodness me,' she said. 'We are an early bird.'

'*We* can't be *an* early bird, Ma. We can be early birds, not *a* bird,' I told her.

'You know what I mean.'

'I do indeed.'

'And very smart-looking too.'

'Got somewhere special to go.'

'Oh?'

'An author. Got to drive to Cricklewood to see an author.'

'Anyone famous?'

'Not yet.'

Ma stretched luxuriously like a cat. 'But you're going to make him famous, aren't you, darling?'

'I might just do that.'

'Of course you will.'

'If you say so.'

I went to Ma's dressing-table and took a sniff at a couple of her perfumes. 'That's nice,' I told her.

'Which one is that, dear?'

'Joy – by Patou.'

'Oh. Yes. Harry gave me that. It's my favourite, I think.'

'You only think?'

'It all depends, dear. On my mood.'

'Oh,' I said. 'You only slap it on when you're feeling joyous?'

'No, dear. I put it on when I *want* to be joyous. It *makes* me happy. That's the whole point of it.'

'I see,' I said, and put a dab behind one of my ears, and twisted my face into an expression of utter sadness. 'Doesn't work.'

Ma laughed happily. 'You *are* an idiot, darling,' she informed me, and poured herself a cup of tea. 'So, you'll be late home this evening?'

'Why should I be late?'

'I just thought – Cricklewood.'

'It's not in Africa, Ma. It's only about ten miles from here.'

Ma looked astonished. 'Really?'

'Yes.'

She frowned. 'It's not a *nice* area, though, is it?'

'I imagine the people who live there think it is.'

'But we wouldn't?'

I grinned at her. '*You* probably wouldn't. Anyway, I'm not going for the scenery.'

'No, dear, but you'll be careful, won't you?'

I can't say why, but Ma's warning struck me as sort of ominous. I nodded. 'I'll be careful,' I told her, and was surprised at how sombre my voice sounded. I went over to the bed and gave her a kiss on the top of her head. 'See you for dinner,' I said.

I was also surprised, by the way, at how easy it was to dump Les Boys. They were parked across the road, and as I came out of the front door I could see one of them nudge the other. They were facing *up* Ritherdon Road so, of course, I walked *down* the road. That meant they had to go even further up the road, turn, and come back down again. Just to annoy them, as soon as I drew level with their car, I looked ostentatiously at my watch and broke into a canter. I knew they'd have to turn into that side road about twenty yards up from my house, and back out on to Ritherdon Road again. I estimated the time precisely. I glanced over my shoulder, and sure enough, they swung into the side road. All I did then was duck down behind the cars parked along the road, and wait for them to come shooting down and whizz past me, making off in the direction of the Underground station. I doubled back, hopped into my car, and was away, chuckling like a lunatic to myself.

Of course, the traffic was horrendous, and to add to my troubles Radio 3 was in one of its esoteric moods, setting my nerves on edge with something quite ghastly by Hindemith. At least, I *think* it was Hindemith – I didn't leave it on long enough to find out. I let Waffling Wogan take over. To tell you the truth I can't stand Wogan, but sometimes he hits the nail on the head, like when he calls Radio 2 'the home of mediocrity'. Still, the music is pleasant enough: hummable and unintrusive.

Anyway, I found Kranze's house without any bother. It was in one of those small roads off Cricklewood Broadway, a road that had seen better times but still managed to be curiously genteel. Maybe it was making a comeback. Maybe the yuppies had moved in. Maybe it would end up being fashionable enough for Ma to admit its existence.

At nine thirty precisely I rang the doorbell – a white button set in a highly polished brass plate embedded in the brickwork surrounding the porch. It made an unpleasant buzzing noise, nothing like the tinkle I had expected. I thought I saw a curtain move in the window to my left, but I might have been mistaken. I didn't have time to think too much about it in any case, because the door opened, and a tall, gaunt woman asked, 'Yes?'

I admit I was slightly taken aback. I don't quite know what I had expected, or if I'd expected anything, but this . . .

She was, at a guess, in her early sixties. But it was her hair that was extraordinary. It was very long and grey. Clearly she had been in the process of doing it: the right side was neatly plaited and pinned to the top of her head, while the left side hung down past her shoulder. It was almost like looking at two people:

one Teutonic, the other a wild harridan. I addressed myself to the Teuton. 'Marcus Walwyn. Mr Kranze is expecting me.'

For a moment she looked puzzled. Then, 'Oh,' she said. 'The publishing gentleman.' She made an effort to smile but didn't quite pull it off.

'That's right.'

'Of course. My husband *is* expecting you. Do come in.'

I went in, feeling a bit like the fly must have felt when the spider offered a similar invitation.

'Let me take your coat,' Mrs Kranze said. 'You just go to the top of the stairs – all the way up – and it's the door facing you,' she told me, and went off down the passage, carrying my coat.

Well, I don't know about you, but I'm the world's worst at imagining what people look like if I haven't met them. I always get it wrong. And I was certainly wrong about Helmut Kranze. I suppose that with his South American connection and all that I saw him as one of those very upright, rigid, lean, tapping the old riding-crop on the boot Nazi types, the ones who stomped up and down the platforms as the Jews were being loaded up for Treblinka. So, when I went into the room Mrs Kranze had indicated, and saw that chubby, cheery little chap, more like your family butcher than anything else, I was dumbstruck. He was only about five foot, as round as he was tall, bald as a coot, and smiling away, coming to greet me with a bouncy stride and a stubby fat hand extended. He spotted my surprise, of course, and said, 'Not what you expected, eh?' in an accent that was certainly more cockney than Coblenz.

'Well, no,' I told him.

He cackled. 'Come and sit down. Come and sit down. Come and sit down,' he said, taking me by the arm in a grip like a vice and steering me towards an overstuffed armchair that had a shawl thrown over it. When I was seated he went to another chair and sat down, his short little legs barely reaching the ground.

It was only then that I noticed his eyes. I thought at first it was a trick of the light, but then it dawned on me that they were, in fact, of different colours, one blue, the other brown. It was most unnerving as he stared at me. The blue one seemed to smile a lot, while the brown one frowned, so it depended which one you were looking at as you tried to gauge his humour, if he was being serious or poking fun at you. He noticed my unease too. 'Throw you, don't they?' he asked, and gave another cackling laugh. 'Throws everyone,' he said, looking very pleased with himself. He was deeply tanned (well, he would be if he'd just come back from South America, wouldn't he?) and the top of his head was peeling. He reached up and tore off a sliver of loose skin. He studied it for a while, rolled it into a ball between his fingers, and tossed it into the fire. I was beginning to feel a shade pissed off with Helmut Kranze. He wasn't measuring up at all to what I required as a mentor, in a manner of speaking. All I needed was for him to pick his goddam nose and chew on the snot for me to really dislike him, and tell him what to do with himself. 'So,' he said. 'The book.'

'Yes,' I said. 'The book.'

'You liked it.' Not a question, that. A bald statement.

'Very much,' I admitted.

'I thought you would.'

A pompous asshole too, I thought, but let the remark pass. I wasn't about to let him rile me.

'Why did you like it?'

'Why? Well, it was very well written for one thing.'

'Hah!' Kranze snorted scornfully.

'Very gripping,' I tried.

'Gripping,' he repeated, like I'd insulted him. 'Why don't you admit it, young man? You liked it because it struck a chord!'

I wasn't at all happy with the way this conversation was going. I have to admit that I was feeling intimidated. I had lost the initiative. I'd never had the initiative. Kranze was in control, and I certainly didn't want that. And he *knew* he was in control which made it that much more humiliating. 'I wouldn't say that,' I answered.

'I didn't expect you to. Not to admit it.'

'It's not a question of not wanting to admit anything, Mr Kranze,' I told him, trying to sound haughty and superior. 'It rang true, if that's what you mean, but it didn't strike any particular chord,' I said, determined to take the wretch down a peg.

It didn't seem to work though. Kranze rubbed his chubby hands together, and his blue eye twinkled. He looked so bloody smug, like someone who knew I was lying, like someone who knew I knew he knew, but was going to overlook my mendacity. 'So, it gripped you?'

'I've said so.'

'Good. Good. But didn't make you *feel* anything?' He was mocking me, I knew.

But it wasn't his mockery that had me worried. It was almost as if he knew what I'd done, knew about Sharon and Darren, and was just teasing me: as if he'd written a script and I, his puppet, had followed it to the letter.

'Didn't it make you want to . . .' he was saying.

I found myself getting really angry. I found myself starting to shake too, which worried the hell out of me. Not violently or anything dramatic like that, not even physically. I was shaking inside, in my mind, and it dawned on me that it wasn't anger at all that I felt, but fear. 'Mr Kranze,' I interrupted, and I still remember that my voice was unusually cold. Indeed, thinking about it now I wonder if there wasn't a hint of menace in it also, as if by uttering his name in that icy manner I suddenly became a threat to Mr Kranze. I had, certainly, wanted to put an end to his probing questions, to take control, but my interruption had an altogether unexpected outcome. Kranze appeared to freeze. His legs stopped swinging. His body became rigid. His eyes glazed. His nice South American tan became a beige. The slightly mad, excited smile that had played on his lips vanished, as though snapped off from a switch in his head. And it was as if something else was switched off too. I swear to God that the room got suddenly cold, as though the coals that glowed a couple of feet away from me had ceased to produce heat. And some of the ordinary objects that decorated the room took on, to my mind at any rate, an altogether more sinister air. Like the large water-colour over the mantelpiece, a pleasant scene of mountains towering over a placid lake, the Tyrol possibly. In the twinkling of an eye it lost its majestic grandeur and became a scene of – well, I hate to say it – of haunting evil, the purple shadings at the foot of the mountains transformed into corners of darkness wherein wailing, demented spirits might hide in the way sinners might conceal themselves in the shadowed side-chapels of great cathedrals. Even the lake, blue and calm, took on a polluted cast. And ornaments (souvenirs from travels abroad, I had supposed), a kris (like RIP's, but smaller and not so finely embossed), an African figurine, a row of Swiss cowbells, for heaven's sake, were changed before my eyes into instruments of witchcraft and torture. Although I know I sat dead still, I could feel myself making the effort to shake myself out of it. Luckily, just as quickly as it had happened, everything returned to normal:

the mountains glowed over untrammelled waters, the ornaments were inoffensive tat. 'Mr Kranze,' I said again. 'I don't know what you're playing at. I—'

'Playing?' Kranze sounded affronted.

'Please let me finish. As I said, I think your novel is very good. Very good indeed – for a first effort.' I put that in so he wouldn't get cocky again. 'There's still, however, a lot of work to be done on it before we could consider it for publication.' I paused for a moment as a clock somewhere downstairs boomed, echoing throughout the house. Instantly it had stopped, Kranze looked as if he was about to try and say something, so I hurried on. 'I do feel, however, that you're – well, that you have expected me to get something rather more from it than what you've written into it. Perhaps, of course, I've missed the point. Maybe you should rework the book, and make additions if there's something more you want to say. Or give it to someone else to read. Someone who would – who would more fully appreciate your intent.'

Kranze was shaking his head violently, looking quite distressed. 'Oh, no,' he said, in a strangled kind of shout. 'No! It is for you.'

I put on my understanding, calming tone. 'You don't really mean that, Mr Kranze. It's not for me. It just happened to come to me. To land on my desk. It could have gone to any one of a dozen other editors. All of whom—'

'That's the point,' Kranze interrupted. 'Don't you—'

'All of whom would have been just as capable as I of editing your work.'

I felt better after giving him that little lecture. It was me who was feeling pretty smug now.

'But you *accepted* it. *You* accepted it,' Kranze was saying. Then, suddenly, Kranze had wrapped his arms about his chest, holding himself tightly, and was rocking in his chair, uttering a low, prolonged moan. I thought he was having a heart attack, or a fit, or something. 'Is something the matter, Mr Kranze?' I asked, feeling really stupid.

'I can't be wrong,' he said, mostly to himself.

'I'm sorry?'

'I can't be wrong.'

'Wrong about what, Mr Kranze?'

'I was so sure.' Again, it was as if he was having an argument with himself, or someone inside him, and I wasn't there for the moment.

'Sure about what, Mr Kranze?' I persisted, although I'd a pretty good idea what he was on about.

Kranze didn't answer immediately. He took a few minutes to calm down and return to his fat little self. Then he stood up, and put his back to the fire, his hands clasped behind him, looking away from me, up at the ceiling. 'You felt *nothing*?' he asked, sounding both amazed and really disappointed.

I wasn't about to give anything away now. Not now

that I'd got the upper hand. 'I don't understand.'

'When you were reading my novel – you felt nothing?'

'Yes. I felt – just like I told you – that it had the makings of a very good book. An excellent thriller.'

Kranze gazed at me mournfully. 'A thriller,' he said vaguely. 'A thriller.'

'I didn't mean that as an insult, you know, Mr Kranze. It's quite a respected genre at present. You mustn't confuse it with the Agatha Christie stuff.'

Kranze gave a small flick of one hand as though to dismiss my explanation as unnecessary, but when he didn't add to that I thought, maybe, I was being dismissed from his presence. Fuck this, I thought, and stood up. 'I'm sorry our meeting has been so—' I began.

'Will you do one thing for me, Mr Walwyn?'

'If I can.'

'Will you read the book once more?'

I gave a sigh. 'Well,' I said dubiously.

'Read it as if it wasn't a novel. Read it as if it were fact. As if everything in there is the truth.'

'I'll certainly *try* and read it in that light, Mr Kranze, if that's what you wish.'

Kranze nodded.

'Very well.'

'Thank you, Mr Walwyn.'

'Give me a few weeks and I'll get back to you.'

'Thank you,' Kranze said again, and turned away, moving to the window, staring out on to the road.

I made my way to the door. I opened it, and then turned back. '*Is* it all true then?' I asked.

'I'd like *you* to decide that, Mr Walwyn,' he told me, without turning round.

I started to get that feeling of unease again, started to feel the control slipping away from me and back to Kranze. I wasn't about to let him get away with that. I gave a scoffing little laugh. 'I don't think anyone could be quite as nasty a character as the one you've created, Mr Kranze,' I told him, and just had time to wipe the smile of contentment off my face before he swung round.

'Don't you?' he asked.

'No. I don't,' I answered, a bit more sharply than I would have liked.

Kranze continued to stare at me for a while, then slowly turned back to take up gazing out of the window again, and I left the room, closing the door firmly behind me.

Outside, on the doorstep, I took several deep breaths of the cold, crisp air. I'd been so anxious to get out of that house that I'd forgotten to find out who the mystery dedicatee, John Speed, was; I'd left without my overcoat, too, but nothing on earth, at that moment, would have persuaded me to go back. As though to emphasise my silliness a shiver went through me as I walked down on to the pavement. I could feel Kranze's eyes boring into me, so I turned and looked up at the window. He was there all right, watching me. Instinctively (and feeling a bit cheeky)

I raised a hand and waved. Kranze waved back, a slow, laboured gesture, like a reluctant blessing.

I can tell you one thing: I was glad to get back into my car, and to hear the voice of Ken Bruce telling one of his woeful anecdotes.

Sergeant Wilson had anticipated an explosion when he told the Inspector that Marcus Walwyn had given them the slip, and had placed a mug of coffee on the desk to lessen the impact. He was surprised when the only reaction was a baleful glare. And that delivered, the Inspector turned back to the notes on his desk which had preoccupied him for most of the morning.

It was close to one o'clock when he finally sat back and took a sip of his coffee. It had gone cold but he appeared not to notice.

'Solved it, sir?' Wilson asked, and immediately regretted making his little joke because the Inspector took the question seriously, and shook his head wearily.

'It's all there, Ray,' he said, shoving some of the papers about the desk. 'All there in front of me and I can't for the life of me see it.'

'You mean you still think there's a connection between Walwyn and that Zanker chap?'

Inspector Birt nodded. 'Got to be. Oh, the methods are different, but the *thinking's* the same. It's only by accepting that – well, if I'm wrong we're never going to . . .' He sighed and closed his eyes.

'You want to talk it through? Might help,' Wilson

suggested encouragingly. 'Does, sometimes, when you talk things out loud.'

The Inspector chuckled sadly. 'I've done that. You should have heard me last night. Up and down the kitchen, ranting to myself.' He gave the Sergeant a canny look. 'You think I'm wrong, don't you?'

'No. I wouldn't say you're wrong exactly.'

'What would you say then?'

'Maybe – maybe you just *want* too much to be right. I mean, yes, sure, there are certain similarities. We both noted those when we read the files on Zanker the other night. But . . . but there's just no way Walwyn could have known the *details* of the Zanker case . . . and even at that we're supposing he's heard of Zanker at all. *I* don't think he has. When you asked him if he'd met someone called Hubert Zanker, he said no, and I believed him. About all I did believe.'

The Inspector nodded. 'Yes. I think you're right, Ray. He was being truthful. He *doesn't* know Zanker, and yet . . . Oh, Christ!' The Inspector slammed his fist on to the desk. 'It *fits*, damn it. Look—' He shuffled through the papers and extracted a page covered with his own haphazard scrawls. He ran his finger down the list. 'Zanker's primary victim was Emily Cox.'

'Because she was threatening to tell his wife they had been having it off together.'

'Whatever,' the Inspector said, sounding peeved at the way Wilson put things. 'He admits that. He also admits that he killed the Wendy Harcourt woman for practice. It's all here in his own words.' Birt referred to another page lying on his desk. 'He says, "I wanted to be sure I did everything perfectly and I saw nothing wrong in practising. Practice, they say, makes perfect." End of quote.'

'And he killed Arthur Cox, Emily's father because—'

'Because—' Again the Inspector read from the report, 'because "he was in the way".'

'And you think Walwyn—'

'I think Walwyn killed Sharon Hayes for practice, and Darren Cornell because he was in the way.'

'So, if we accept that, Karen Scott is his primary victim?'

The Inspector sucked through his teeth. 'I don't know.'

'Doesn't seem likely, sir. I mean, as far as we can establish he's got absolutely no motive for killing her. On the contrary, he seems to fancy the girl if you ask me. Fancy her a lot.'

The Inspector nodded slowly. 'Too much?'

'Maybe.'

'That could be a motive.'

The Sergeant looked dubious. 'A bit tenuous, that. It's asking a lot for a jury to believe he killed two people just because he had hot pants for Karen Scott.'

'I *know*,' the Inspector snapped.

'Besides, Scott told us he never really made any

serious passes at her. Said he was the perfect gentleman.'

'I *know*,' the Inspector said again, wearily this time.

'It's not as if he's exactly frustrated either. He has that girlfriend up in Bray – the one his mother expects him to marry.'

'God, Ray, don't rub it in.'

'But you might be right.'

Inspector Birt suddenly laughed. 'I've got to hand it to you, Ray. You make everything I thought sound like rubbish, and then you tell me I might be right.'

'Well, you might be, sir. He could be some sort of nut who's infatuated with Scott. He *could* be. But – sorry about this – but it still doesn't explain any Zanker–Walwyn connection.'

'No. It doesn't, does it.'

'Could just be coincidence, I suppose.'

Inspector Birt shook his head. 'I think not.'

'Well, why don't we do what you suggested – go and see Zanker?'

The Inspector said nothing.

'He might just—'

'I dread seeing him again, Ray,' the Inspector admitted.

'I thought you sort of admired him?'

'His intelligence, maybe. But the man – I don't think I've ever hated anyone so much in my life. In fact, I know I haven't.'

Sergeant Wilson gave a small smile. 'I'll look after you, sir.'

'Hah! But who'll look after you, Ray?'

Inspector Birt stood up and stretched. Then, abruptly, he made up his mind. 'All right, Ray. Let's do just that. First thing tomorrow morning, let's go see Mr Hubert Zanker.'

Luckily Ma had one of her migraines that evening, so I didn't have to entertain her. She went to bed about seven, and I went to my room and locked myself in. I put a Bruckner CD on (his *Grosse Messe*) and lay on the bed. My plan had been to spend the evening thinking about Karen, you know, rehearsing everything in my mind as to what I would say and do tomorrow evening. But that had been before I met Kranze. Now, lying there, only Kranze came to mind. To be truthful, as you might have guessed, he had proved something of a disappointment. I've told you already what I thought he'd *look* like and that I'd been proved way off the mark, and I'd been totally wrong about him in the most important way, too. I mean, from his book anyway, I'd expected someone calm and erudite, a great thinker, someone who would take me under his wing, perhaps, and educate me in matters homicidal. No. That's not what I wanted. That's just stupid. I had wanted someone I could confide in, someone who would share the excitement of what I had done, who would be flattered I had used his book as a guide, someone

with whom I could compare notes as it were, someone with whom maybe, maybe, maybe I could, at
some future date, commit another perfect murder.
But there was no way I would have confided in that
crackpot in Cricklewood. Wouldn't tell him the time
of day let alone anything about my clever extermination of Sharon and Darren.

Still, the novel was there. Brilliant. So brilliant, the
vague thought now struck me, that maybe the silly
sod hadn't written it at all. Maybe that Brünhilde of a
wife of his had written it. She certainly seemed more
the type!

And then – and then – my question, '*Is* it all true
then?' and his enigmatic answer, 'I'd like *you* to
decide that, Mr Walwyn,' loomed into and filled my
consciousness. I wondered if I'd been mistaken in
imagining the book to be factual. I wondered, too, if
it was *my* actions that made it true. Perhaps that is
what he meant. And perhaps he wasn't quite so mad
after all.

I swung off the bed and got undressed. Then I
padded along the hallway to the bathroom and gave
my teeth a good scrub. As I was looking at myself in
the mirror (wiping the toothpaste from my lips with a
flannel), something else struck me. Something else
Kranze had written in the novel: 'It may seem
strange, dear reader, but murder can be a very
pleasant exercise. So pleasant that it can become
habitual.' I took another, harder look at myself, and
wondered. I admit I was quite shocked when it

dawned on me that he was right – about it being a pleasant experience at any rate. I realised I really *had* enjoyed both murders, particularly Darren's. And so, was he right about the other bit? Was I looking at an habitual killer? Certainly not, I told myself. Definitely not.

And yet later – well, you know that moment, the moment when you're not quite asleep yet, but not quite awake either? That's the state I was in when I found myself searching my mind for someone else to kill.

Poor Ma seemed the most likely candidate as I drifted off, but that just proves I wasn't hooked.

Nineteen

Saturday started with me having a touch of the Sigmund Freuds: it had snowed overnight and about an inch of it settled so everything was white, and my mind turned to things virginal again. Like I've told you, I'm not stupid, and I knew Karen and Darren were having it off (that type of person, Darren, always does *have* to have it off, being incapable of anything remotely like a platonic friendship; no words, you see, can't talk). But it sort of got fixed in my mind that with Darren departed, somehow (and this was absolutely in my mind) Karen got her virginity back and was, of course, keeping it for me. I did have another thought, but it's quite vulgar, if you'll excuse me. I thought that Darren's prick was probably so small anyway, and mine so formidable, that it would be like deflowering a virgin in any case.

It was going to be a long day, I knew. There was no way Ma would venture out in such weather, not even to Fortnum's (it's always Fortnum's, by the way, to

273

those who actually shop there; Fortnum and Mason's
to the yuk tourists and those who would like to shop
there but can't afford it). 'All that slush, darling,'
she'd say in exactly the same way as she'd say 'all
those people, darling', like neither had any right to
intrude into her life. My worry was that she'd decide
to have a blitz on the house and enrol my help – not
by asking me or anything as overt as that: by sighing
and giving the odd little moan like she was really
killing herself on my behalf. She did that from time to
time on a wet Sunday, redusting and repolishing
everything the daily, Mrs McLeod, had done every
day during the week. That was another of Ma's
hobby-horses: the inferior quality of present-day
servants. She'd harp back to the days when *her*
mother had a brace of 'nice country girls' for 2/6 a
week plus their keep, not the wretched ethnic refu-
gees she had to tolerate, although what made her
think Mrs McLeod was ethnic is anyone's guess.
Unless the Scots *are* ethnics. Maybe they are. Harry
Rutherford once said in his supercilious way,
'They're not quite like us white folk.' Maybe he was
right.

But I needn't have worried. When I brought Ma
in a cup of tea at about nine, she decided she was
feeling 'a trifle faint', which meant she'd been
slurping the gin. So, I told her to stay where she
was, and said I was going to work on my book. I
knew that would keep her out of my hair since, as
the brilliant author she was determined to believe I

was, I could not possibly be disturbed.

'Oh, darling. How is it going?'

'Quite well, really,' I lied. 'But I'm at a particularly tricky bit just now.'

'Oh, dear,' Ma said, like I'd told her about starvation in Ethiopia. 'What a shame.'

'I'm going to spend the morning working on it.'

'Don't you worry, darling. It will work itself out,' Ma said, and I had to smile to myself because that was *exactly* what she said when the Ethiopian famine was first mooted. 'I'm sure it will work itself out,' she'd said, and gone back to whatever it was she'd been doing – making up her shopping-list for Fortnum's, I think.

Needless to say, I spent the morning poring over Kranze's novel. I thought I might have second thoughts about it, now that I'd actually met Kranze. See it in a different light, I mean. But once I got into it again any doubts I might have had vanished. When I'd finished it I found myself laughing aloud, just like Kranze, in the book, ended up laughing at the police because, naturally, they never caught him. I could actually hear his mad cackle echoing around my bedroom, and I thought about practising that manic laugh, and maybe using it sometime myself, when Inspector Birt and his ludicrous chum finally gave up, for example.

The furthest thing from Hubert Zanker's mind was laughter as he eyed Inspector Birt and Sergeant

Wilson with something akin to utter loathing.

'Long time, Hubert,' Birt said, deciding to try the personal approach.

Zanker blinked once but said nothing.

Inspector Birt looked about the room, nodding to himself. 'Nice and comfortable,' he said in a low voice, meaning only to think it.

'What is it you want?' Zanker asked.

Uninvited, the Inspector sat down. 'Your help, believe it or not.'

Zanker gave a scornful half-laugh.

Sergeant Wilson ostentatiously pulled a notebook from his inside pocket. 'Still on licence, I see, Mr Zanker?' he said, making it a question.

Zanker ignored him.

'It could—' Sergeant Wilson started to say, when Inspector Birt interrupted him.

'Tell me about Marcus Walwyn,' he said suddenly, watching Zanker carefully.

Zanker gave a slight twitch. 'Hah,' he said.

'You *do* know him?' the Inspector persisted.

'I didn't say that.'

'No, but—'

'Been up to no good, has he?' Zanker demanded, suddenly appearing almost jovial.

'I didn't say that,' the Inspector decided to say. 'So you *do* know him then?'

'I didn't say that,' Zanker said again.

The Inspector sat forward. 'Don't play games with me, Hubert. Do you know him or not?'

Zanker gave him a shrug. 'In a manner of speaking.'

'Meaning?'

'I don't *know* him.'

'You've met him?'

'Once.'

'When?'

Zanker gave a thin smile. 'Yesterday.'

'Yesterday?' the Inspector revealed his surprise.

Zanker nodded gleefully. 'He called on me yesterday.'

'Why would he call on you?'

Zanker rubbed the top of his head furiously with one hand, keeping his odd-coloured eyes fixed on the Inspector's face. 'Why should it concern you?' he asked. Then he cackled. 'He *has* been up to something, hasn't he?'

'It's no laughing matter,' Sergeant Wilson said.

'Oooh,' Zanker said, mockingly. 'He *has* been naughty then.'

'He's a goddam killer like yourself, Zanker,' Wilson exploded.

'Thank you, Sergeant,' Inspector Birt said coldly, clearly annoyed. He turned back to Hubert Zanker. 'He's a suspect,' he explained.

'Why come here? To me?' Zanker asked.

'Because – because there are certain similarities between your . . .' the Inspector paused and gave what appeared to be an embarrassed little cough, '. . . your *modus operandi* and his.'

277

'Indeed?' Zanker asked.

'Indeed,' the Inspector said.

'And you think—' Suddenly Zanker was on his feet, his eyes flashing. 'And you think I was helping him?' he demanded angrily. 'You bastard, Birt. You think just because—'

'Sit down, Zanker,' the Inspector ordered.

Slowly Zanker sat down, but his body remained tense as if he was about to spring into frantic action again at a moment's notice. Small beads of spittle formed on the edges of his mouth, and he wiped them quickly away with the back of his hand.

'Now,' Inspector Birt said quietly, as if nothing had happened. 'Tell me why Marcus Walwyn came to see you yesterday?'

'Because he's editing my book.'

Inspector Birt exhaled, and kept his mouth open for several seconds.

'Your book?' he asked quietly.

'My book,' Zanker reiterated.

'And what book might that be?' the Inspector enquired, making the question sound vaguely mocking.

'A novel I've written.'

'A novel?'

'A novel.'

'Based on your . . . your . . .' The Inspector floundered.

'My exploits,' Zanker said in a matter-of-fact tone.

The Inspector leaned back in his chair, frowning,

clearly with something on his mind. 'How much of this – I mean, is it fiction or fact? How much of it is – how much do you draw on your – your exploits?' he asked, saying 'exploits' with some distaste.

Zanker stuck out one pudgy hand and wiggled it to indicate fifty-fifty.

'You describe the murders?'

'Oh, yes.'

'And the fact that the *first* murder was what you called "a trial run"?'

'Yes.'

'So in what way does it differ?'

Zanker gave a wicked grin. 'My hero gets away with it,' he explained.

'Ah.'

'You've got a copy of this book, I suppose?' Wilson asked.

'Of course.' Then his eyes widened. 'Don't tell me – so *that*'s what our young friend Marcus has been up to. Good heavens!'

'We'll want a copy of it.'

'For what reason? Surely it's permissible to write—'

'We'll want a copy,' the Inspector said firmly.

'Very well,' Zanker said, but made no move to do anything about it.

'Well, go and get me one then,' Inspector Birt said.

Zanker stood up and trundled across the room to a large cupboard that stood in the corner.

'Incidentally,' Inspector Birt said, 'how does your

hero manage to get away with it?'

Zanker took a copy of the manuscript from the cupboard and turned, answering as he made his way back to his chair. 'He didn't make the mistakes I did,' he said coldly.

'Cleverer than you, eh?' Wilson asked.

'No. Cleverer than you,' Zanker said. 'Than the police,' he corrected himself.

'Easy when it's fiction,' Wilson said.

'Really?' Zanker asked. Then he shrugged. 'We'll have to wait and see about that, won't we? Young Marcus seems to have you pretty well baffled, I'd say.'

'Are you seeing him again?' the Inspector asked, standing up and tucking the manuscript under his arm.

'I'd say so.'

'When?'

'When he's decided how he can improve my work. When he's edited it.'

'Needs improving, does it?' Wilson asked.

'*He* says so.'

'And when does he hope to have that done?' the Inspector wanted to know.

Zanker shrugged. 'He didn't say.'

Inspector Birt walked across the room, and stood over Zanker. 'Right. Now I want you to listen to me, Hubert. I want you to listen carefully. You are *not* to tell Walwyn that we've been to see you. You are *not* to tell Walwyn we know anything about this book. I swear to God if you in any way let him know anything about either our visit or our knowledge of this book I'll have you for conspiracy, or for aiding and abetting, or for something. I'll have you, one way or another. Is that clear?'

'Quite clear,' Zanker said, a curiously cunning smile playing in his eyes.

'As I said, if you do—'

'Inspector, I have no intention of telling him.'

'Good.'

'Not because of your threats – which, to tell the truth, don't worry me in the least.'

'They bloody well should,' Wilson interrupted.

'But because it would ruin the whole point of the book,' Zanker said, repeating, 'The whole point of the book.'

'And what's that supposed to mean?' the Inspector demanded.

Zanker gave him a look filled with hatred and mockery. 'Goodbye, Inspector,' he said, and closed his eyes.

'The Inspector asked you—' Wilson began, but Inspector Birt put a hand on his arm, and shook his head.

'We'll be back, Hubert,' he promised. 'One way or the other, we'll be back.'

Zanker opened his eyes briefly, and smiled. 'Always a pleasure to see you, Inspector,' he said, the smile drifting from his face only after the two men had left the room.

★ ★ ★

You'll remember I told you how I'd seen Karen fiddling with her broken charm bracelet on the Tube, and how she'd seemed upset as she tossed it back into her handbag? And perhaps you'll remember, also, that I said I went window shopping on the day I found out where Karen worked, killing time until she got off work. I also mentioned that I bought something, and that I'd let you in on that secret later. Well, what I bought, as if you haven't guessed, was a charm bracelet, a really good one. Actually, when I bought it, it was charmless, but you'd think I was really some sort of freak if I said I bought her a charmless bracelet, wouldn't you? Anyway, it was only charmless for a short while since I also got her a little gold gnome to hang on it. Don't ask me why I chose a goddam *gnome*. There were other things on offer – hearts, and crosses, and dogs, and cats, and even an Eiffel Tower – but I chose the gnome, and was very pleased with my selection, maybe because it was sort of ambiguous.

Anyway, I decided to take the bracelet with me that evening, and *maybe* give it to her if everything worked out all right. I didn't wrap it up in fancy paper or anything like that. I just slipped the box into my jacket pocket, and thought I'd produce it at an appropriate moment, making the generous gesture seem ever so casual. I also kept it in the back of my mind that if things *didn't* go as planned, if giving a gift appeared to be, well, over the top, I could always give it to her for Christmas. Nothing like thinking ahead.

'Darling, you look *so* handsome,' Ma said when I came downstairs, ready to go out and meet Karen.

'Thanks, Ma. You feeling better?'

'Thank you. Yes.' She was in the drawing-room, reclining like Sarah Bernhardt on the settee.

'Harry coming round this evening?'

'He said he might drop in for a drink.'

'Good. Don't like to think of you here by yourself on a Saturday evening.'

Ma gave a little titter. 'You don't have to worry about me, dear.'

'I know I don't have to *worry*, Ma,' I told her, and took the comb from my inside pocket and ran it through my hair once again.

'Somewhere special, I take it,' Ma said.

I shook my head. 'Not really.'

Ma gave me one of her sceptical looks.

'Just a couple of drinks with Nick Putty and his wife.'

'I haven't met him, have I?'

'Who, Nick? No. You will though. Must have a party here sometime soon.'

Ma brightened. 'Yes. What a good idea, dear. Let's do that. Maybe Christmas week.'

'We'll see. Anyway, must go.'

'Enjoy yourself, dear.'

'I'll try.'

'And do drive carefully.'

'Not driving, Ma. Drinking. I've phoned for a taxi.'

'You *are* a good boy.'

'Oh, the best, Ma. The best.'

For some reason Ma took that seriously. 'Yes, dear. You really are. You've been quite wonderful to me since your father died,' she said, and started to look weepy so I went over to her and kissed the top of her head.

'I won't be all that late,' I told her. 'Probably see you when I get home, but if you're asleep I won't wake you.'

The front doorbell rang. 'That'll be my taxi.'

'Bye, dear.'

'Bye, Ma.'

So, there I was, sitting in the taxi, going down Ritherdon Road. I was really tempted to wave to the two goons sitting in their unmarked Vauxhall, but I decided not to, decided to treat them with proper disdain. I was feeling a bit sadistically sorry for them really. It was bitterly cold, and sleeting quite heavily. I'd booked a table in the Brasserie of L'Escargot, and in my mind's eye I saw the poor sods tramping up and down outside while Karen and myself enjoyed ourselves. The table I'd booked was the one I always used, the one in the corner by the window, so I'd be able to look out and see them. If I felt really cheeky I might just raise my wine-glass to them if I caught their eye. Make them really pissed off. You wouldn't get

Inspector Birt or Nosferatu out in that sort of weather, that was for sure. I wondered what the Inspector *was* up to. Tearing what was left of his hair out, probably.

Twenty

It was as if the years had fallen away, as if he was once more a young and eager detective constable, as if, almost, he was being given a second shot at life. Sitting there on the settee in the over-heated front room, his feet defiantly propped on the restored and varnished mahogany coffee-table, a tumbler of whisky and water on the arm beside him, Inspector Birt had been mesmerised by Zanker's novel. Clever that: Zanker/Kranze. Well, not all *that* clever, but it explained the reason Walwyn had truthfully said he had no idea who Hubert Zanker was. And, to give him his due, Zanker had stuck pretty much to the facts, until the final three chapters at any rate. And he had eschewed the temptation to make the police look like plodding dolts if only because by so doing he could make himself appear that much more wily and intelligent. Yet, what intrigued the Inspector most was the fact that he could have been reading about Marcus Walwyn rather than Hubert Zanker. It was uncanny. It was also the problem: if Walwyn continued to follow the novel, if, as in the book, he stopped now, he would be well nigh impossible to incriminate, just as Zanker's main character had been impossible to catch. In real life Zanker hadn't stopped, hadn't been able to stop, and had been caught. But his hero . . . that was another kettle of fish.

Inspector Birt picked up his glass and swilled the whisky round and round, staring at it. Somehow, God alone knew how, Marcus Walwyn would have to be goaded into making the single error that would betray him. The Inspector drank deeply, feeling the whisky burn its way to his stomach. Karen Scott was the key. She was, in effect, the primary victim although clearly, at the moment, Walwyn had no intention of killing her. What if, though . . . The Inspector gave an involuntary shudder. He glanced at the clock on the mantelpiece. It said ten minutes to four which meant it was twenty past four since the clock always ran half an hour late for some reason he had been unable to fathom: precisely half an hour late. Never any more, never any less.

'What made me a cut above your average murderer was that I knew precisely when to stop, when to call enough, and leave the police floundering.' That was what Zanker had written. And if Walwyn did know that now was the time to stop he would certainly have them floundering. The Inspector wished Wilson was with him. He thought about telephoning, even rose from the settee as if to make for the phone, but changed his mind and stretched, arching his aching back. A vague idea of getting Zanker to help passed through his mind, but was quickly dismissed. The only advantage he held was having the book and Walwyn being oblivious to that fact. One false move on Zanker's part and Walwyn would cotton on. He was a bright lad, no question of that. An arrogant son of a bitch too, and it was his arrogance that Birt was now convinced would be his downfall. His pride, that was what had to be played on: damage his miserable pride and he might just make the mistakes. If not . . . the Inspector preferred not to think about that for the moment. He bent down and gathered up the manuscript, tapping it on the table until the pages were neatly in place. He finished his whisky, and carried the empty glass into the kitchen. Pride cometh before a fall, he thought to himself, and laughed somewhat bitterly. Then another thought struck him. What was it Paterson had said when he phoned in at the end of his stint? Lovers, came to mind. Like lovers. That was it. He's said they were eating in a restaurant in Soho, looking happy – just like lovers. The Inspector rinsed his glass under the tap and left it to dry on the draining-board. For a moment he wondered if there had been a conspiracy between the two – Karen Scott and Walwyn. It would certainly explain . . . He shook his head. No. The Scott girl was too . . . too . . . he couldn't think of the word he wanted. Too open, maybe. Too frank. Innocent, almost. He shook his head again. He walked back to the sitting-room and lay down on the settee, propping a cushion behind his head. There was only one way to go. He closed his eyes. It would mean taking Karen Scott and Paul Cornell into his confidence. That could be tricky. But . . . He'd talk to Wilson about it later. See what he thought. He wriggled his body more comfortably into the couch, and fell asleep.

We were both early, which was a good sign. I got to the café about ten to six, and Karen arrived five minutes later. She looked really pretty, and I could see she'd made a special effort just to please me. I thought about kissing her on the cheek, but decided not to. I didn't want her to think I was being forward just yet. So, we just shook hands although I did hang on to her hand for a bit longer than maybe I should have, but she certainly didn't seem to mind. 'You look lovely,' I told her. That's a tip for you: always tell a girl she looks lovely even if she looks like a dog, and you'll have her eating out of your hand. They can't resist flattery. Maybe because they don't get much of it in this day and age.

'Thank you,' she said, and gave me a happy look with her big doe eyes.

I held out my arm, and she slipped hers through it. 'Anything special you want to do?' I asked.

She shook her head, and looked up at me as if to say I'm happy just being with you, Marcus.

'Well, I thought we'd go and have a drink and then

go out for dinner. I've booked a table.'

'That would be lovely.'

'Right. Let's go then.'

We strolled along to the Savoy and went up to the American bar for a drink. I ordered her a White Lady and a Jack Daniels for myself. I sat opposite her, not beside her, just so she'd really feel at ease. It was like taking a child to the zoo for the first time. She was totally fascinated, looking at everything and everybody, and I know she was impressed when I dismissed the waiter with a casual wave of my hand when he brought the change, like the fiver tip I gave him was a mere bagatelle.

'It's terribly expensive,' she said.

I smiled. 'It's the Savoy,' I told her. 'People who come here don't think about the cost. They don't have to.'

'I feel out of place.'

I smiled at her again. 'Don't be silly.'

'I do. Really.'

'You're with me, Karen,' I told her. I don't know why I said it, or what I really meant by it, but it seemed to work.

'Yes,' she said, and gave me another of her lovely smiles.

'Well, then, no need to feel out of place,' I said and smiled back charmingly.

We left the Savoy at ten to seven, and took a taxi to Greek Street. Lisa, who ran the Brasserie (but who's gone now, now that they've revamped the place, I hear), was on duty and welcomed us with her usual big smile. 'Ah, Mr Walwyn,' she said, and took us to the table I'd booked.

Karen was enthralled. 'It's the first time I've ever been to a real restaurant,' she confessed.

'Really?'

She nodded. 'McDonald's was where Darren and me used to go.'

I made a face.

'It's all we could afford.'

'Oh, I didn't mean—'

'I know,' she said, and touched my hand with her fingers. 'It's really lovely here,' she added as if to make up for upsetting me. 'You must eat here a lot.'

'Why do you say that?'

'Well, that lady knew you.'

'Lisa? Yes, well, I do like it here. Down here, not upstairs. What they call the proper restaurant is upstairs. It's where all the so-called celebrities go. Just to be seen. The food's better down here, *I* think.'

'What celebrities?'

'The usual. Jonathan Ross. Melvyn Bragg – creeps like that.'

'I've heard of Jonathan Ross,' she said.

I ordered us a couple of vodka martinis to be going on with, and we sipped those while we waited for the food. Karen had smoked salmon to start with (which she clearly didn't like a lot but ate all the same) and I had six escargots which I adore. Then we both had noisette of lamb which was delicious. We had a bottle of Chardonnay too, which went down a treat. We didn't have any pudding. By the way, always remember to call it 'pudding' or you'll give yourself away: only real upstarts call it 'sweet' or 'dessert'. We didn't speak a lot while we were eating, just sort of chatted about nothing, the way people do. We had coffee to finish off with.

'You enjoy that?' I asked.

'It was wonderful. Thanks, Marcus.'

'My pleasure.'

'You've been so kind to me.'

'Don't be silly.'

'You have. Really, you have.'

'It's easy to be kind to you, Karen,' I told her. 'I just wish . . .' I started and then stopped, making what I was about to say a bit more dramatic.

'Wish what, Marcus?'

'Nothing.'

'Tell me.'

'Oh, I just wish we had met under – well, different circumstances.'

Her face clouded. 'Yes.'

'Anyway,' I said, raising my glass, raising it high enough for the two detectives out in the street to see too, 'Here's to us.'

For a moment she had a puzzled expression, but she raised her glass anyway. Then she said, 'Marcus, I don't want you to think—'

'Shhshh,' I said.

'It's just that—'

I leaned across and put a finger on her lips to silence her. When I took my finger away she gave me a really sad look. 'Hey, come on,' I said quickly. 'We're supposed to be enjoying ourselves.'

'Oh, I *am* enjoying myself, Marcus. But—'

'But nothing.' I reached into my pocket and pulled out the box with the bracelet inside. 'I got that for you,' I said, and slid it across the table.

'For me?' she asked, genuinely surprised.

'Who else?' I asked, with a great big smile. 'Go on, open it.'

Like a child at Christmas she opened the box, and gave a little squeal of delight. 'Oh, Marcus, it's lovely.'

I saw Birt's two boys staring in at me, so I said, 'Don't I get a kiss or anything?' and leaned towards her. She kissed me on the lips, and I was tempted to wink at the lads over her shoulder. She put the bracelet on. 'I have one of these but it's broken,' she said.

'Yes, I know.'

'You know?'

'Yes. Saw you on the Tube trying to put it on one morning.'

As soon as I'd said that I knew it had been a mistake. She gave me a strange, penetrating look, and frowned briefly. 'I thought you said . . .' she began.

'Said what?'

She smiled at me. 'Nothing. Never mind. Just me being silly. You must have been watching me very closely, though.'

'Not really. Just happened to notice you that morning.'

She toyed with the bracelet. 'It's really lovely,' she said again.

'I'm glad you like it.'

'You shouldn't buy me expensive things like this, though.'

'Why not, for heaven's sake?'

'Because, well, because we're not . . .' She stopped and laughed timidly.

'Not what, Karen?'

'We're just friends.'

'I see.'

'Marcus – you're ever so nice, but – well, I haven't got over Darren yet. I . . .'

It was quite difficult for me not to show my annoyance, but I managed to hide it okay, although I knew a damper had been put on the evening.

'So, who says just friends can't give pressies, eh?'

'You know what I mean.'

'Sure I do. Don't you worry. I can wait, you know.'

'Oh, Marcus – don't. Please don't.'

I was really angry by now. I swallowed hard before saying, 'Don't what, for heaven's sake?'

'You know I like you a lot but – but not that way.'

'I see,' I said, trying to look shattered instead of furious.

'Give me some time, will you?'

'All the time you want,' I told her.

'You're sweet,' she said.

'Oh, sweet as a nut,' I answered.

She laughed at that, nicely. 'I mean it, Marcus,' she told me. 'Really, I do.'

Of course, just because she was being *nice* about rejecting me made matters worse. And the fact that she was fobbing me off made me want her all the more. I was getting quite horny under the table, and I knew I had to be really careful. 'Are you saying you don't want to go out with me again? Is that it?'

'Oh, no. That's not it, Marcus. I just don't want you to think . . .'

I didn't want to hear what I wasn't supposed to think. I finished the last of the wine in my glass. 'Let's drop it, will we? Let's start again, okay? We're two friends having dinner together, nothing more, right?'

She gave me a lovely, appreciative smile. 'Right,' she said.

'Good.'

But it was anything but good, and it was pretty much downhill from then on. To make matters worse, I couldn't really understand what had gone wrong. I couldn't think of anything *I'd* done or said. I'd been nothing but nice and kind to her, and what did I get for my troubles?

We left the Escargot at about nine thirty. Mind you, once we got outside she took my arm again and snuggled up to me against the wind, which was quite nice, but I really wanted to get rid of her now. I wanted to think things out on my own. I wanted to work out why things had gone sour, and, of course, to plan a renewed strategy. I wasn't about to give up that easily.

Anyway, without asking her, or saying anything to her, in fact, I hailed a taxi, and I must admit it was some small compensation to see she was disappointed when I opened the door for her and said, in a fairly off-hand way, 'I enjoyed this evening, Karen.'

'So did I, Marcus. Really I did,' she said, and got into the taxi.

I shut the door, and gave the taxi-driver twenty quid, but I didn't tell him where to go. Then I stood back and waited for the taxi to drive off.

Karen opened the window. 'Can I call the little gnome Marcus?' she asked sort of wistfully.

'Call it anything you like. Call it Darren if you want,' I told her, and turned away.

I could see her looking at me out of the back window as the taxi moved off towards Shaftesbury Avenue. She looked pretty sad. Not half as sad as I felt though. Well, not so much sad as bitter. Maybe I'd pushed too hard, but I didn't really think so. She was just using me, that's all. That's what I decided to think anyway although now, I know, it was unfair. Anyway, it was at that moment, standing there in the cold on the corner of Greek Street on that Saturday night, that I think I had my first feeling of hate for

Karen. I do know that later, after I got home and
took to my bed, I thought again about Kranze's
phrase, 'It may seem strange, dear reader, but murder can be a very pleasant exercise', and it was now
Karen who figured largely in my mind instead of Ma.
I definitely knew that if I wasn't going to have Karen,
nobody would. Not any new boyfriend. Not the
deceased Darren. I'd certainly see to that.

Twenty-one

Inspector Birt had made up his mind by Monday evening, but he said nothing about it to Sergeant Wilson on the drive to the station, perhaps because he was worried the Sergeant might dissuade him from his plan of action. Yet he had decided to be adamant, regardless of what anyone said, regardless, too, of the very real danger his strategy represented. So, he was in a querulous, testy frame of mind when he addressed the team assembled in the Incident Room.

'Right, you lot,' he began. 'Sit down, shut up, and listen.' He looked around for a chair for himself, and nodded his thanks curtly as Sergeant Wilson brought him one. He sat down and leaned forward, his hands clasped and resting between his knees. Carefully and methodically he told the team exactly what he intended to do. He explained why he intended to use this particular ploy. He answered questions willingly and without his usual impatience. He asked for opinions, and when they were given he discussed them, arguing if they differed from his own until he had proved his point. It was only when he was completely satisfied that everyone appreciated the dangers involved that he stood up, and said, 'And that's it, gentlemen – and ladies,' he added with a thin smile to the two WPCs. And with that he walked quickly from the room, followed by Wilson.

'You're taking one hell of a chance, aren't you, sir?' the Sergeant asked as he closed the door and leaned his back against it.

'I've no option, Ray.'

'And if it doesn't work?'

'It's *got* to work.'

'But if it doesn't?'

'It *will*.'

Sergeant Wilson shook his head. 'I hope you're right.'

'So do I, Ray. So do I.' The Inspector sat down behind his desk, and folded his hands behind his head, closing his eyes.

'Sir?'

The Inspector snapped open his eyes and raised his eyebrows.

'Nothing.'

'Say it, Ray,' the Inspector said wearily.

'You know I back you in everything you do.'

'But?'

'But I just don't think you're right in—'

'Why didn't you say so in there then?'

'I didn't want to—'

'Embarrass me?'

'Undermine you,' Wilson corrected.

'Ah.'

The two men remained silent for several moments, eyeing each other. Then the Inspector said, 'Sit down, Ray,' and when Wilson was seated, Birt continued, 'I spent the whole weekend reading Zanker's book, and it's all in there. All of it. Walwyn has been using it as a sort of textbook. If we allow him to stick to it, we'll never catch him. He'll stop now. That will be an end to it. We've nothing on him. We simply *have* to goad him into deviating from the text and making a mistake. And the only way we can do that – I honestly believe this, Ray – is by using the Scott girl and Paul Cornell.' The Inspector paused, but instantly held up a hand as the Sergeant looked as if he was about to interrupt. 'I'm not going to try and *force* either of them to help. That's a promise. I want simply to put it to them and see what their reaction is. If they agree, well and good. If they don't . . .' the Inspector shrugged and sighed, 'then we'll have to think again.'

Sergeant Wilson crossed his legs, and tugged gently at the corner of his moustache. He gave a grimace that said he wasn't altogether convinced, but he didn't speak, and looked mildly startled when the Inspector said, 'Murder can be a very pleasurable exercise.'

'I'm sorry, sir?'

'That's what Zanker says. And I think Walwyn

enjoys killing. He's not *afraid* to kill. It's an intellectual exercise for him.'

'Great.'

'Zanker insists that the trick is knowing when to stop. And he's absolutely right, you know. If Walwyn was to stop now . . .' the Inspector shrugged again. 'What I want to do is make it impossible for him to stop now.'

'Using Scott and Cornell.'

'They're the only weapons I have.'

The Sergeant sighed. 'All right.' he said finally.

'You mean you agree?'

'I mean I'll back you.'

'Good,' the Inspector said. 'Now we can start doing something.' He gave the Sergeant a smile. 'Right. I want both Scott and Cornell here this evening. Get Paterson to take a WPC with him – Williamson, if she's free – and bring in Scott. I want to speak to her *before* I talk to the two of them together. But I want it made clear to her that this is – what's the word – shit, I can't think. I want her to feel at ease. When she gets here, put her in the Rape Victim Room. It's better in there. More homely. As for Cornell, you might have to pick him up at work. I don't want any heavy-handed stuff. Tell whoever goes for him to lie if they have to, just so his boss and his workmates don't think we're taking *him* in – okay? They can say there's been an accident – any damn thing they like. Just make it clear *he's* in the clear, and that he's not helping us in any investigation. You know what they're like. Last thing I want is for Cornell to be seen as a grass.'

The Sergeant nodded. 'Right.'

'And have someone with him all the time. Get him tea. Talk to him. Put him absolutely at ease – if that's possible under the circumstances.'

'Right,' the Sergeant said again, with the trace of a smile.

'And you better warn your wife, Ray. It's going to be a long night.'

'You're going to have to tell them Walwyn is the one you suspect,' the Sergeant pointed out, ignoring the Inspector's remark for the moment.

'I know.'

'Cornell, he's going to want—'

'Not after I've explained things to him.'

'You hope.'

'Yes. I hope. What the hell else is there for me to do, but hope?'

The Sergeant gave a small snort. 'Not a lot.'

'Precisely.'

I had a really miserable Sunday. All I could think of was Karen, and how she'd treated me. It had been in my mind that after a lovely evening on Saturday we'd have seen each other again on Sunday, gone somewhere, somewhere crazy, like the zoo maybe, and laughed and been really happy. But instead I had to endure one of Ma's Sunday lunches, those monthly

ones when she had half a dozen of her cronies in, and
sit there like a zombie listening to their stupid
chatter, chatter that usually ended up by them all
discussing *my* future and wanting to know when I was
going to get married and settle down. 'Not ready to
settle down yet,' was my stock reply, and Ma, to be
fair, usually backed me up. 'Marcus knows what he's
doing,' she'd say. 'He's not going to rush into anything, are you, dear?'

So, I was glad when Monday came and I could go
into the office. At least there I wasn't getting pushed
into nuptials. I was left pretty much alone, and I
could really think about what had gone wrong. To be
perfectly honest I suspected it had been my fault. I'd
probably expected too much too soon. But I also felt
Karen could have been a bit more forthcoming.
Bloody friendship. Just great, that. You know, I even
thought about kidnapping her. Just a crazy idea.
Something to pass the time. I didn't have any intention of actually doing it, but I enjoyed fantasising
about it. It helped me get through the morning at any
rate.

And come lunch-time I was in a better frame of
mind, so I decided I'd go up to the café and see her.
Maybe even apologise, if that was what she wanted.

As usual I left it quite late so that the café wouldn't
be too busy.

'Hello, Marcus,' Karen said.

'Hiya,' I said, and sat down. 'Coffee and a ham
sandwich, please.'

'Marcus . . .'

I looked up at her innocently.

'Back in a minute.'

So far so good. She was on the defensive, which was what I wanted. I watched her as she went to get what I'd ordered. Funny, you can tell when people are nervous even from the way they walk, and Karen was certainly nervous. It was in her voice, too, when she came back and put the coffee and sandwich on the table. 'Marcus, I'm so sorry.'

I looked surprised. 'For what?'

'For Saturday.'

I pretended to be lost. 'For Saturday? What about Saturday?'

'I was awful.'

'No you weren't,' I told her. 'You were great. I was the one who was awful.'

'No you weren't,' she now told me, and suddenly we were laughing.

'This could go on all day,' I said. 'Yes you were, no you weren't.'

'I'm forgiven?'

'Nothing to forgive,' I said.

'Hey, Miss!' someone shouted.

'Must go,' Karen said.

I grabbed her hand. 'Tell him to piss off,' I said.

She giggled. 'I can't do that.'

'Pity,' I told her, and let go of her hand.

She left me and went over to the yob who'd shouted. She took some money off him and went to the till. Then she brought him back his change, and came back to me. I noticed she wasn't wearing my bracelet. 'Didn't like the bracelet, then?' I asked.

She looked puzzled for a moment. 'Oh. Of course I liked it. I love it.'

'Why aren't you wearing it then?'

'Not to work, silly. It's *far* too nice to wear to work. It's for special occasions.'

I liked that. It really pleased me. But I just said, 'Oh.'

'I was thinking about you all weekend,' she said.

'What were you thinking about me?'

'Only nice things.'

I bathed her in a smile. 'I was thinking about you too,' I admitted, but I didn't give her any clue as to what I'd been thinking.

'I hope you're going to ask me out again.'

'You want me to?'

She nodded, nicely shy. 'Yes.'

'Just as a friend, of course.'

She blushed.

'Sorry,' I said. 'Maybe this weekend?'

She nodded. 'I'd like that.'

'Maybe go to a club. You like dancing?'

'I love it. I'm not very good at it, though.'

'Okay. I'll arrange something. But I'll see you before that anyway.'

'Good,' she said, and sounded as if she really meant it.

Two old biddies came into the café, and Karen had

to leave me to serve them. I ate the sandwich and drank my coffee. Both were finished when she came back. 'Anything else?'

I gave her a wicked grin. 'Now that you mention it—'

She blushed again.

'Just joking.'

'I know.' She took a long hard stare at me. 'I'm getting very fond of you, Marcus. You're so – so *kind*.'

'That's my middle name, you know. Marcus Kindness Walwyn.'

'I'm serious.'

'So am I.'

We stared at each other for quite a while, and I knew in that second that I had her hooked. Now all I had to do was reel her in. By the weekend I'd have her in bed. I'd have her loving me just like I'd always planned. That terrible feeling of hatred I'd momentarily had for her vanished. I ached. 'Better make a move,' I said, and was surprised my voice was so hoarse.

'Must you?'

'Got to work. Earn a crust, as they say.'

'When will I see you?'

I thought about that. 'Thursday,' I said. 'I'll come in at lunch-time on Thursday.'

'Not tomorrow?'

I shook my head. 'Can't tomorrow. Got too much on. Too much business,' I lied.

I stood up, and kissed her lightly on the cheek.

'See you Thursday,' I whispered.

She nodded. 'Be good.'

I looked shocked. 'I'm *always* good,' I told her, and we both laughed again.

She was still laughing as I turned at the door and waved.

Well, I can tell you I was floating when I got back to work. I passed Camp Carl in the passageway, and he noticed it too. 'Who's a happy boy then?' he asked.

'Me,' I told him, and blew him a kiss.

'Promises, promises,' he said with a sigh.

'Never know when your luck's in, Carl.'

'Yours certainly seems to be.'

'I think it is. I think it is.'

'Nice for some.'

'*Very* nice.'

'Where the hell are they?' the Inspector wanted to know, pacing the office, and checking his watch.

'They'll be here, sir,' Sergeant Wilson told him. 'It's only just after five.'

The Inspector glowered at him.

'You want a coffee?' asked Wilson.

'I need a drink,' Inspector Birt said. 'Yes. Please, Ray. A coffee.'

And minutes later, when he came back with the coffee, Sergeant Wilson was smiling. It irritated the Inspector. 'For God's sake stop smirking, Ray,' he snapped.

'Karen Scott is downstairs.'

Inspector Birt stopped dead in his tracks. His eyes narrowed. He took a deep breath. 'Come on then,' he said, and made for the door.

'Your coffee?'

The Inspector gave him a withering look.

'Just asking.'

As luck would have it Harry Rutherford called round in the evening. Ma wasn't expecting him, so she left me to entertain him while she made herself presentable. I didn't know how long that would take, so I decided not to waste any time. 'Harry, you wouldn't do me a favour, would you?' I think he must have suspected I was going to touch him for a loan since he put on his judicial face, getting himself ready to refuse. 'I don't want a loan, Harry,' I said, with just the right amount of sarcasm.

'Ah,' he said, relieved. 'Yes. If I can.'

'You wouldn't take Ma away for the weekend?'

He looked really surprised. 'Take your mother – *this* weekend?'

I nodded.

'Well, I don't know . . .'

'It would really help me,' I told him, and looked about the room like someone making sure no one was listening. Then I adopted my conspiratorial tone, and told him, 'I've got this date, and—'

'Ah,' Harry interrupted. 'And you want the house to yourself?'

'Exactly,' I said, and gave him a lewd wink.

'Away Saturday, back Sunday?'

'Just the ticket.'

'Oh, I think that could be arranged.'

'You're an angel,' I told him.

'But not a word to your mother.'

'Not a whisper.'

'All right.'

'Thank you, Harry. Anytime you want me out of the way, just ask.'

'Yes,' Harry said dryly.

'I mean it.'

'I'm sure you do.'

'Sure who does what?' Ma wanted to know, sweeping into the room, looking very presentable.

'Harry was just saying he was sure I find writing my book very difficult,' I explained.

'Isn't it exciting, Harry? Marcus writing a book.'

'Very exciting,' Harry agreed.

'It's such a wonderful talent, I think. I wish *I* could write,' Ma said.

'Well, you know what they say, Ma. There's a book in everybody.'

'I'm sure that's nonsense.'

'You don't know until you try.' I was just waffling on to give Harry a chance to get himself back on an even keel. I made a face at him now.

'Oh. Yes. I just dropped in . . . really . . . to ask . . . are you doing anything special this weekend?' he asked Ma.

'I don't *think* so,' Ma said. 'Am I, Marcus?'

'*I* don't know, do I?'

'No. I don't think I am. Why?'

'I thought we might . . . I mean, I thought we might . . . well,' Harry was saying, and I really wanted to kick him. 'I thought I might take you out to dinner,' he blurted finally, and I felt like strangling him. Even Ma was surprised, disappointed too.

'Dinner?' she asked.

'Yes,' Harry said. 'In Paris,' he blurted, and I could have kissed him.

Ma really liked that idea. She beamed. 'Oh, Harry, what a lovely idea! Dinner in Paris, how romantic.'

'Well, you know, fly over Saturday morning, have dinner, stay the night, fly back Sunday,' Harry said, and gasped at the end of it.

'That would be lovely,' Ma said warmly.

'That's really nice of you, Harry,' I said.

'Good,' Harry said.

'You'll have a drink while you're here, of course?' I asked.

I think Harry realised just then what a commitment he'd made since he started to bluster again. 'Eh, well, no. No, I won't, thank you.'

'Oh,' I said.

'You're sure, Harry?' Ma asked.

'Quite sure.'

'Well, I'll leave you two romantics alone then,' I said, making Harry go red, and Ma say, 'Really, Marcus!'

So, the road was clear for Saturday night. All I had to do now was plan it properly. No more mistakes. Make it an evening never to be forgotten, for Karen anyway.

The room set aside for victims of rape was small and warm and intimate. It was decorated in greys and soft pinks. There was a two-seater couch and an armchair, and a long, low table with half a dozen up-to-date women's magazines on it. There was even a vase of flowers, albeit silk ones. Karen Scott and WPC Williamson sat on the couch, and were talking quietly to each other when Inspector Birt and Sergeant Wilson came in. Williamson stood up immediately, and made as if to leave, but stopped and sat down again when the Inspector said, 'No. Stay, please,' and settled himself into the armchair. 'I'm sorry about this, Karen,' he began. 'I hope you'll bear with me.'

Karen Scott nodded. 'I just don't understand why—'

'I'll explain everything to you in a moment. Just a few questions first, I'm afraid. Nothing but questions, eh?'

Karen smiled nervously.

'Mr Walwyn. Marcus. Peter. What do you call him?'

'Marcus. He told me his name was Marcus not Peter.'

'Right. Marcus. You've seen him a couple of times

312

since our last meeting, I think?'

Karen nodded.

'I'd like you to tell me about what happened.'

'Nothing happened.'

'No. I mean tell me what you talked about. What you did.'

'Oh.' Karen Scott screwed up her face and thought for a minute. 'You've been watching me?'

'Please. Just tell me about your meetings with Marcus Walwyn.'

Karen Scott pushed her hair back from her face, and sat forward, her knees together, her hands resting on them. 'Well, he came to the café about a week ago and told me he'd been to see you. He said you told him about Darren. He was very upset about that. Said if he could help me in any way all I had to do was ask.'

'You went to a pub with him,' Sergeant Wilson said.

'Yes.' Karen looked uneasy all of a sudden.

'Who's idea was that?' Wilson asked.

'His, I think. Or maybe it was mine. I don't know. I can't remember. I was . . . I wanted to talk to someone. Maybe it *was* my idea.'

'That's fine, Karen,' Inspector Birt said. 'Just relax. You've nothing to worry about. So, you went to the pub and talked – right?'

Karen nodded. 'That's right. He was very nice. Very concerned and understanding. He . . . I can't explain it, Inspector. He was just so nice.'

313

Now the Inspector nodded. 'Go on.'

'Well, we ended up making a date to go out at the weekend. Maybe I was wrong to do that, but I wanted to go out. I hadn't been anywhere since . . . since . . . you know, since Darren died. So we made a date and then we left.'

'You went home?'

'That's right.'

'Alone?'

'Yes. Alone. Marcus got me a taxi. He paid for it too. He was really kind.'

'Good. You're doing really well, Karen,' the Inspector told her. 'Then, last Saturday, you met him again, isn't that right?'

'Yes. We met at the café. At six. He took me to the Savoy first, for a drink.'

'The Savoy, eh? You must have enjoyed that.'

'It was amazing.'

'I'll bet,' Sergeant Wilson said.

Inspector Birt ignored Wilson's remark, but WPC Williamson gave a thin smile. 'You walked there?'

'That's right.'

'And after the Savoy?'

'He took me to dinner. A restaurant in Soho. The Escargot.'

'Very nice,' the Inspector commented.

'Yes,' Karen said, but there was a slight hesitation in her voice, and the Inspector jumped on it.

'It *was* very nice, wasn't it?' he demanded.

'To begin with.'

'Ah. Not all the time?'

'Well, yes. No. I mean, I don't really know what went wrong. He wanted to . . . I thought we were just friends but he . . . he didn't *do* anything, he just sort of took it for granted we were more than friends.'

'And you told him you didn't want any of his—'

'I just asked him to give me time, that's all.'

'And he didn't like that?'

'He got – not angry exactly – upset. I felt awful.'

'Why was that, Karen?'

'Because he'd been so kind. He gave me the most lovely charm bracelet. To replace my broken one, he said. And—'

'Just a minute, Karen. Did you have a broken bracelet?'

'Yes. He'd seen me trying to fix the clasp on the Underground. That's why he bought me the new one.'

'You don't remember when you'd tried to fix your bracelet on the Tube, do you?'

'Oh, ages ago. Months ago. In the summer sometime, I think.'

'I see. So, to get back to Saturday, you had a row?'

Karen Scott shook her head. 'Not a row. Everything just sort of went cold. You know. Not as friendly as it had been.'

'And after your dinner? What then?'

'He put me in a taxi and sent me home.'

'He didn't go with you?'

'No.'

'He paid for the taxi, though?'

'Yes.'

'He didn't say anything?'

'Well, yes. I wanted to try and make things up. I didn't want to go off leaving him all upset. He'd put a little gold gnome on the bracelet so I told him I was going to call it Marcus. I thought he'd be pleased.'

'But he wasn't.'

Karen shook her head. 'He said I could call it anything I wanted. Darren if I felt like it.'

'Ah,' the Inspector sighed. Then, as if the thought had just struck him, he asked, 'Have you ever told Marcus where you live, Karen?'

'No. I don't think so. No, I'm sure I haven't.'

'And when he put you in the taxi – he gave the driver some money, right?'

'Yes.'

'Did he not tell the driver where to take you?'

Karen Scott stared unblinkingly at the Inspector for a few moments. Then she frowned. 'No,' she said. 'I did. I remember I did. I remember the driver turned his head and asked me where to. When I told him he had a bit of a chuckle, and said, "I thought you'd be going further for this," he said, and he showed me a twenty-pound note.'

Karen still looked puzzled. She twisted her fingers, and looked from the Inspector to the Sergeant, and back to the Inspector again. Inspector Birt smiled encouragement at her. 'You're doing just fine,' he told her. 'Now. Lunch-time today,' he began.

'I must have told him,' Karen Scott said suddenly.

'Sorry? Told him what?'

'Where I live.'

'Why do you say that, Karen?'

'Because . . . I *must* have told him. The other time . . . the time he came to the café and we went to the pub after . . . *that* time he *did* tell the taxi-driver where to take me.'

The Inspector sucked his teeth. 'You're sure of that?'

'I'm sure.'

'Quite sure?'

Karen nodded. 'Absolutely sure.'

Inspector Birt looked up at Sergeant Wilson and gave him a huge smile. Then he turned back to Karen, getting serious again, but before he could say anything, Karen asked, 'Is it important? If I told him where I live or not, I mean?'

'It might very well be, Karen. Nothing for you to worry about, though. It's just that every little bit of information helps us.'

'Inspector?'

'Yes, Karen?'

'You don't think Marcus had anything to do with . . .'

The Inspector forced himself to smile reassuringly. 'We've got to find out as much as we can about *everybody*,' he said, adding quickly, 'now about lunchtime today. He came to the café again, didn't he?'

Karen Scott nodded.

'And how was he?'

'Fine.'

'Friendly?'

'Yes, friendly.'

'Like nothing had happened?'

'Nothing *did* happen, Inspector.'

'I meant like you'd never had that little tiff.'

'Yes. He was fine,' Karen Scott said again. 'He asked me to go out with him again this weekend.'

The Inspector nodded.

'You agree?' Sergeant Wilson asked.

'Yes. I *like* him. He's . . . I just like him,' Karen said quietly, and jumped as someone knocked on the door.

Sergeant Wilson went to the door and opened it. Someone outside said something to him in a low voice. 'Right. Thanks,' the Sergeant said, and closed the door again. He came across to the Inspector and bent down, whispering in his ear. The Inspector nodded, and said aloud, 'Go bring him up, will you, Ray?'

'It's not Marcus, is it?' Karen Scott asked suddenly.

'No, Karen. It's not Marcus. Would it matter?'

'No. Just . . .' Her voice tailed off.

'Tell me,' Inspector Birt said.

Karen Scott waited until Sergeant Wilson had left

the room. 'I just wouldn't want him to think I was talking about him behind his back.'

'You're not afraid of him, are you, Karen?'

'Of course I'm not. I've told you – he's really nice to me.'

'Yes. Yes, of course. You told me that. Anyway, it's not Marcus. It's Paul. Paul Cornell.'

Karen looked astonished. 'Paul? Why—'

Inspector Birt held up his hand. 'I'll explain everything to you as soon as Paul comes up. That's a promise.'

'Would you like a cup of tea now?' WPC Williamson asked.

Karen Scott shook her head.

'Inspector?'

Birt also shook his head. 'You might try and rustle up a couple of chairs, though,' he said.

WPC Williamson stood up. 'You're sure you don't want anything, Karen?' she asked, adding, 'All right,' as Karen shook her head once more.

Alone with Karen Scott, Inspector Birt wondered if he was doing the right thing. She looked so very vulnerable sitting there, her shoulders hunched, her head down. He would be pretty vulnerable himself also, he reflected, if anything went wrong. He smiled briefly at Karen as she looked up at him for a moment. There was always the chance that neither she nor Cornell would agree to his plan, of course. Then what? He cleared his throat to dismiss the thought from his mind, and was pleased when the

WPC came back into the room with two plastic chairs – an added distraction.

'Thank you,' he said.

'You want me to stay, sir?'

'Please.'

WPC Williamson sat down on the sofa beside Karen again. She reached out and patted her on the hand. 'Don't *worry*,' she whispered, and the Inspector just had time to nod his approval when Sergeant Wilson returned to the room with Paul Cornell.

'Karen!' Paul Cornell said.

'Hello, Paul.'

Paul Cornell rounded on the Inspector. 'What the fuck is—'

'Mr Cornell – please,' Inspector Birt interrupted, waving the WPC from her place on the sofa and Paul Cornell into it with a single economical movement of his hand. 'Thank you,' he said pointedly when they were seated, and he was touched at the way Cornell put his arm about Karen's shoulder by way of protection. It also mildly surprised him, although why he should assume that the surly young man in the black leather biker's jacket with the aggressive air should be incapable of affection was beyond him. Something about not judging the book by its cover passed through his mind, and perhaps because of this he was particularly soft-toned and gentle when he next spoke. 'I want you both to regard anything I say to you now as in the strictest confidence,' he said. 'You are not to repeat any of it once you leave this room.

Speak to no one, is that clear?' He paused, and waited, looking at Karen Scott until she nodded, then transferring his gaze to Paul Cornell. 'Mr Cornell?'

'All right,' Paul Cornell said, albeit grudgingly.

'Thank you,' the Inspector said, and allowed a small smile of gratitude to struggle across his lips. 'To begin with, the reason I've had you both brought here is because I want to ask for your help. Without your help I don't think we'll be able to catch the man who killed Sharon and Darren. He—'

'You know who it is?' Paul Cornell demanded.

The Inspector nodded. 'Yes.'

'You've arrested him?'

'No. No. Not yet.'

'Why the fuck not?'

'Because, because quite simply, we don't have any proof. A lot of what we call circumstantial evidence but no proof. If we arrested him now and went to court there's every chance a jury would let him off.'

'Who's the bastard?' Paul now demanded.

The Inspector sighed. 'It's someone Karen knows. His name is Marcus Walwyn.'

Karen Scott shook her head. 'It can't be,' she said.

'Who is he, Karen?' Paul Cornell wanted to know.

'Just someone who comes into the café.'

'You've been seeing him?'

'No, Paul. I just—'

'Mr Cornell,' Inspector Birt interrupted. 'Just listen to me, will you? It's my belief that Karen is in some considerable danger from this man. He is infatuated with her. From two small things Karen told us this evening, for example, we know he's been watching her for months. We know, too, that he's gone to the trouble of finding out where Karen lives. He probably did that to put the note on your brother's bike. I suspect he killed Darren because he was in the way.'

'But Sharon? Why Sharon?' Paul asked.

'That's rather more difficult to explain, I'm afraid,' the Inspector said. He didn't want to say that Sharon had been murdered just for practice. 'I suspect he felt she was in the way too – being Karen's best friend. Anyway, now that both Darren and Sharon are no longer a threat, he feels, I believe, that he can – well, that his path is clear to pursue Karen.'

Inspector Birt suddenly felt annoyed with himself. He wasn't making a very good job of things. He didn't want to go into all the business about Zanker's book, yet without so doing it was almost impossible to explain Marcus Walwyn's actions. He was very grateful to Karen when she asked, 'You said you wanted us to help?'

'Yes,' he said simply.

'How?' Karen asked.

'By goading him into making a mistake.'

Karen shook her head. 'I don't understand.'

'By making him so angry he'll lose control and—'

'But how – I mean, how can we help with that?'

Inspector Birt took a deep breath. 'I want you, Karen, to reject him. Tell him you're just not interested in him.'

Karen gave a small, shy laugh. 'I can't see *that* making him all that angry.'

'Oh, yes it will. I can assure you it will. Everything he's done so far – the two murders, the plotting and planning – all that will have been for nothing. That will make him very angry indeed. His pride, you see, will be sorely hurt. It's his pride that's important to him. Your rejection will make him furious.'

Paul Cornell wanted to know more. 'Hang on a tick. So, Karen rejects him and makes him angry. What does he do then? What's this mistake you're on about?'

The Inspector was aware it was make or break time. He looked away from Paul's eyes for a moment, and pursed his lips. But he couldn't bring himself to say what needed to be said. He glanced across at Sergeant Wilson for support.

'He'll try and kill you, Karen,' Sergeant Wilson said.

Instantly Paul Cornell was on his feet. 'Fuck that,' he shouted, taking Karen by the arm and dragging her to her feet also.

'He wouldn't try and kill me,' Karen said in a tiny, bemused voice.

'He won't be getting the fucking chance,' Paul Cornell told her.

Inspector Birt found his voice. 'He *will* try, Karen,' he said quietly. 'He'll try. And that's when we'll get him.'

'Karen, for Christ's sake, don't listen to this nutter,' Paul Cornell was saying.

'Paul – please,' Karen said, and sat down again. She held Paul's hand, tugging it gently. 'Sit down, Paul,' she added. Then she looked at the Inspector. 'You *sure* it was Marcus who killed Sharon and my Darren?'

Inspector Birt nodded.

For some time Karen remained silent, stroking Paul's hand as if it was a small, comforting animal. 'I suppose we'll have to help him,' she said finally.

'We don't have to do nothing,' Paul Cornell told her angrily.

'But if it means—'

'You killed too? Great. Just fucking great.'

'Karen won't come to any harm,' Sergeant Wilson said.

'You're going to see to that I suppose, are you?'

'Yes.'

'Fuck off.'

'What sort of thing would we have to do?' Karen asked.

'For fuck's sake, Karen!'

'Paul, please.'

'I had thought that . . . maybe . . . well, that you could tell him you'd decided to go out with . . .' The Inspector gulped. 'With Paul,' he concluded.

'Oh, thanks. And have the shit gunning for me too?' Paul Cornell demanded. 'That's all I fucking need.'

'You'd be protected.'

Paul Cornell gave a derisive sneer. 'Yeah. Oh, yeah. I know all about your crappy police protection. Didn't protect Sharon, did you? Or my brother?' Inspector Birt tried to sound reasonable. 'We didn't know about Marcus Walwyn then. Once we did find out we've had him – and Karen – under twenty-four-hour observation.'

'You *have* been watching me,' Karen said.

'All the time.'

'Maybe, Paul we should—'

Paul Cornell was on his feet again, zipping up his leather jacket defiantly.

'You can help these bastards if you want, Karen. Forget about me, though. But I'll tell you one thing – I'll be watching you too, and if that shit comes within a mile of you, I'll kill the fucker myself.'

The Inspector sighed. 'Then we'd have to do you for murder, Paul,' he said. 'That would be a waste, wouldn't it?'

'Don't be stupid, Paul,' Karen said, and seemed to have a more calming effect on the young man than the Inspector. 'I just mean maybe we owe it to Sharon and Darren,' she said almost to herself, and started crying gently.

'See what you've done?' Paul Cornell demanded.

He sat down again beside Karen and put his arm about her once more.

'I'm all right, Paul,' Karen said. Then she looked at the Inspector. 'You really wouldn't let him do anything to me, would you?' she asked.

'No, Karen, we wouldn't.'

'How you going to stop him?' Paul wanted to know. 'You can't be with Karen all the fucking time.'

'We can, as it happens. If Karen agrees, WPC Williamson there will move into the flat.'

Paul Cornell started to laugh. 'You met Karen's mum?' The Inspector nodded.

'No more chance of her letting a cop into her house than a bloody Paki.'

'I think she'll agree when we explain. Anyway, WPC Williamson could be Karen's cousin or something, and from the moment Karen leaves the house, all the while she's working, to the moment she returns home again she'll be followed by two of our officers. Twenty-four hours a day. She'll never be out of our sight. And the same would apply to you, Paul except . . .' the Inspector added with just the hint of a smile, '. . . except we won't move a WPC into your home.'

'Oh, very fucking funny.'

'Paul . . . maybe—' Karen began.

But Paul Cornell had made up his mind. He was on his feet again. 'You're off your bloody head, Karen,' he said. 'But if you've made up your mind you can do what you like. I'm off, though. Fucked if I'm getting involved.'

'Paul,' Karen pleaded.

'Forget it,' Paul Cornell said, and left the room, slamming the door behind him.

Immediately Sergeant Wilson was on his feet, looking at the Inspector with raised eyebrows. Birt nodded. 'Yes. And be quick. Make sure they're both on motorbikes.' He turned back to Karen Scott when Wilson had left the room. 'Just a precaution. In case Paul decides to do anything stupid.'

Karen gave a tiny smile. 'He won't do anything stupid. Paul never did anything without Darren's say so. He's still not able to do much for himself. He relies on me a lot now, you know. He's so lonely,' she added. 'So really lonely. Darren and Sharon and me were all he had, you see.'

The Inspector nodded. 'We'll see he doesn't come to any harm,' he said, and watched as Karen Scott stood up, readying herself to leave. 'I'm sorry you couldn't see your way to—'

'Help? Yes. I'm sorry. I just—'

Suddenly WPC Williamson interrupted. 'My goodness,' she exclaimed. 'I completely forgot, Inspector. That message you were expecting from Scotland is on your desk.'

The Inspector looked baffled.

'It's marked urgent. Maybe you should—'

'Oh. Yes. Right,' the Inspector said. 'You'll excuse

me a moment?' he asked and, still looking puzzled, left the room.

He didn't go to his office, though. He paced the corridor, glancing often at his watch, giving himself five minutes. When he returned to the room, Karen and WPC Williamson were sitting side by side on the couch, and Williamson had a look of satisfaction on her face. 'Karen's decided to help us, Inspector,' she said.

The Inspector smiled and sat down. 'Thank you, Karen,' he said. 'I really appreciate that. Unfortunately your help isn't any good without Paul's.'

Karen smiled. 'Of course Paul will help. He'll do it for me. There was just no way he could agree to help the police. He couldn't do that.'

'Oh, I see,' Inspector Birt told her with an understanding smile. 'The police.'

'Yes,' Karen said. Then, 'So you better tell me what you want me to do.'

The Inspector hesitated. 'You are quite sure about this, Karen?'

'What do you want me to do?'

The Inspector leaned forward. 'When do you see Marcus again?'

'Thursday. He said he'd come to the café for lunch on Thursday.'

'Right. On Thursday, just act as if nothing had happened. As if we hadn't had this conversation. Be your usual self.'

'I'll try,' Karen said, with another of her tiny smiles.

'Good girl. Now, if he mentions Saturday again, about your going out with him, see if you can put him off. Tell him to come back on Friday and you'll make arrangements then.'

Karen nodded.

WPC Williamson asked, 'Are you quite sure, Karen, you'll be able to get Paul to help?'

Karen nodded again.

'He really is very important to the Inspector's plan. Are you sure?'

'Yes. I'm sure. You don't know Paul like I do. He'll do anything I ask. I know he will.'

'Good,' the Inspector said, giving the WPC a glance which could have been one of gratitude. 'All right,' he went on. 'When Marcus comes on Friday, I want you to act really happy. Tell him you want to go out with him, but tell him, too, that you've got a big surprise for him.'

Karen Scott looked puzzled, but nodded anyway, returning the smile that WPC Williamson gave her.

'Arrange to meet him . . .' the Inspector was saying, hesitating before suggesting, '. . . in that pub you both went to. Would that do?'

Again Karen nodded. 'Yes.'

'Now, on the Saturday, I want you to bring Paul with you, and tell Marcus the big surprise you have for him is that you and Paul are getting engaged.'

Karen Scott stared at the Inspector as if she thought he had gone slightly cracked. Then she burst out laughing. 'Paul will go mad,' she said.

'Can you get him to agree to it?'

'I told you. Paul will do anything for me. It won't stop him going mad, though. I think he's a bit in love with me. Or thinks he is.'

'But you can get him to go along with the plan?'

'Oh, yes.'

'Right. Now, Karen, once you've told Marcus that you and Paul are getting engaged – I've no idea what Marcus will do. I can't see him doing anything violent there and then. He's far too clever for that. My guess is that he'll put on an act and pretend to be delighted for you both. Whether he'll still want to go out with you that evening or not, I can't say. Probably not. But it's from the moment you tell him about yourself and Paul that you have to start being really careful. Don't do anything or go anywhere out of the ordinary without letting us know first. You'll be followed all the time, but – well, for example, if you're taking the Underground don't leave it until the last minute to get on the train, just in case our men couldn't make it. You know the sort of thing I mean?'

'I think so.'

'Good girl.'

'And—' Karen began, glancing towards WPC Williamson.

'WPC Williamson will move in with you tomorrow night, if that's all right.'

'Fine with me.'

'And with your mother?'

Karen giggled. 'She'll kick up hell to begin with.

But she'll agree in the end. Leave her to me.'

The Inspector nodded. 'Good.'

'It's Sarah, by the way,' WPC Williamson said.

Sergeant Wilson came back into the room, and gave Birt a curt nod. The Inspector nodded back. 'Good,' he said, then turned to Karen. 'Well, that's about it. WPC – Sarah, will be your main contact, Karen. Tell her everything – all right?'

'Yes,' Karen said quietly, and stood up.

The Inspector stood up also. 'Most importantly – if Paul refuses to help, tell Sarah immediately so that we can make other—'

'Paul will help.'

Inspector Birt exhaled heavily. 'Thank you, Karen. Thank you very much.'

'You won't let him – Marcus – do anything to me, will you?' Karen asked suddenly.

On a sudden impulse Inspector Birt moved across to Karen Scott and put an arm about her shoulder. 'No, Karen, we won't let him get within a mile of you. I promise you that.'

Karen gave him a smile. 'Let's hope your plan works then.'

'It will. I'm sure it will.'

Karen gave a deep sigh of resignation. 'Goodbye, then.'

'I'll see you out,' WPC Williamson said.

'See Miss Scott *home*, would you – Sarah?' the Inspector said.

'Yes, sir.'

'Thank you.'

Inspector Birt waited until Karen Scott had gone through the door. Then, 'Thank you, Williamson,' he said.

WPC Williamson gave him a smile and a nod.

'That was good work.'

'We have our uses, sir.'

Alone with Sergeant Wilson, Inspector Birt collapsed back into the armchair. 'Give me a cigarette, Ray.'

'Eh? You don't smoke.'

'I *know* I don't smoke. I used to. And I want one now.'

Sergeant Wilson passed the Inspector a cigarette, and held the lighter while he lit it. 'What do you think?'

Birt blew a thin stream of smoke from his lips. 'I'm afraid to think, Ray. Never been so afraid in all my bloody life.'

Sergeant Wilson lit a cigarette for himself, and sat down on the sofa, stretching his long legs out in front of him, crossing his ankles. 'There's no way he'll be able to get at her, boss,' he said.

Inspector Birt didn't seem so sure. 'It'll only take some tiny error on our part—'

'There won't *be* any errors. Look, we'll have Williamson in the flat, and two men outside all the time. There'll be at least one of us in the café all the time she's working there, and two more outside. She'll be followed everywhere. The slightest sign of a move from Walwyn and they'll be on him like a ton of bricks.'

The Inspector nodded. 'You're right, Ray. I know you're right. But—'

'No buts, sir. Everything is covered.'

'For Cornell too?'

'For Cornell too.'

'You're sure?'

'Quite sure.'

The Inspector looked at his half-smoked cigarette in disgust, but took another long draw anyway. Then he stood up. 'All we can do is wait then.'

'That's about it.'

'And pray, I suppose.'

'I'll leave that to you, sir.'

'Hah. Typical. Leave the hardest bit to me.'

Twenty-two

When I got in to my cubby-hole on Thursday morning there was a message from Kranze on my desk. It said, 'Helmut Kranze phoned. He says it's urgent.' The 'says' was underlined which will give you an idea of what we in publishing think of authors: we never really believe anything they say. Got to prevent them getting the idea that *we* need *them*. Much better to have them think the reverse – that they need us. So, I decided Kranze's urgency could wait, and I didn't call him back. I really didn't want him fussing me about his novel. I had much more important things on my mind. Karen. I told myself I'd leave returning Kranze's call until I'd got everything nice and settled between Karen and myself. Anyway, I'd already told the sod that I'd be in touch in a few weeks, and a few weeks was what I figured I needed to have my relationship with Karen running smoothly. Still, I didn't want any notes about Kranze lying around, so I folded it up and shoved it in the top pocket of my jacket, along with a worthless betting-slip – some nag

I'd backed in the Mackeson on Heather's advice.

I did a bit of work that morning too, even gave one novel my 'has possibilities' imprimatur, and sent it upstairs to the glamorous Natalie Curren since it was the romantic sort of slush she liked to deal with. But all the while I had my eye on the clock, urging the hands to get a move on. I'd probably have gone insane if Camp Carl hadn't come in with some extra mail, and stayed for a chat, telling me about some rough trade he'd picked up in the Golden Lion, and how the stars had come out, as he put it. He could be very funny, could Carl. Doesn't give a shit what anyone thinks, and really enjoys trying to shock people. Anyway, the time came when I could go for lunch without raising too many eyebrows – got to be careful about that: there's always some bastard ready to whisper in the right ear that you're skiving off. Carl was angling to come with me (I think he fancied me a bit, more than a bit, a lot, but he'd never have dared to say so in case it spoiled our friendship: I was, I think, the only one in the house he could have a bit of a camp with, and he knew what he said to me wouldn't be spread all over the place) but I told him no. 'Sorry, sweetheart,' I told him. 'Got myself a date already,' making a joke of it so as not to hurt his feelings. That's something I try very hard to do: not to hurt people's feelings unnecessarily. Only morons do that, in my opinion, people who are so weak they have to take the piss out of other people to make themselves feel important.

Now, this isn't hindsight or anything, believe me, but as soon as I walked into the café I knew something was wrong. No. Not wrong. Different. I still couldn't tell you what made me know that. I just felt it. It had nothing to do with Karen. She was sweet. She came over as soon as she saw me and said, 'Hiya,' and I said, 'Hiya,' and ordered something which she trotted off to get me. And when she came back with it, I asked, 'What's new?' and she said, 'Not much, what's new with you?' and I told her 'Nothing'. And it wasn't until I'd finished whatever it was I'd ordered that I asked her if everything was still on for Saturday, and she said, 'Yes, I think so.'

'Only think so?'

She gave me a funny smile – coy, sort of. 'I'll know definitely tomorrow. Can you come in for lunch then?'

'Yes, I can come in tomorrow.'

'Good. We'll make arrangements then.'

'Suits me,' I told her although it didn't really suit.

Was that it, her putting me off until the next day? Was that what made me feel uneasy? I don't think so. I'm sure I felt something was different long before we got to that conversation. I'm very sensitive to – what's the word? – I can't think . . . vibes, will do, but I told myself I was just being *over*sensitive, and a lot of my worries vanished when she let me kiss her on the cheek as usual, and gave my hand a little squeeze.

And I suppose it could have been a hangover from

that feeling that made me even more uneasy on the Friday. I got really confused with myself. I mean, I wanted Karen to be nice to me and everything, but that Friday, when she was *really* nice, I kept telling myself she was being *too* nice, like she was buttering me up for some big let-down. She bounced across the café to meet me, and *she* kissed *me* on the cheek, smiling like I'd never seen her smile. 'What's got you in such good humour?' I asked.

She sort of preened. 'Don't you like me being happy?'

'Of course I like to see you happy. I just wondered what brought it all on.'

'Maybe *you* did. Coming here.'

'Oh, yeah?'

'Well, you're certainly part of it.'

'Just part of it, eh? What's the other part?'

She bent over and pressed a finger to my lips – her way of telling me not to be asking questions, I guess. 'I'll tell you all about it tomorrow,' she promised. 'I've got an enormous surprise for you,' she added, stretching her arms out like a lying fisherman to show me the enormity of the surprise.

'Why not tell me now?'

'Tomorrow,' she insisted.

I shrugged. 'Guess I'll just have to wait then.'

'You most certainly will,' she told me, and flounced off, looking ever so pleased with herself. But she wasn't *being* herself.

I didn't have too much time to dwell on that though, since she was back at my table again pretty soon, asking me if everything was all right.

'Oh, just terrific. Better than the Escargot even.' She giggled at that.

'Where are we meeting tomorrow?' I asked. 'Here again?'

She wrinkled her nose. 'No,' she said.

'Where then?'

She thought about that. 'What about that pub? The one you took me to the *first* time we went out,' she said, stressing the first like it was pretty significant to our relationship.

'Okay. If that's what you want. Or we could make it the Savoy if you like.'

'No. The pub.'

'Right. What time?'

'Seven?'

'Seven it is. Now, that surprise you were on about—'

'Tomorrow,' she insisted, making a little face at me. 'You'll have to learn patience, Marcus.'

'Oh, I'm very patient.'

'Well, then, you won't mind waiting.'

'Not as long as it's a *nice* surprise.'

'I think it's wonderful,' she told me, her eyes dancing.

'Then I guess I will too.'

'I *hope* you will. I'll be very upset if you don't.'

'We wouldn't want to upset you, Karen, would

we? I'll just have to like it – even if I don't,' I said with a grin.

She patted my cheek. 'That's a good boy,' she told me, and I half expected her to offer me a goddam bone.

In fact, it all really annoyed me. So much so that I went back to work earlier than I need have done, just waving to her, and nodding as she blew me a kiss and mouthed, 'Tomorrow at seven.' I nodded again.

There was another message from Kranze when I got back, this one marked 'really urgent'. So, I rang him, but the line was engaged, so I left it. Time enough for that on Monday. Anyway, if it was *that* urgent, he could call me again.

I've never been one for believing in omens and all that bullshit, but maybe I should have given them consideration that Saturday morning. If ever life conspired to keep me in bed all day it was then. It was a right shitty morning, bitterly cold, sleeting, and with a wind that came direct from Siberia. And the central heating had gone on the blink during the night, so I swear to God when I went for a quick pee an icicle did its damnedest to form on the tip of my penis. I dashed back to bed, leapt in, and pulled the blankets up over my head, telling myself I wasn't going to venture out again for a week. I should have listened to myself. But we never do, do we? I eventually emerged about lunch-time, and set about getting the house ready to receive Karen. There was a lot to be done, but with Ma in Paris, and the house to myself, I enjoyed doing all the chores, singing along to some of the songs on Radio 2 (Ma's preferred station – 'they play such nice songs, darling, songs you can sing to, not those awful noisy things where people just shout at you'), and even putting on one of Ma's frilly aprons and having a right good giggle to myself when I thought of what Camp Carl would have said had he seen me. I gave my room a real going over, dusting everything, hoovering, even plumping up the cushions. I changed the sheets on the bed, and made sure the right CD was ready in the player: Billie Holiday – the *Lady in Satin* one. I thought about putting some flowers on my table but decided against that. A bit over the top, I thought. Too poncy.

When I'd done everything I could think of I ran myself a bath and lay in it for over an hour, topping it up with hot water every so often, soaking. Soaking all my cares away, I said to myself, with a little help from some Herbal Radox and a dab of Ma's Floris bath gel. I'd only just got out of the bath when the man came to fix the central heating, looking none too happy about having to work on a Saturday, I can tell you. Surly bastard. Acted like he was doing me some sort of big favour. I didn't give him an excuse to hang about, didn't offer him any tea or anything, just showed him where the works were and left him to it. To be fair, he didn't take that long about it, about an hour in all. He left about five o'clock. I checked the kitchen to make sure he hadn't made a mess, and poured myself a weak Jack Daniels. It was five thirty when I finished my drink, five forty-five when I shaved, six o'clock when I started dressing, and half past six when I left the house. And despite the weather (still pissing down and an east wind blowing that would cut you in half) there was a spring in my step, my tail was up, and not even seeing the two apes sitting cosily in the car opposite could dampen my spirits. Indeed, it was enough for me that one of them had to leave the snugness of the car and follow me on foot. I bet he was raging, particularly when I hailed a passing taxi and whizzed off leaving him getting drenched, waiting for his dozy mate to pick him up.

I don't know if you've ever tried to get into the West End early on a Saturday evening. If you haven't, you're lucky. It's really murder. The traffic has to be seen to be believed. You wonder where all the cars come from – everything from those vulgar stretch limousines taking tourists who fancy themselves to the theatre (the *English* theatre, darling), to our ethnic brethren in their customised Minis and Cosworths, high as kites, out for a cruise, man, their radios blaring. Anyway, it's not all that far from Balham to Leicester Square but it took us the full half-hour to get there, so by the time I'd scuttled along to the pub it was two minutes past seven.

I didn't see Karen at first, probably because I

was looking for her to be by herself, so I went to the bar and got myself a half of lager. I took a sip and started to gaze about the place the way you do. I can still remember myself sort of freezing when I finally spotted Karen sitting in one corner with this other man. A whole pile of things went through my head: I'd got the wrong day; it wasn't Karen, just someone who looked exactly like her; I was asleep and dreaming, having a nightmare in fact. But it was the right day, it was Karen, and I was wide awake. I turned back to the bar and stared down into my drink, trying to think. Then I heard, 'Marcus?' called tentatively behind me. I turned round. Karen was standing there, smiling up at me like she hadn't a care in the world. 'It *is* you,' she said. 'Didn't you see me?'

'Oh, Karen. Hello. No. No, I didn't. Where are you sitting?'

'Over there. In the corner. With Paul.'

You know, I really wanted to hit her: one good swipe across the face and storm out. 'Paul? Who's Paul when he's at home?'

'Paul Cornell. Darren's brother. Come on over and meet him. I know you'll like him.'

I hated the bastard without meeting him, but I followed her over to the table. I didn't sit down immediately, just stood there looking down, only half hearing what Karen was saying. 'Marcus, this is Paul. Paul – Marcus.' Something like that. I remember nodding. I don't think I could have spoken even if I'd wanted to. My throat was as dry as a bone.

'For goodness sake, sit down, Marcus, why don't you?'

I sat down, and heard myself say, stupidly, 'Sorry I was late.'

'That's all right,' Karen said, giving Paul a coy little look and sort of snuggling up to him.

I noticed she wasn't wearing my bracelet. 'So,' I said, and then couldn't think of anything else to say.

Karen gave a little laugh. 'So,' she said, and tittered again. Then, 'Say something, Paul,' she said.

'Nothing to say,' the brute said.

'Strong silent type, eh?' I asked.

Karen giggled at that. 'Exactly,' she said, and snuggled a bit closer to him, brushing her cheek against his leather jacket, and gazing into his face for a moment. 'Will we tell him, Paul?' she asked.

Paul Cornell shrugged, but never took his eyes off me.

'Tell me what?' I asked, trying to sound both interested and casual.

'Well,' Karen said, deciding to be dramatic, pausing after the word for effect. 'You remember I said I had a surprise for you?'

I nodded.

The bitch decided to keep me in suspense. 'You tell him, Paul,' she said.

What happened from then on is still a bit hazy in

my mind, but it went something like this, like a play I was watching:

It:	Karen and me are getting married.
Me:	Oh, yeah?
Karen:	Yes. Paul asked me the other day.
Me:	And you accepted?
Karen:	Of course. Isn't it wonderful?
Me:	Terrific.
Karen:	I knew you'd be pleased.
Me:	I'm really pleased.
Karen:	Thank you, Marcus.
Me:	You deserve each other.
Karen:	Thank you.
Me:	Always said the working class should stick to the working class.
It:	Huh?
Me:	You heard.
Karen:	Marcus!
It:	Fuck this—
Karen:	Paul—
Me:	Nothing like an ape marrying a slag. Match made in heaven if you ask me.

All hell broke loose after that. It was on his feet in a

flash, sending the drinks flying as he lunged across the table to grab me. But I was much too quick for him, of course. I ducked back, got up, grabbed my chair, and brought it down on his back with all the strength I could muster. Karen screamed. It moaned and rolled on to the floor. I shouted something like, 'And fuck you too, slag,' and walked with some dignity out of the pub.

When I got outside I started running. I wasn't running away or anything. I wasn't running away from what I'd done. I was, I think, just running to try and get all the anger and hate out of my system, as if hate and anger could be got out of the body wrapped in drops of sweat. Mostly I was angry with myself for letting that creep make me act in exactly the way I hadn't wanted to act. I know I could have been really cold and undramatic about the whole thing if he hadn't lunged at me and made me defend myself. And I hated him more than I hated Karen, although I wasn't exactly thrilled with her either.

I was halfway to Piccadilly Circus before I stopped to catch my breath. All of a sudden I felt weak. I thought for a minute I was going to faint: violence has that effect on me. *Unnecessary* violence that is. I leaned my hand against one of the shop windows and bowed my head. I felt sick, really sick, like I was going to puke. I'm sure that if I'd eaten something I would have puked.

'All right, mate?' someone asked.

I nodded but didn't look up.

'Sure?'

I nodded again.

I started to feel cold inside. Like my guts were freezing while my flesh was burning hot and perspiring. Then I must have blacked out.

I honestly don't know how I got home, but home I got, and I was there when I came to my senses again. It was only twenty to nine so I hadn't exactly dallied in the West End. Also, sometime between actually getting home and coming to, I had, apparently, gone mildly berzerk. My room was a shambles. Just about everything that could be smashed was smashed. The CD player looked like I'd hurled it across the room: it was in bits on the floor and there was quite a dent in the wall a few feet above it. All the bits and pieces that had been on my table were scattered about, just as if I'd swept them off with my hand. I'd even ripped the bed sheets to shreds, and a couple of strips hung from the light-fitting like some sort of macabre bunting. Yep, it certainly was a mess. And so was I, I can tell you. You know that expression – so-and-so just isn't himself? Well, that's exactly how I felt. I simply wasn't myself. There's no other way I can put it.

Mind you, I felt a bit of an idiot when I realised what I'd done, and a worse one as I started trying to tidy up. But all the time I was really seething inside. Christ!

I got fed up trying to straighten everything out, and

had just sat down to roll myself a soothing joint, when the phone rang. I immediately thought, that's her, that's the bitch ringing up to apologise, to tell me what a fool she'd been, to say she simply could not understand what had made her see anything in that leather-clad yob, to beg me to come back into town, and take her out as promised. A whole load of things like that raced through my mind, and I'd started steeling myself to be quite cold and reserved when I picked up the phone. It wasn't her though. It was bloody Kranze. That really annoyed me. 'Look, Mr Kranze, I don't discuss work when I'm at home. I—'

'Marcus, you've got to stop,' was Kranze's opening remark.

'Stop what?'

'Don't fool about, Marcus. You've got to stop. Now. Stop now. They know.'

It was all a bit scary, but I wasn't about to let Kranze know that. 'What the hell are you talking about, Kranze? Stop what, for Christ's sake? Who the hell knows what?' I shouted at him. Actually, I thought I was going off my head again. I thought I was hearing things that weren't really being said. In a nutshell, the whole evening was becoming surreal.

But Kranze wasn't letting up. 'The police. They know, Marcus. They've been here. They've got the book.'

You'll have to forgive me, but the only way I can describe it is by saying I honestly felt a cold hand squeezing my heart. And I got a searing pain in my head, like my brain had cramp.

'Marcus? Are you still there Marcus?'

I don't remember answering, but I must have said *something*, because Kranze went on, 'Now listen to me, Marcus. You've been brilliant up until now, but now is the time when you *must* stop.'

Astonishingly I heard myself say, quite simply, 'I can't.'

I heard Kranze sigh down the telephone. 'You'll be caught, Marcus. You'll be caught and ruin everything.'

Someone said, 'No, I won't. They'll never catch me. Not now,' and it really took me a couple of minutes to realise it was myself speaking.

For some reason I was sitting on the floor by now, my legs pulled up under me, just like the frigging gnome on the bracelet I'd given Karen. I remember rocking myself back and forth, don't ask me why though. I said to myself, 'I *hate* her,' and was surprised at how vicious I sounded. But I hadn't said it to myself, it seemed, because Kranze wanted to know, 'Who is it you hate, Marcus?'

'Her.'

'Who's that?'

'Karen. Karen bloody Scott.'

'Why don't you tell me about her, Marcus?'

So, that's what I did. I told him everything about Karen, right from the beginning. About how I'd first seen her. About how I really wanted her to like me, just like me, not love me like I loved her. And I told

him about Sharon and Darren too. About how useful
his book had been when it came to getting rid of
them. 'I'd never have thought of using Sharon for
practice,' I told him, and he gave another little sigh
which I think meant he was flattered, that's what was
conveyed to me in any case.

'Tell me all about it, Marcus,' he said.

So I did that too. Told him how I'd killed Sharon in
the kitchen and dumped her body near Windsor. I
told him too that I'd put my mark on her just like
he'd said I should in the book – just like he said was
permissible anyway.

'What mark did you use, Marcus?'

'Just a little cross. Between the eyes at the top of
her nose.'

Kranze made a gurgling sound as if he had enjoyed
that. 'No other mark?'

'No.'

'Go on, Marcus.'

So I went on, telling him the lot. Somewhere in my
head I knew I was being stupid. I mean, it could have
been a set up: my phone could have been bugged, or
Kranze could have been recording everything to use
against me later, but by that stage I really didn't care,
I just didn't give a damn to quote Rhett Butler. And
when I told him how I'd put the note on Darren's
bike and lured him to Bray, he said, 'Brilliant,' and
added, 'and you were able to do that without being
seen?'

'Oh, yes.'

'Brilliant.'

'It was quite easy, really.'

'Tell me why that was, Marcus.'

So I gave him a picture of Hatfield Close and explained how people sat outside the flats in the hot weather.

'And you just mingled?'

'That's right.'

'Weren't you afraid that man – Darren – might be keeping an eye on his bike and see you from the window?'

'Couldn't do that. Too high up, you see. Fifth floor.'

'Oh. That was his flat?'

'No,' I told him, and I remember being irritated. '*Her* flat. Karen's.'

'I'm sorry, Marcus,' he apologised, so I guess he spotted my annoyance. 'You're so much more clever than I am. You thought of everything.'

'Yes. Yes, I did.'

'So why ruin it all now?'

'Because she's not going to treat me like that.'

'I know, I know, Marcus. It is wicked,' Kranze told me. 'It's just such a shame if – Marcus?'

'What?'

'Will you do one thing for me?'

'What's that?'

'Will you sleep on it and telephone me in the morning?'

Well, I hadn't planned to do anything about Karen

that night, so it was easy enough for me to agree. 'All right,' I said.

Kranze sounded very relieved. 'You're quite right, of course, Marcus,' he then said. 'She cannot be allowed to treat you like that – just play with your emotions. But . . . well, the important thing is that you don't end up paying dearly for—'

'You mean by getting caught?'

'That's right.'

At that point I remember just letting myself topple over, and I lay there on the floor, my legs pulled up in what they like to call the foetal position. On one hand I was feeling great. Relieved. Like as if I'd been to confession or something. Better, in fact, since I knew Kranze had understood everything I was going through. Priests don't. Don't understand, I mean. Not supposed to anyway. Not supposed to have done half the things we sinners confess to. On the other hand, though, I was feeling really miserable, and something happened that I'm a bit ashamed of, and I can't explain why it happened either. I started to cry. Sobbing to myself.

'Are you all right, Marcus?' I heard Kranze ask.

'Yes,' I told him. 'Just lying down.'

'I thought I heard—'

'Getting a cold, I think,' I interrupted quickly.

'Ah,' he sighed. 'You better just lie there and get some sleep,' he advised, so I presume he thought I was tucked up in bed.

'Yes,' I agreed, and shut my eyes.

I'm pretty sure Kranze went on talking for quite a while after that. I seem to remember his soothing voice droning on, but I can't be sure. I could quite easily have been dreaming it. Anyway, it's irrelevant. I *did* fall asleep there on the floor, and if hearing Kranze talk was a dream, it was the only dream I had.

Twenty-three

They came at half past three. None of your polite knocking on the door and could we have a word with you, Mr Walwyn, though. They kicked the door down and had surrounded me when I came to. It was that oaf Wilson who was master of ceremonies. 'Marcus Walwyn,' he intoned, and was getting a lot of pleasure out of it, I can tell you, 'we're arresting you on suspicion of murder. You are not required to say anything, but anything you do say will be taken down and may be used in evidence against you.' That's what he said to me. 'Get him out,' he said to a pair of his mates. And I wasn't even fully awake when they handcuffed me and took me outside to a car, and shoved me in. You know, the really strange thing is that I wasn't all that worried. Part of me was saying that this wasn't happening at all, saying that I was still upstairs in my room having a nice kip and just dreaming all this melodrama. Another part of me, a more practical part, I presume, was saying it *was* happening but that they were just chancing their

355

arm, trying to scare me into admitting everything. It wasn't until the car turned into the police station forecourt that I thought maybe I'd been right, maybe fucking Kranze *had* done the dirty on me, maybe he *had* recorded everything and passed it on to the police. But I didn't have too much time to dwell on this since I was hauled out of the car the minute it stopped, and frogmarched into the station. They took my handcuffs off and put me into an interview room with a constable built like a prize-fighter for company, standing with his back to the door, gaping at me. 'Any chance of a cup of coffee?' I asked him, but I might as well have been talking to a brick wall. He didn't even bat an eye. 'Tea?' I tried. 'Cocoa?' I gave up after that. I leaned back in the chair and closed my eyes. I was delighted with how cool and calm I felt. In fact, by the time Inspector Birt and the ubiquitous Wilson came in I found myself quite looking forward to the proceedings.

The Inspector looked really awful. Like death warmed up. His face was truly grey, and his eyes were sunken and bloodshot. If I'd thought he was capable of it, I'd have said he'd been crying. Wilson looked his usual pig-ignorant self though, and it was he who slotted the tapes into the machine and recited the little spiel they have: giving the time of the interview and naming those present. He asked me to state my name, which I did, willingly. Then he came across to the table and sat down beside the Inspector. 'Very nicely done,

Sergeant,' I told him, but he ignored me.

'Mr Walwyn,' the Inspector said. 'You're entitled to have your solicitor present if—'

'Should have told me that before you put that thing on, shouldn't you?'

'You haven't been questioned yet. Do you want your solicitor here?'

'Shit, no. What do I want a solicitor for? I haven't done anything, have I?'

'That's what we want to find out.'

'Fire ahead.'

So the Inspector fired ahead, using the gentle ploy to begin with, sounding really sorry for me when he asked, 'Why, Marcus, why did you have to kill her?' My mind started racing at that. I tried desperately, without showing it, of course, to think of what they might have found to link me with Sharon. I couldn't think of anything, though. 'I don't know what you're talking about, Inspector,' I said finally.

The Inspector gave a small sigh, shaking his head as though begging me not to take him for a fool. 'We *know* you killed her, Marcus.'

'Oh, well, that's all right then,' I said. 'Let's go to trial,' I added with a pleasant enough smile.

The Inspector gave another sigh. 'If that's how you want it,' he said, and gave the Sergeant a sideways glance – his cue to be a star.

'Where were you this evening?' Wilson asked.

'What time this evening, Sergeant?' I asked politely.

'From six thirty on.'

I gave him my most charming smile. 'Well, as you know perfectly well, Sergeant, I left the house at six thirty and took a taxi to Leicester Square – didn't your mates tell you?'

The Inspector nodded. 'They told us.'

'And then?' Wilson asked.

'Went to a pub, didn't I?'

'You did,' the Inspector agreed. 'You met Karen Scott and Paul Cornell.'

'That's perfectly true, Inspector.'

'You had a fight with Cornell,' Wilson told me.

'A slight difference of opinion,' I called it.

'You had a fight with him,' Wilson insisted.

'If *you* want to call it that.'

'You attacked him with a chair.'

'I *hit* him with a chair, Sergeant. Self-defence. *He* was about to attack *me*. Ask Karen if you don't believe me.'

Although I've no idea why he would want to, I could have sworn Wilson was going to lean across the table and whack me. His face went a wonderful purple colour, and speckles of saliva formed on his lips. He ran his tongue over them and wiped them away. The Inspector on the other hand, just briefly closed his eyes, and took a deep breath. He asked, 'And then?'

'Then I went home again.'

The Inspector nodded. 'And then?'

I got annoyed. 'And then, and then, and then,' I

said, getting shirty. 'And then – nothing. I stayed at home,' I said, and when neither of them made any comment on that, I added, 'You *know* I stayed at home, Inspector. You've had those goons outside the house for weeks, for Christ's sake.'

At first I thought the Inspector just didn't like hearing his good brave men referred to as goons. He whacked his hand hard down on to the table, making both me and Wilson jump. Then in a very clear and cold voice he told me, 'Karen Scott was murdered this evening, Marcus. And you did it.'

Well! What can I tell you? I honestly haven't got the words to describe what the Inspector's statement did to me. I thought for a moment it was some sort of joke, a really sick joke, the sort of joke the police are famous for pulling when they're trying to fit someone up. But then I noticed the Inspector's eyes, and knew what he'd told me was true. 'Karen's *dead*?' and I could feel the blood draining from my face. Literally. 'Karen's *dead*?' I asked again.

The Inspector nodded.

'And you wouldn't know anything about it, of course?' Wilson said, with one of his snidey little snorts.

I ignored the ignorant slob. 'Killed?' I asked the Inspector.

He nodded again.

'But where?'

'In the lift going up to her flat,' he told me, watching me like a hawk.

I could feel myself starting to shake now. Karen

dead. It just wasn't possible. 'Was it Paul?' I asked.

'It was you,' Wilson said.

'Listen, you fat son of a bitch—' I began, but Inspector Birt intervened. He spoke very quietly when he asked, 'It was you who killed her, wasn't it, Marcus?'

'I never touched her,' I said.

'Hah,' Wilson snorted.

'Her killing had all the hallmarks of—'

'I swear I never touched her,' I told the Inspector. He didn't look as if he believed me. 'Look, I swear to God I never saw her after I walked out of that pub. You must know that. Jesus, you've got apes following me morning, noon and night.'

'You could have given us the slip.'

'How could I?'

'You did before.'

'When?'

'The morning you visited Mr Zanker.'

'I've told you, Inspector, I don't *know* anyone called Zanker.'

'Kranze?'

I was getting confused. 'What about Kranze?'

'He's Zanker.'

I started to laugh. 'Kranze is Zanker?'

'That's right.'

'Well, what d'you know!'

'You've been using his book as a guide.'

'I've been *editing* his book, Inspector. I'm an editor.'

'You're a reader,' Wilson pointed out with a smirk.

'Same difference.'

'You murdered Sharon Hayes as practice,' Inspector Birt said.

I said nothing.

'You murdered Darren Cornell to get him out of your way.'

I still said nothing.

'And you murdered Karen Scott because she rejected you in favour of Paul Cornell.'

I jumped to my feet and started screaming at them. 'I didn't! I didn't! How many times do I have to tell you? I never saw her after I left the pub.'

'Sit down,' the Inspector said.

I sat down.

Then Wilson started. 'You murdered Sharon Hayes for practice.'

I looked away.

'You murdered Darren Cornell to get him out of the way.'

I glared at him.

'And you murdered Karen Scott because she preferred Paul Cornell to you.'

'Bullshit,' I told him.

Then Inspector Birt started the same old rigmarole again. I just kept shaking my head. Back to Wilson, and off he went, repeating the accusations. I didn't bother to react at all to him.

'You must really have hated Karen,' Inspector Birt said.

'I *loved* her.'

'Until she ditched you,' Wilson put in.

I just gave him another glare.

'She was so pretty, wasn't she, Marcus?' the Inspector asked.

I nodded.

'So young and so pretty.'

The bastard. He knew what he was doing all right. I started to cry a bit. I just couldn't help it. My eyes just filled with tears and they rolled down my cheeks.

'Why don't you just tell us about it, Marcus. It will make things so much easier for you.'

'I didn't kill her,' I sobbed. 'I didn't kill her.'

'All that mutilation,' the Inspector said, shaking his head.

I choked. 'What mutilation?'

'On her forehead. The cross.'

'You mean like Shar . . .'

The room went deadly quiet. Inspector Birt just stared at me. Wilson pointed his forefinger and thumb at me like a gun. 'Gotcha,' he said.

I tried, for a while, to bluff my way out of it, but it was a waste of time. They'd kept the business of the cross on Sharon's forehead a secret. But, like I said, I tried anyway, and came up with answers of a sort when they asked me how I knew Sharon had a mark on her face.

'Must have read it in one of the papers,' I said – I think that's the usual answer given, isn't it?

The Inspector shook his head. 'It wasn't in any of the papers.'

I shrugged. 'Maybe Karen told me.'

The Inspector shook his head some more. 'Karen didn't know.'

Wilson said, 'Nobody knew except us and whoever killed her.'

'That's it – *you* must have told me when I came in that time.' It was pretty pathetic, I know. Wilson gave a sort of guffaw, and Inspector Birt shook his head. 'Come on, Marcus,' he said. 'Just admit it, will you? We're all tired. You must be exhausted. Just tell us . . .'

He was right, of course. I was absolutely exhausted. Drained, more like. It came into my head that probably they *had* been fooling me about Karen, telling me she'd been murdered just to get me unsettled and make an admission. And the bastards had succeeded, of course. I didn't really care about that, though. I don't honestly know why but it just didn't seem all that important. 'Karen's not dead really, is she?' I asked the Inspector.

He never moved a muscle. 'Sharon, Marcus. What about Sharon?'

'Yes. All right,' I heard myself say. It was really weird: it was as if I knew that by telling them about Sharon and Darren it would guarantee Karen's well-being.

'You admit killing her?'

'Yes. Now, what about Karen?'

'And Darren Cornell?'

Jesus, he was really bleeding me. 'Yes!' I screamed at him. 'Yes, I killed that stupid moron too. What about Karen?' My voice sounded really strange, and I was thumping the table with my fist, not hard, not making all that much noise. I was honestly expecting him to smile at me now and tell me that, yes, they had been pulling the wool over my eyes, that Karen was safe and well, that it had all been a wicked plot to get me to confess. But he didn't. 'Why don't you tell me about Karen, Marcus?' he said.

I remember I gave a loud sort of moan, and thought I was going to fall off my chair. 'I don't *know* anything about Karen,' I was saying, and I was crying again, sobbing. 'She's not dead, is she?' I heard. 'I don't want her to be dead,' I heard too, but I might have just been thinking it.

Then Sergeant Wilson asked, 'How did you get into the lift without us seeing you?'

That started all sorts of things rattling about in my brain. It wasn't so much what he asked, but how he asked it. Then it dawned on me. Clearly, they had all sorts of security set up to protect Karen, and he was hoping I'd tell him something that would get him off the hook. They weren't interested in Karen's death at all: they just wanted to save their own backsides. It's crazy, I know, but suddenly all I wanted to do now was thwart them. I kept my head down for a few moments. I stopped crying. I got myself together. Then I looked up and stared Wilson straight in the face. I gave him my most enigmatic, knowing smile, a smile that said, that's something you'll never find out, you big, fat shithead.

'We'll take a break here,' Inspector Birt said.

I was still staring and smiling at Wilson, and he was staring and glowering back.

'I said we'll take a break here,' Inspector Birt repeated.

Reluctantly Wilson blinked, and got up to switch off the tape-machine. 'We'll have a statement written up for you to sign and then you'll be formally charged,' Inspector Birt told me.

'With?'

'The murders of Sharon Hayes and Darren Cornell.'

'Not Karen Scott?' I asked with as much sarcasm as I could muster.

'No,' Inspector Birt said.

'Not yet,' Sergeant Wilson said.

'Not ever, mate,' I told him.

Twenty-four

I'm not going to bore you with all the business of being on remand and being hauled back and forth to court like a sack of potatoes for one thing and another. It's enough to say it wasn't the best time of my life. I was treated well enough, though, with due respect, I felt, although why they insisted on putting a blanket over my head every time I left the wagon to go into court I don't know. I didn't want it. I wanted to have a look at the morons queuing up to gawp at me. But no, the blanket had to go on like it was part of some macabre ritual.

But the trial was interesting. Good old Harry Rutherford put up a valiant defence, dredging up every weird and wonderful excuse he could to try and save me. Even tried the Munchausen Syndrome by Proxy which is pretty fashionable, and spiced that with Post Traumatic Stress Disorder, saying RIP's suicide had left me terribly scarred, but, like I told you at the beginning, he was fighting a losing battle. Not counting my confession (which Harry tried to make out had been tricked out of me) the police didn't really have too much evidence against me. One thing came out that gave me a little laugh – to myself, mind. You remember when I picked Sharon up she'd just bought a duvet? Well, they found that stupid duvet in the boot of my car. I'd totally forgotten about it, and it had been lying there all the time. Amazing. Still, when it came to Harry's turn he managed to make the police look like a gang of incompetent idiots which pleased me no end, especially since I could see Fat Wilson out of the corner of my eye, see him getting more and more furious, on the verge of apoplexy it looked like.

Ma never came to see me while I was on remand. She never came near the trial either, but that was because I told Harry to persuade her not to. It would have been far too nerve-racking and degrading for her, and with Ma you never knew, she might just have caused a scene (you can see her, can't you, having a go at the prosecution, screaming, 'How dare you disbelieve my son?') and found herself plastered all over the front page of the *Sun* or something. But I'll tell you who was there: Camp Carl, bless his cotton socks. That surprised me. He came along to the trial every single day, always sitting in the same place, giving me his camp little waves and shy smiles when he caught my eye, encouraging me sort of. I really appreciated that. None of the other creeps from work came. Probably thought it would be degrading to be associated with the likes of me, although I've since heard that there was a meeting at which the midget Consuella Kelly suggested it might be a bright idea to try and get me to write a book about the whole thing. Some tough bitch she is!

I suppose it's the same for anyone who finds themselves in my predicament, but I actually got to the stage when all I really wanted was to have the whole charade over and done with. I wanted the judge to pronounce his sentence and pack me off for as long as he wanted. I yearned to be left in peace. That was all. He did sentence me eventually, but it took the best part of four whole weeks for him to get round to it.

I don't know if you know anything about murder trials — if you're not one of those ghouls who troll along to the courts for kicks, I don't suppose you will; but the day the verdict is delivered is like the first night of a very expensive West End production. Everyone is on edge and expectant. Everyone gets all dressed up too: the members of the jury, the accused, and even the gawpers in the gallery. A right Lloyd-Webber of a day it is. Harry saw to it that my very best suit was brought in, and a white shirt, and what he called a sober tie. Dressing up does something for you, doesn't it? I think it does anyway, and I felt perfectly calm and appropriately interested when I was taken to court on that final morning.

I remember there was this little gasp and some muttering from the gallery when I was brought in, looking smart and clean and very handsome.

Although they *know* it isn't true, people have this ridiculous idea in their minds as to what a murderer *should* look like: ugly as sin, with a squashed nose and cauliflower ears: someone repellent who it's *easy* to dislike. It really throws them when someone like me turns out to be the guilty party. Anyway, I decided as a final gesture to give the poor sods their money's worth, to make their day. I looked about me with an air of dignified composure. I raised my eyes, and stared at the gallery, allowing a small, wan, little-boy-lost smile to play on my lips. I have to tell you, though, that the smile sort of froze when I spotted Helmut Kranze sitting up there in the front row. He was just about the last person I expected to see there, for obvious reasons. But he was there all right, and he smiled at me, surreptitiously, and nodded his bald head, and made a small secretive gesture with his hand, like he was patting me on the back, I felt. Applauding me, maybe. Applauding both of us.

Anyway, after a lot of palaver and a couple of false alarms, the jury came back, and none of them looked at me so I knew I was for the chop. There's hardly any need to tell you they found me guilty, but though I'd expected that, it still came as something of a shock. I was very gracious about accepting their decision. I nodded in agreement to them, and gave them an encouraging smile. I'd have been quite happy to retire from the court at that moment, but the judge wanted his say, of course. He had a field day. Really went to town on me, rambling on about what a shocker I was. All crap, really. But it was as if he'd rehearsed the whole thing and was going to have his moment of glory even if it bored the rest of us to death. I was brutal. I was sadistic. I was a danger to the public. I felt like doing a Camp Carl and saying, '*Moi*?' in astonishment, but I thought better of it. I was conscienceless, calculating and cruel. You name it, I was it. When he'd got all that off his chest – ending up by calling me a fiend and my acts heinous – he gave me life, naturally. I don't think he liked me much.

They don't half tell you a load of crap about prison. You can take it from me that it's really quite nice in here. They do everything for you, just about, and though the food isn't what you'd call spectacular, it's quite edible, and anyway I've always believed if you've got a brain it's possible to get used to anything. Believe me: all that business about losing your liberty being so hard to bear is just so much rubbish. All you really lose is your *physical* liberty, and that's no big deal. Your mind still has its freedom, and that's what counts. Of course, the physical side of things is what most of the morons in here think about all the time. They keep semi-erotic pictures torn from cheap magazines stuck up on the walls of their cells, and have their stupid fantasies. They're mostly inadequates. All they live for is the visits they get from their wives and girlfriends, and you can hear the springs of their bunks going hell for leather the night after those visits. Disgusting, I call it. Luckily I don't have visits myself. Heather writes to me sometimes. I think it adds spice to her cravings just to imagine she's having it off with a real live killer. But she doesn't come down to see me. Not that I'd want her to. She'd probably start trying to grope me under the table, and really embarrass me.

I did get one visit that really surprised me, about three months after I'd been sentenced and sent here. Know who from? Inspector Birt, that's who. Ex-Inspector Birt, actually. I'd heard on the grapevine that he'd retired, but I also heard that was a bit of a euphemism. I have to say I got quite a shock when I saw him. He'd aged terribly. He looked like a tired old man. I mean, a really *old* tired man. He looked sad too, and somehow incomplete without that cretin Wilson hanging on to his tail. And it took what seemed like an age for him to get round to the reason for his visit.

'Hear you've retired,' I mentioned.

He nodded.

'Going to grow roses then?'

He smiled a bit, and shook his head.

'I thought that was what all retired policemen did – grow roses.'

'Not this one.'

'Not stamp-collecting, I hope?'

He shook his head again.

I sighed. 'You're going to get awfully bored,' I advised him.

'Probably.'

'Leads to an early grave, that does,' I said.

He was listening, but not listening, if you know what I mean. Watching me.

'How about writing your memoirs? You know, *Inspector Birt's Most Puzzling Cases*? Reckon I'd get a mention?'

'Probably.'

'And I'd edit it for you for free.'

He chortled at that. 'Thank you,' he said, and then, suddenly, went very serious again. 'Marcus, will you tell me something – off the record?'

'Depends, doesn't it?'

'You did kill Karen Scott, didn't you?'

I felt really sorry for him. He so desperately needed to know. As though if he didn't know for sure he'd be like one of those ghosts who wander about until someone does the right thing and takes the jinx off them, letting them settle. And, what the hell, it made no difference to me now. Besides, he'd got me in a good mood. 'Tell you what – I'll answer that if you promise there'll be no other questions.'

He nodded agreement.

I grinned at him. 'Yeah. All right. I killed her,' I lied.

His old watery eyes softened, and he gave me half a smile. I was glad I'd done him that favour. But he was shaking his head then, like someone still bemused and amazed. 'How *did* you get into the lift? Past my men and into the lift?'

I waggled an admonishing finger at him. 'That's another question. You're only allowed the one.'

'I just thought . . .'

'Got to keep some secrets, don't I?' I replied. 'You know, carrying my secrets to the grave. You can use that in your memoirs. Great ending to your chapter on me: "But Marcus Walwyn carried that secret to his grave" – just what editors like. Mystery. Great stuff, mystery, isn't it?'

He stood up.

'Clever though, wasn't I?' I added, just to tease him. I didn't want him to have a completely carefree retirement, did I?

He gave me a baleful look. 'I wouldn't say *that* clever, Marcus.'

'No?'

He gazed about the room, and then at me. 'You're locked up in here, aren't you? And will be for a very long time.'

That annoyed me. There I was, trying to be nice to him and all the bastard did was taunt me. 'Yeah,' I told him. 'But you're locked up in here,' I said, tapping my head. 'For ever,' I added.

Last month I landed myself a cushy job in the library, probably because I'm about the only one in here who can read the titles of the books properly. You'd be surprised at how many people can't read or write. I think that's a serious problem. No wonder the poor sods can't get work. No wonder, either, that they turn to crime.

But I've started helping some of them to improve themselves, making them take out simple reading and writing books (the sort you and me had in kindergarten) along with the other rubbish they want – comics mostly. The Flintstones are very much in demand right now. And I recommend reading to those few who can read. Make them see there's more to literature than sex and violence. I'm plugging Malcolm Lowry and Cormac McCarthy at the moment. I make myself useful, you could say. It passes the time agreeably.

It's the nights that prove a bit difficult. I've no idea why it is, but darkness seems to make everyone very tense, very morbid too, very depressed. It makes them dwell too much on the outside, and that's fatal, of course. The trick is to forget you ever had another life, but they can't seem to do that like me. You can hear a lot of sobbing going on after lights-out, and screams too when it all gets to be too much for some poor bastard.

You want to know what I find myself thinking about? It's not Ma, or home, or Heather, or the murders, or even Karen – she seems unreal now, seems like a dream, like she never really existed at all except in my mind. Like an image I once had. An image that crumbled. No, what I think about is old Helmut Kranze for some reason. Think about him a lot. Mostly about the secretive smile he had on his face in court. About the little gesture he made. It's not that I want to think about him. I don't really. He just pops into my head every so often, usually just as I'm about to fall asleep, like he was doing it on purpose so he'd be with me all through the night. And sometimes (quite often, to be truthful) I can actually hear his weird cackle rattling around in my head. Sometimes, too, it's not in my head, but bouncing off the walls of my cell. I never quite seem to make out what it is he's laughing at, but there's definitely an edge to that cackle. It's sort of sinister, and triumphant, and like he's expecting me to join in. It's a bit like he thinks we've succeeded in putting one over on someone. But that's not quite it. More like *he's* pulled a fast one, and got away with it.